PRAISE FOR JACI BURTON
AND HER NOVELS

"Jaci Burton's stories are full of heat and heart."
—*New York Times* bestselling author Maya Banks

"A wild ride."
—#1 *New York Times* bestselling author Lora Leigh

"Jaci Burton delivers."
—*New York Times* bestselling author Cherry Adair

"One to pick up and savor." —*Publishers Weekly*

"Jaci Burton's books are always sexy, romantic and charming! A hot hero, a lovable heroine and an adorable dog—prepare to fall in love with Jaci Burton's amazing new small-town romance series."
—*New York Times* bestselling author Jill Shalvis

"A heartwarming second-chance-at-love contemporary romance enhanced by engaging characters and Jaci Burton's signature dry wit." —*USA Today*

"Captures everything I love about a small-town romance."
—Fresh Fiction

"Delivered on everything I was hoping for and more."
—Under the Covers Book Blog

"A sweet, hot small-town romance." —Dear Author

"Fun and sexy." —Fiction Vixen

TITLES BY JACI BURTON

• • • • •

THE
Best Man
PLAN

JACI BURTON

JOVE
New York

A JOVE BOOK
Published by Berkley
An imprint of Penguin Random House LLC
penguinrandomhouse.com

Copyright © 2020 by Jaci Burton, Inc.
Penguin Random House supports copyright. Copyright fuels creativity, encourages
diverse voices, promotes free speech, and creates a vibrant culture. Thank you for buying
an authorized edition of this book and for complying with copyright laws by not
reproducing, scanning, or distributing any part of it in any form without permission.
You are supporting writers and allowing Penguin Random House to continue to
publish books for every reader.

A JOVE BOOK, BERKLEY, and the BERKLEY & B colophon
are registered trademarks of Penguin Random House LLC.

ISBN: 9780451491282

First Edition: July 2020

Printed in the United States of America
3 5 7 9 10 8 6 4 2

Cover photo by Claudio Marinesco
Cover design by Rita Frangie
Book design by Alison Cnockaert

This one's for my sister. Because sisters are secret-keepers, shoulders to cry on and sometimes pains in your butt, but they always have your back. They are your forever lifeline in a crisis. Thanks, Sissy, for everything.

CHAPTER

· · · · · ·

one

ERIN BELLINI SHOUTED out from her office at Red Moss Vineyards.

"Mom. Have you talked to the caterers?"

Her mother didn't respond right away. It was her most annoying quality. While she waited, Erin jotted down several things she needed to remind her bridesmaids about. Her two sisters were onsite so she had them covered, but she made a note in her planner for the rest of the bridesmaids.

Erin's mother, Maureen, made an appearance in Erin's office. "You don't need to yell at me, Erin. You could have just sent me a text. And yes, caterers are confirmed. Which I already told you this morning."

"Right. You did. For some reason I hadn't checked it off the list. Sorry." She typed an X in the spreadsheet on her laptop as well as marking it off on the page in her planner. She looked up at her mother. "And my dress is back from alterations, right?"

"It's in your closet." Her mom made that face, the one where her lips went straight and her eyes narrowed and you knew you were being scrutinized. "You're not getting nervous, are you?"

Erin smiled and took in a deep breath to center herself. "I never get nervous. Because I have everything organized. In my planner. In my spreadsheet. In the notes on my phone."

Her mother smiled. "Right. Yes, well, that's you, honey. I'm going out to the vineyards to check on your dad. Call if you need me."

"Okay."

She should call Owen, her fiancé, to make sure he remembered he had to pick up the tuxes. Or maybe she should call Jason, Owen's best friend and the best man. Owen was always scattered and busy and he'd likely forget. Thankfully he had her to organize everything for him.

She picked up her phone and found Jason, then pressed the call button.

"Busy here, Erin."

She shook her head at Jason's gruff brush-off. They'd grown up together, had known each other forever. "I need you to pick up the tuxes."

"What?"

"The tuxes, Jason."

"I'm knee-deep in cow shit right now, Erin. You don't mean now, do you?"

"No. I mean tomorrow." She heard mooing. "You delivering babies?"

"Pregnancy checks."

"Oh. Cool." Jason was a large animal vet, so he was always on the run. He was part of a practice in town, but he also worked the local ranches.

She was scrolling through her e-mails when she saw one from Owen. Huh. That was odd. Owen never e-mailed her. He either called or texted. She frowned and clicked on it.

"I thought Owen was doing the tux thing," Jason said.

"Owen is likely up to his elbows in hops or wheat or whatever it is that brewers do. Or he's making sure the brewery won't go up in flames without him when we're on our honeymoon. You know how he is."

"Fine. I'll handle it. Anything else?"

"Yeah." She was trying to concentrate on Owen's e-mail and forgot she was on the phone with Jason.

"Erin. Anything else?"

Her blood went cold. Everything in her went cold, despite the warm May day.

She read the e-mail again. It was a breakup e-mail. Two days before the wedding, and Owen was breaking up with her.

"In a freaking e-mail? He's breaking up with me in an e-mail?"

"Who's breaking up with you?" Jason asked. "Owen is?"

She was getting married in two days. Correction. Apparently she was *not* getting married, because exactly two days before their wedding Owen had broken up with her. Via e-mail.

She felt dizzy and sick to her stomach. She leaned over and put her head between her legs.

"Erin. Are you there?"

"Did you know about this?" she asked, trying not to faint or throw up.

"Hell no, I didn't know. Did he call you?"

Erin straightened, the dizziness making her feel as if she'd just downed a bottle of Bellini's best prosecco in one gulp.

Two days. They were getting married in two days.

This had to be a mistake. But as she looked at the e-mail again, the word "mistake" was written in the same sentence as the words, "us getting married."

"Ahhhhhhhhh!" she screamed, long and loud, then yelled, "That son of a bitch. I will kill him. He broke up with me in an e-mail, Jason."

"He didn't," Jason said. "Are you sure?"

She straightened, shoving her laptop as if that was somehow the same thing as slapping Owen. "Oh, he did. And I'm sure. I can read a damn e-mail, Jason. I gotta go." She ended the call and stared at her lists, tears pricking her eyes as the future she'd envisioned with Owen dissolved right in front of her.

All because of an e-mail. An e-mail! How could he be so cold?

"I will kill him. I. Will. Kill. Him."

She was breathing too fast and she knew it. She was going to hyperventilate if she didn't calm down. She pushed herself out of her chair and forced herself to pace the floor of her office, centering her breathing, holding the tears back, resisting the urge to crumple on the floor and sob like a baby.

How could he do this to her? To them? They were perfect together.

Oh, no. She would not cry. Not over him.

"Who are you going to kill?" Honor asked, running in. "You screamed. What's wrong?"

Torn between betrayal, hurt and utter fury, she couldn't even answer her younger sister. She finally managed to find her voice and pointed at her laptop.

"Owen dumped me. In an e-mail!"

Honor gasped. "He did not." She yelled out the door. "Brenna, get in here now!"

Brenna sauntered in. "What's up?"

"Owen dumped Erin. In an e-mail, apparently."

Erin reread the e-mail again, making sure it said what she thought it did. Maybe she'd misinterpreted it.

But, no. There was no misinterpreting "I'm sorry" and "We're not right for each other" and "We shouldn't get married." She felt her sisters' hands on her shoulders as they leaned over her to read it.

"That son of a bitch," Brenna said.

"I can't believe he'd do this," Honor said. "It just doesn't seem like Owen at all. Did he say anything to you that sounded like he wanted to back out?"

Erin swiveled around in the office chair to face her sisters. "No, he didn't say anything to me because apparently he was too busy packing for Aruba. For our honeymoon. He's taking *our* honeymoon trip by himself."

Brenna crossed her arms and narrowed her gaze. Erin felt a little vindicated by the fury in her older sister's eyes. "I will personally destroy him."

"You won't get the chance," Erin said. "Because I get the pleasure of doing that."

"Dad might kill him first," Honor said, looking worried. "Although, knowing Mom's temper, you might have to hide the kitchen knives."

Erin stood and started to storm out of the office, but then turned. "Nobody gets to kill him but me."

Their mother walked in right then, a smile on her beautiful face.

"Who are we killing now?"

Mom was used to the three sisters always plotting someone's demise. Oh, but she didn't know how bad this was. This was really bad. This actually felt murderworthy.

"Owen dumped me, Mom. And he's already left for Aruba without me."

Their mother just stared at her, dumbfounded for a few minutes. "What? He did what?"

She took her mother's hand and led her to the desk, showing her the e-mail Owen had sent. She read it. Then read it again and lifted her head to stare in confusion at Erin.

"This makes no sense, Erin. He loves you."

Erin snorted. "Apparently not. He said he tried to talk to me but I wouldn't listen. I don't even know what he's talking about, because he most certainly never talked to me about ending our engagement. And the rest of it is all blah blah blah whatever where he didn't want to hurt my feelings." She pointed to her laptop, to the life-altering e-mail. "Like *that* wouldn't hurt my feelings? He couldn't even face me, the coward."

"Are you sure he didn't talk to you about this?" Honor asked.

"Honor!" Erin said. "Whose side are you on?"

"Yours, of course. I just . . . it's just that we all know Owen. He'd never hurt you like this."

Erin waved her hands at her laptop. "He just did."

Honor sighed and shook her head. "You're right. I'm sorry, of course you're right. He's a terrible person. A coward for not facing you."

"Bastard coward," Brenna added. "So now what do we do? Everything's ordered for the wedding. Flowers, cake, caterer, music. Nothing can be canceled at this late date except the venue here at the vineyard, of course. He couldn't have gotten his cold feet six months ago?"

At Erin's stricken look, Brenna added, "Or, never? I mean, who wouldn't want to marry you? You're beautiful and talented and smart and any guy would be lucky to have you."

"Damn right he would," her mother added.

Erin didn't understand it. As her mother and sisters talked amongst themselves, she turned to face the window, looking out over the vineyards, rows and rows of grapes growing, promising a prosperous future.

She sighed and went over the past year in her head. Owen had proposed in his apartment. She hadn't been too surprised because they'd talked about marriage for a year. They'd planned the wedding. Everything had seemed fine.

And sure, she'd been preoccupied with her work here at Red Moss Vineyards, plus all the wedding planning, but Owen had been equally engaged with his work. They were both successful in their jobs. Owen had started up a craft brewery in Oklahoma City. Erin handled the business aspect of the family winery. They were both super busy but they made time for each other.

They'd known each other since they were kids. They'd been in love, dammit. She rubbed her stomach, aching inside at the loss of the future they'd planned together.

She couldn't pinpoint one time where warning bells had clanged in her head, where she might have stopped and thought that maybe he was having second thoughts.

And now she had a wedding in two days and no groom. And no refunds at this late date, either.

Fury replaced the hurt, pure anger wrapping an icy wall around her shattered heart.

Well, screw that. And screw him, too.

She'd have her revenge. And a party to remember.

She pivoted to face her mother and sisters, lifting her chin in defiance. "We're going to have the reception without him."

Her mother shot her head up and stared at Erin. "What?"

"You heard me. Everything has already been paid for. Since we own the winery and the wedding venue, we have the spot reserved. We'll never get our money back for anything else. So let's throw one hell of a party here on my non-wedding day."

Honor came over and put her arm around her. "Oh, honey, don't you think that's the last thing you'll want on the day you were supposed to get married?"

"Maybe. But if he thinks I'm going to cancel, then spend that day crying over him, he's wrong. Dead wrong." Erin shrugged. "Let's party our butts off on my non-wedding day. We'll call it the Bellini spring party instead. What do you think?"

"I'm in," Honor said. "Whatever you want, you get, as far as I'm concerned."

Brenna nodded. "Agreed. It's your day, Erin. You get to do whatever you want to do. I'm in, too. Mom?"

Their mother sighed. "Wait till your dad hears about this. I'm not convinced he won't fly to Aruba and personally drag Owen back here to marry you."

Erin lifted her chin. "I don't want to ever see him again, let alone marry him."

It took a few beats for her mother to answer. "Okay, then. We'll throw the best party this venue has ever seen."

And Erin would drown her heartbreak in the finest wine the Red Moss Vineyards produced.

It would be one hell of a party.

JASON CALLUM DROVE the dirt road like the fires of hell were on his heels.

He'd tried calling Owen's number three times. Each time, his phone went directly to voice mail. Owen often turned his phone off when he was working back in the brewing area, but he knew for a fact that his best friend was off work for the next two weeks.

Jason glared at his phone. "Because you're supposed to be getting married in two days, asshole."

He tossed his phone on the console of his truck.

He should have never backed off three years ago when Owen said he wanted to ask Erin out.

Then again, it hadn't been like Jason was going to do it. He and Erin had been friends since they were kids. Just friends.

You like her, dumbass. You've always liked her. You just didn't have the balls to do anything about it.

He gripped the steering wheel, trying to bite back the curse words that wanted to escape from his mouth.

This whole thing was his fault—indirectly, but still his fault.

Three years ago, Jason could have told Owen to back off, that he was interested in Erin. Instead, he'd told Owen to go for it and had swallowed the feelings he'd had for her himself.

Of course, he hadn't realized how strong those feelings were until he'd had a front-row seat to watch Owen falling in love with Erin.

And who wouldn't? She was strong-willed and smart and capable and beautiful and the way she laughed could instantly make a guy fall crazy in love.

So what the hell was Owen doing?

He turned down the long drive of the Red Moss Vineyards.

He hoped like hell he'd heard Erin wrong, that this was some kind of colossal mistake. Because his best friend wouldn't do this to Erin, wouldn't up and cancel the wedding with only two days to go. That just wasn't Owen, and Jason knew him probably better than anyone.

He pulled the truck along the side of the main house and got out, brushing off dust and animal hair that clung to his worn jeans. He'd changed out of the boots that he'd been working in and slid into another pair so he wouldn't track cow shit into the Bellinis' house. He walked up the wide wood stairs and onto the oversized porch. He knew he didn't have to knock. He'd known this family for as long as he could remember. He'd played out back with the Bellini girls when they were all kids.

He walked through the front door and followed the sound of Johnny Bellini's booming voice, some of it in English and some in Italian.

"Dad, you're not going to kill him," Honor said.

"*Bastardo*. He disgraced my daughter. That is just not done."

Erin rolled her eyes. "I am hardly disgraced. Pissed? Yes. Disgraced, no. And second? By the time I'm done talking to everyone about what he did to me, it'll be his reputation that's ruined."

"Hey," Jason said, stepping into the room. "I was on the phone with Erin and I heard. I came right over to make sure you were okay."

His gaze shot to Erin, who looked as upset as he'd ever seen her. Erin was never flustered, never upset, never out of sorts. She was the one sister who always had her shit together.

Today she definitely didn't have it together. Her dark raven hair was piled high in a crown on top of her head and the pencil she'd stuck into it threatened to topple the entire shebang. Her normally sharp green eyes were clouded, as if she was on the verge of tears.

Jason wasn't sure he'd ever seen Erin Bellini cry. Not even when he'd pushed her off the slide when they were eight years old. She'd just gotten up, brushed herself off, then calmly walked over and punched him right in the jaw.

He figured that's when he'd first fallen in love with her.

Now she just looked sad. But damn, she still looked beautiful, and he had no right to think that.

"I'm not okay, Jason." She walked over to him and leaned against him.

He put his arm around her and held her close. "I'm sorry, Erin."

He'd do anything he could to take this pain away from her, including kicking the shit out of his best friend.

"Have you heard from him?" she asked.

"No. I tried calling him on my way over and his phone went right to voice mail each time."

"Damn. Has he said anything to you?"

"About calling off the wedding? No. You know I'd have talked him out of it. What was he thinking?"

She tried to smooth her hair into place, then walked back into the living room. "I don't know. I wish I could talk to him."

"No. You will not ever speak to him again," Johnny said. "I, however, have a lot to say to him."

"Johnny, calm down," Maureen said.

"What about his parents?" Honor asked. "Has anyone called them? Aren't they supposed to drive in tomorrow from Dallas?"

"They are," Erin said. "I hadn't even thought about calling them."

Jason pulled out his phone. "Let me do that. I'll just step outside."

The phone call with Owen's dad was short, but just about as much of a punch to the gut as hearing Erin scream. When he hung up, he saw Erin standing just outside the front door.

"They know?"

He nodded. "But not for long. They just got off the

phone with him about an hour ago. They're in shock, Erin. They didn't know anything before now, either."

She walked forward and took a seat on the front step, cradling her arms around her knees. She lifted her gaze to his. "Did he tell them anything about why?"

He took a seat next to her. "Just that he changed his mind, he knew what he was doing was wrong and would make a lot of people unhappy, especially you, and that he flew to Aruba because he needed some distance."

She sighed, and Jason felt the weight of her sigh as if he carried it himself. "I don't understand any of this. Why didn't he just talk to me?"

"I don't know. Why didn't he talk to *me*? I'm his best friend. If he had second thoughts, you'd think he'd want to sound them out with someone. It seems to me like he didn't talk to anyone. Not you, not me, not his parents. So I don't get it, either."

"Yeah, none of this makes sense to me, Jason. Owen and I always talked everything out. I mean, maybe we haven't done a lot of talking lately, but with the wedding planning, my job, his job, we've both been busy." She swept a stray hair away from her face. "I thought everything was fine. He'd told me he was fine. Clearly he wasn't. Couldn't he have said something to me? Like, 'Hey, Erin, I don't want to get married'? That would have been a great start."

Jason read the anguish on her face and he wanted to pull her close, to comfort her. But he also read the tension in her body and knew now wasn't the time.

Damn. How could his best friend do this to . . . his other best friend?

Erin straightened. "Well, anyway, screw him. I've decided we're still going ahead with the reception."

"What?"

"You heard me. Everything is paid for and we won't get our money back if we cancel anything. So we're going to have one hell of a party."

"You don't have to do that, Erin. Everyone will understand if you want to cancel."

"But see, that's the thing. I don't want to. I might not be getting married, but I'll have the best damn non-wedding reception this town has ever seen. And I'll expect everyone to be there. Well, not Owen's family, of course. But everyone else should come. You'll come, won't you?"

If there was one thing he was sure of about Erin Bellini, it was her determination. And he could tell from the look on her face that she was determined not to spend this weekend acting like the jilted bride. But there was no way to know how this non-wedding party of hers was going to play out. So he would be by her side. He wasn't going to be another guy who let her down.

"Hell yeah, I'm coming. And I'll wear the damn tux, too."

He got up and held his hand out for her.

She grinned and slipped her hand in his. "Good, because you and I, Jason? We are going to dance Saturday night."

He was counting on it. Owen may have screwed her over, but Jason was going to make sure that Erin had the best night possible.

CHAPTER

······

two

WEARING HER WEDDING dress to the party was definitely out, for obvious reasons. Erin would donate it because though she would get married someday, she'd never
wear that dress.

It was a stellar dress, too. It would make some bride
very happy.

But it was dead to her now. So was her reception dress.
Too bad, because it was a knockout, too. A pale blush-
pink, chiffon, knee-length beauty with spaghetti straps,
it was tight at the top and flared out at the knee. Perfect
for dancing, showed off a little skin, but still—sexy as
hell.

She'd bought it to romance her new husband.

Dammit.

She stared into her closet and tapped her foot. Then
the sparkle of silver caught her eye and her lips lifted.

She pulled a silver metallic dress out of her closet. The
dress was skimpy and short and scandalous and would
show off a ton of skin.

Totally inappropriate for a wedding. Then again, this wasn't a wedding, was it?

She'd feel decadent in it, just the kind of dress she needed tonight. She had a pair of spiky silver heels that would show off her legs. She'd wear it to drink and dance and eat and forget all about Owen.

She stared at the wedding dress hanging over the back of her closet door. For the past two days she hadn't allowed herself any emotion, any upset over Owen's sudden change of heart.

But now, she was preparing herself for her non-wedding reception—no, she refused to use the word "wedding" in this event any longer. This was officially called the Bellini Party now.

She sighed and thought of all the sympathetic looks she was going to get tonight, and how now she'd forever be known as "the bride who basically got left at the altar."

Ugh.

Not that she was concerned too much about that of course. She was a Bellini, and Bellinis were made of strong stock. Her parents had always taught her to be resilient and courageous and never hide from anything.

Tonight she would embrace that wholeheartedly.

She was a fierce, capable woman. She would weather this and come out stronger on the other side.

Her gaze caught the wedding dress again. Without thought, she pulled off her robe and grabbed the dress off the hanger, knowing she shouldn't, but unable to stop herself. She slipped into the dress, zipped it up as far as she could without help, then slid into the beautiful sparkly shoes she'd bought to go with it. She'd never wear these shoes, either.

She turned and looked at herself in the mirror.

She hadn't had her hair done in the style she'd rehearsed

with her hair stylist. She'd planned on a partial updo, with one lock cascading down her shoulder. She wouldn't wear her mother's necklace or her grandmother's earrings. She wouldn't face Owen and say the vows she'd written. They were damn good vows, too. She'd taken weeks to write them. Had Owen even bothered to write vows?

Probably not. How long had he known he was going to bail? Days? Weeks?

"Why didn't you talk to me, Owen?" she said to her reflection. "Why didn't you tell me you were so unhappy?"

How could she have missed the signs? She was good at reading people.

Apparently, she wasn't as good as she thought. Because she'd clearly missed one big whopper of a sign in her fiancé.

She inhaled a shaky breath and reached up to calm her erratic heartbeat.

Okay, so tonight she'd be brave and fierce. But right now her heart was broken.

She sank onto the edge of her bed, staring down at her hand, where her sparkling engagement ring mocked her. She pulled the ring off and set it on her nightstand, rubbing the spot where her finger felt suddenly so naked, so exposed and vulnerable.

She tried to push the tears back, but couldn't, so she allowed them to fall and her heart to open up to all the emotion she'd held inside since she'd first read that e-mail.

Oh, this hurt.

She didn't think she could feel this much pain, but as she lay on the bed and curled up into a ball, she grabbed Mr. Brown, the teddy bear that had always given her comfort when she was a little girl. She wrapped her arms around him and wished for Mr. Brown to ease her pain.

Not even Mr. Brown could make her feel better. She had thought she could cry it out for a few minutes and be done, but once the waterworks started she couldn't hold back the floodgates.

This really sucked.

Brenna came in and smoothed her hand over her brow, then laid down next to her, spooning her.

"You have to let it out, honey," Brenna said. "When a man hurts you like that, the only thing you can do is cry."

"I don't want to cry over him," she managed in between sobs.

"I know." Brenna smoothed her hand over her hair. "But once you cry all these tears over how much he hurt you, you never have to cry another one over him again."

She sniffed. "That sounds okay."

So Brenna held her and Erin cried. Then Honor came in and climbed onto the bed and held her, too. And then Mom came in and laid Erin's head in her lap and wiped her tears and let her blow her nose, and she cried some more until she gave herself a headache. Until she had no more tears to shed. Not today, anyway.

"Okay, enough. I'm done." She sat up and her sisters slid off the bed. She took the dress and shoes off and Brenna and her mom put them away. That felt a little bit like closure, anyway. And maybe the crying had helped to release some of the pain.

Honor left the room and came back with some iced tea for all of them. Erin took several long swallows, feeling dehydrated from all the tears.

"Great," she said, swiping at her eyes with a tissue. "Now I'm going to have puffy eyes for the party tonight."

"No, you won't," Brenna said. "I have a gel mask in the freezer that'll get rid of that puffiness in no time."

"You still look pretty," Honor said, sliding her hand over Erin's hair.

"You always know the right thing to say," Erin said. "But honestly, I'm a wreck."

"All my girls are beautiful, even when you cry," her mom said. "But Brenna's right. A mask on your eyes will get rid of the puffiness. And God knows, Erin, you needed to cry it out."

Erin nodded, then turned to Brenna. "Is that what you did when your marriage to Mitchell ended?"

Brenna nodded. "For days. And days. And then I never cried again. You need to get it out of you, Erin, or you'll end up breaking down at the grocery store one day. Or the hair salon."

"I know. And I do feel better now. Still sad, but better."

"I imagine you're going to feel sad for a while," Honor said. "You planned a life with Owen. And he let you down."

She took a deep breath, then let it out. "No more talking about Owen. Is everything set for the party tonight?"

Her mother nodded. "Everything's set. Nearly everyone reconfirmed their attendance. Obviously, some of the people Owen works with won't be attending. And some of his closest friends and his family said they won't be here."

Some of Owen's friends were her friends, too. That one stung, but she understood. It would be awkward on both sides and the only thing she wanted tonight was fun. "That's fine. I expected that."

"But Jason's coming," Brenna said.

Erin smiled. "He told me he'd be here. I mean, he was my friend before he was Owen's friend."

"This much is true," her mom said. "Anyway, I have to go supervise the table setup. You sure you're all right?"

She smiled up at her mother. "Fine and ready to party."

"Good." Mom leaned over to kiss her cheek. "It'll get better, *cailín leanbh*."

She smiled at her mother calling her "baby girl," as she often did with her daughters. "Thank you, Mom."

After her sisters left her room, she got up and went into the bathroom, staring at her tear-streaked face in the mirror.

Her hair was a mess, her eyes were swollen, and she looked just like everyone was going to expect—a bride whose groom had left her.

Well, she wasn't going to give them the satisfaction. She went in search of the mask that Brenna had told her was in the freezer, grabbed it and tried her best to lie still on the bed. But lying still forced her to think, and her head filled with thoughts about getting married and packing for her honeymoon. And walking down the aisle next to her dad, with Owen standing there at the other end waiting to marry her.

She felt the prick of tears again and inhaled. She pulled the mask away long enough to turn on music. Loud, heart-pumping music. To hell with relaxation. She needed something that would keep her brain occupied, that would make her want to sing and would keep her from dwelling on things she couldn't change.

She moved her head back and forth while she waited for the mask to do its job, and the only thing in her head now was how much fun she was going to have tonight.

So much damn fun.

CHAPTER

......

three

JASON FELT STUPID wearing the tux, but if it was what Erin wanted, then that's what she was going to get. At least her dad was wearing one, too, and so was Finn, a friend of the family who also worked on the vineyard.

The ceremony was supposed to take place outside, followed immediately by an hors d'oeuvres and wine bar near the grapes.

Obviously, there wasn't going to be a ceremony, but Erin's dad told him everything else was going to happen just the way they'd arranged it.

"Erin insisted," Johnny said with a shrug, tugging on the collar of his tux. "At least it's not a hundred degrees out here."

"She told me she wanted May because it wouldn't be too hot yet like it might be in June."

Johnny laughed, his cheeks puffing up. "Yeah, my girl isn't the sentimental type. She couldn't have cared less about that whole June-bride thing. She was just afraid it might rain on her weddin' day."

The day had dawned bright and sunny without a cloud

in the sky. It would have been a perfect day for a wedding. Too bad his best friend had turned out to be a total dick.

He and Owen were going to have words when he got back from Aruba.

Owen must have left his phone off, because Jason had tried calling him again, and the calls still went straight to voice mail.

Jason took a sip of wine. *You can run, buddy, but you can't hide forever.*

He ran into Finn Nolan at the bar. Finn looked even more uncomfortable in his tux than Jason felt.

"How long do we have to wear these suits?" Finn asked.

"Eh, you can suck it up for one night. For Erin."

"Yeah, I guess so. She's like my little sister. If I had a sister. Which I don't. But, you know, if I had sisters, she'd be one."

Jason laughed. "What time did you start drinking today?"

"Noon. Weddings aren't my thing. Too much frilly shit and standing around and not nearly enough whiskey."

"I hear that." Jason paused. "You have whiskey?"

"Dude, I'm Irish." He pulled a flask from his coat pocket and handed it over to Jason.

Jason took a swig and let the liquid burn its way down his throat, then screwed the top back on and handed it back to Finn. "Good."

"Hell yes it's good. Made it myself."

"Yeah?"

"Yeah. Johnny's letting me experiment in one of the barns."

"So now you've got a winemaking and whiskey business?"

"Well, I don't make the wine. I'm just a carpenter and

I help Johnny out. The whiskey's just for fun. And okay, maybe someday. Ya know?"

Finn Nolan had lived here since his senior year of high school. His mom and Maureen Bellini had been friends back in Dublin when they were kids, and when Finn turned eighteen his mom passed away. With no other living relatives, Maureen brought him over to finish his last year of high school and attend college, so he lived with the Bellinis and started working at the vineyards. He and Jason had become friends at school and often hung out together, along with Owen.

"Well, you make some fine whiskey, Finn."

"Thanks."

"This is a damn hot mess that Owen got us all into."

Jason turned to see his other best friend, Clay Henry, also dressed in his tux for tonight. Clay and Jason and Owen had all grown up together, had hung out and gotten in trouble and had one another's backs for everything.

He didn't have Owen's back for this, though.

"Have you talked to him?"

Clay shook his head. "Tried to call him a few times, but all my calls go straight to voice mail. Now his mailbox is full."

"Same." Owen was going to have a lot to answer for when he got back home. First, he would have to answer to Erin, of course.

Jason gathered Clay, Finn and a few of the other guys together, determined to make sure that tonight was all about Erin. He also wanted to be sure that the guests didn't hit her up with comments like "I'm sorry" and "Oh, poor Erin" or pummel her with questions about Owen that she didn't have answers for. So he told the guys to greet everyone as they came in and make sure they didn't ask those questions, and just had a good time and enjoyed the food and the music and one another. That way Erin could enjoy tonight.

The Bellinis had done an amazing job of decorating the vineyard, making it look nothing like a wedding and more like a party. Colorful lights were strung all across the front entrance to the vineyard, and the barn was lit up with bright lights and spring flowers. There was seating for plenty of people, and there were bars set up both in the barn and around the vineyard, so people could walk and enjoy the spring weather and still stop and get something to drink.

Music was playing, something lively and entertaining. Definitely nothing romantic, and Jason would bet Honor Bellini had everything to do with that. As the wedding planner, she'd made sure to obliterate anything having to do with a wedding reception so her sister wouldn't have to even think wedding. She'd done a great job.

Now that the guys were greeting the guests, he planned to hit up one of the bars.

But then he saw Erin walk out of the main house and stopped dead in his tracks.

She wore something silver that sparkled. It was short—sinfully short, showing off magnificent legs that were accented by heels he had no idea how she maneuvered in. Her raven hair was down, long waves falling over her shoulders. And as she walked down the steps, she took his damn breath away.

Owen was the dumbest fucker on the planet for letting Erin get away.

He went over to her and couldn't help but let his gaze roam over her. From a distance, she blew him away. Up close, the dress was hardly a scrap covering her magnificent body. If she was out to prove a point to her nonexistent fiancé about what he was missing, she was proving it. She looked nothing like a bride tonight. She looked like a seriously sexy single woman who had no intentions of getting married.

And there were a lot of single guys here tonight.

Shit.

"What do you think of the dress?" she asked.

"That's barely a dress, Erin."

Her lips lifted. "It covers the vital parts."

"As long as you don't move too fast."

She laughed, and her eyes sparkled in the flicker of torchlight.

"I need champagne," she said. "Care to escort me to the nearest bar?"

"Happy to." He held out his arm and they walked toward the barn.

"You look seriously hot in your tux."

He was sweating in the damn thing, more due to the sight of Erin in her almost-dress than anything else. "Thanks."

"Thank you for wearing it."

"Anything for you. I want you to have a good time tonight."

They made it to the bar and she grabbed a glass of champagne, took a sip, then another. "Oh, I intend to have a very good time tonight."

And he intended to stay close.

IT HAD TAKEN everything within Erin to muster up the courage to come outside and greet her guests. Fortunately, her sisters had surrounded her, as well as her parents. She'd fully expected to have to do a round of "Oh my God, Erin, what happened?" explanations, along with having to endure hours of "I'm so sorry" and "How could he do that to you," but, shockingly, no one had said a word other than to tell her she looked beautiful, the vineyard and barn looked amazing and they were happy to be there.

Something was up. She didn't know what it was, but someone had gotten to all the guests in advance and told them not to say anything to her about Owen. Not that she minded. In fact, she was utterly relieved.

"Where did you get that dress?"

She smiled at her friend Alice Weatherford. Erin and Alice had become fast friends after Alice had been snowbound at their house last winter. And then Alice had fallen in love with Clay Henry, who'd also ended up stuck in the house along with them during the snowstorm. The two of them had had a whirlwind romance, and even though Alice had a matchmaking business in LA, she commuted back and forth between LA and Clay's neighboring ranch.

"I found it at a shop online, fell madly in love with it and ordered it about six months ago. It fit me perfectly and I've been saving it for a special occasion."

"This is a great occasion to wear it, because you look like a sex-bomb queen lording it over your subjects tonight."

Sex-bomb queen? That wasn't her intent, but she appreciated Alice's take on it. "Ooh, thanks. Now I feel even better."

Alice laid her hand on Erin's arm. "You should feel better. It looks like half the town showed up for you. And the place looks incredible. I love the colorful lights. And the barn. And those lobster crostinis were to die for."

"We had a great caterer." She'd spent months testing out various caterers to find the best one, trying out various appetizers and main courses to make sure they'd end up with one both she and Owen liked. Of course, Owen didn't care. He'd told her he just wanted her to be happy.

Am I happy now, Owen? How did that work out?

She brushed the thought aside. Not tonight. Tonight Owen Stone didn't exist. He might never exist again.

She needed more champagne. Fortunately, they'd thought ahead. No, *she'd* thought ahead, since she'd done all the planning for this wed— this event, and didn't want people waiting in line at a single bar, which was why there were several. So she walked to the one only a few feet away and grabbed another glass. So convenient. She wandered around with the glass in her hand and visited with several of her friends, some family members, all who were being so friendly and polite and no doubt wondering what was going to happen now that she and Owen were no longer going to get married.

She knew exactly what was going to happen. She was going to move on with her life and put this all behind her, because what good would it do to dwell on it? She couldn't change what had happened, and thinking incessantly about it would only make her miserable. Erin didn't believe in being miserable. She believed in being active and happy and planning for the future. The past didn't belong in the future. She was busy with the business aspect of both the winery and the weddings at the vineyard, and come Monday, when she wouldn't be on her honeymoon, she'd go back to being busy again.

Life would go on. And while her heart hurt like crazy right now, eventually it wouldn't hurt anymore.

Simple, right?

"How's it going?" Brenna asked, coming up to walk with her.

"It's going about like I expected it to go, except no one's asking me any questions."

"That's good. Did you see that Joaquin Gonzales brought Amber Redmond as his date tonight?"

Erin's eyes widened. "He did not."

"He did. And his ex-girlfriend, Beatrice, is here with Carver Armstrong."

"Shut the front door." She'd been so wrapped up in herself she hadn't even paid attention to the typical party drama, which was always the best thing about a big bash like this.

Joaquin and Beatrice had just broken up last week after two years of dating. So there had to be some serious revenge dating going on tonight.

Brenna slipped her arm in Erin's. "Let me show you."

"Okay." She could use some drama that wasn't about her.

Brenna led her into the barn and around the side wall. "We'll stop here. They're over at tables five and seven."

Erin's gaze traveled right over to where Beatrice was currently shooting daggers at Amber so hard that Erin was surprised actual flames weren't flying out from her eyes. And Joaquin's shoulders were so tensed up it appeared as if he might climb over his table and leap onto Carver's.

"I think that maybe Joaquin and Beatrice aren't over each other yet," Erin said.

Brenna laughed. "You think? My guess is one of two things will happen. By the end of the night Amber and Carver will end up leaving together and Beatrice and Joaquin will reconcile, or there's going to be a huge fight."

Erin's lips lifted. "The fight would be more entertaining, but probably not the best thing for either couple."

"And potentially way more expensive for us."

"True." Erin looked over at Brenna. "This is just like high school. Beatrice could always get a guy riled up. I don't know that she'll ever settle down."

Brenna nodded. "She does like the drama."

Erin finished her champagne. "That she does. But she can also be super sweet, so I don't know. Joaquin's a hothead, but he's adorable. Who wouldn't fall madly in love with those dark brown eyes and that long hair?"

"They are a well-matched couple. I don't know why they broke up in the first place."

"Beatrice told me she's tired of waiting for Joaquin to commit. But you know how she is."

Brenna nodded. "Impatient. She wants what she wants when she wants it."

"Yes. So I guess we'll see what happens."

Erin hoped her friends would be able to work things out. In the meantime, she was on the hunt for another champagne. Brenna went to check on the wine for dinner.

The champagne had certainly helped to alleviate any jitters Erin had earlier. Now she felt like she was floating on a cloud of numbness, exactly where she wanted to be. She wandered outside to enjoy the fresh air, which was where she noticed Clay and Finn greeting some incoming guests.

That was nice of them. She also noticed them talking to them for a while, as if explaining something, and then her friends nodded and smiled and shook the guys' hands before wandering down the walkway toward the barn.

Then the realization hit her. Oh. That's why no one was asking her about Owen. They'd been given a debriefing before being allowed into the party.

Interesting. And she'd bet money she knew who had organized this little greeting party.

"You lost?"

She turned to see Jason standing there. In the torchlight, he looked magnificent. Then again, when didn't he look that way? He was tall, lean and utterly gorgeous, with raven black hair that was always a little shaggy and in need of a trim. His face was smooth, his jaw angular, and his eyes so dark and mysterious. And those lips, full and extremely kissable. How had she missed how sexy he was?

Because her attention had been focused elsewhere.

She took a quick glance at her left hand, that naked spot on her finger where just yesterday an engagement ring encircled it.

But she was free now. Free to do . . . whomever she wanted, actually.

"I am most definitely not lost."

Those full lips of his rose into a smile. "Good."

She tilted her head to the side, motioning to the guys behind her. "You did that?"

"What?"

"Talked the guys into greeting the guests."

"Oh. Yeah. I thought it would be a nice touch."

"You also told them to tell everyone not to mention Owen."

He shrugged. "Don't know what you're talking about, Erin."

"Uh-huh. I think you do." She finished her glass of champagne.

"You know what I think?" He took the glass from her hand, grasped her hand in his and started walking.

"What?"

Before she knew it, they were in the barn, and he placed her empty glass onto the bar, then led her onto the dance floor.

"I think you need to dance."

He pulled her against him, his body firm, his hand warm against her back as he led her across the floor. She realized she'd never danced with him before. She'd never felt him like this, either, felt the touch of his hand in hers, the way his other hand swept up and down her back, the assured way his feet moved her across the floor.

The music was a love song. She liked it—a guy telling a woman how beautiful she was, and how perfect he was for her. She sank into the lyrics, the way Jason glided her across the floor. Fortunately, there were other people dancing so she didn't feel like she was on display. She could enjoy the feel of Jason's arms around her.

This felt new, and a little bit exciting. And something she deserved after what she'd been through the past few days. She lifted her gaze and focused on Jason's face.

She'd never noticed the way his gaze met hers, with such unabashed . . . heat.

Wow. Being in Jason's arms had lit a fire under her that she so desperately needed right now.

The song wrapped around her, enveloped her, making her feel things she hadn't felt in a long time. She realized she'd been invested in her wedding and planning and flowers and dresses, and she'd been running a hundred miles a minute and hadn't taken any time to even feel excited, to feel any romance. Was that what had gone wrong? Had she pushed the romance aside to become some kind of bridezilla with her own wedding?

The only thing she could remember feeling lately was the utter devastation over being dumped, and sinking into that embarrassment and devastation.

Now, though? Now she felt something here in Jason's arms and it was damned exciting.

When the song ended, they stayed where they were.

"It's your night, Erin," he said, his hand smoothing along the bare skin of her back, making her tingle in places that hadn't tingled in longer than she could re-member. "You can have whatever you want."

She thought she'd had everything she wanted. She'd been wrong about that. But in this moment, new doors were opening for her, and she planned to walk through them.

"What if I want you?"

His brow arched. "On the dance floor? In front of all these people?"

She laughed. "I think I've caused enough gossip for the rest of the year."

She walked off the dance floor and Jason followed. On the way out of the barn, she grabbed another glass of champagne.

"How about something to eat?" he asked. "There's some amazing food."

"Did you eat?" she asked.

"A little."

She turned, walking backward as they made their way toward the vineyards. "You should go eat some more."

"Yeah? And where are you going?"

She had no idea, other than she needed to keep moving. Standing still meant she might actually stop and think about what would happen tomorrow after this was all over with.

What *would* happen tomorrow?

Don't think about it. Don't stop.

Plus, the evening was beautiful. No wind, the sky was clear, the stars were out, and she felt numb, and also kind of awesome. She couldn't feel her nose anymore, thanks to the champagne. Wasn't that amazing?

She kicked off her heels and wandered into a row of grapes. "I never wanted to grow grapes. It seemed like a lot of work. But I like keeping track of the money aspect, and what grapes we're growing, how much we bottle and the client aspect of the wine business. Same with the wedding side."

She took a sip of champagne. "I didn't want to manage the planning of the weddings. Honor's good at the people part of that, and dealing with florists and caterers and jittery brides-to-be. But I like doing budgets and schedules and ensuring we make money. So my sisters do all the work, and I take care of the business side."

"Seems to me you do plenty of work. Juggling between the winery and the wedding business keeps you plenty busy."

"I guess." She stopped and tilted her head back. "The stars are beautiful tonight. Would have made for a nice wedding day."

"He's an ass, Erin. He doesn't deserve you."

She inhaled, then let it out. "No, he sure as hell doesn't."

She finished off her glass and let her hand drop to her side, then turned to Jason. "We should have sex."

His lips curved. "Here? In the vineyard? I dunno, Erin. That's a damn nice dress you're wearing. I'd hate to see it get dirty."

She knew what he was doing. "I don't mind dirty."

She heard his sharp inhale, liked the sound of it, liked even more that it had to do with her. When was the last time she'd felt desired? Owen had been distracted. They hadn't had sex in . . .

She wrinkled her nose. Hell, she couldn't remember. That was pretty bad, wasn't it? People who loved each other should have sex. Even people who didn't love each other had sex. Sex was fun. She should have sex now that she was single again. Lots of fun sex.

She leaned against Jason. "I'm desirable, right?"

"Damned desirable, Erin."

"Let's leave and go somewhere else. Get naked."

"I don't think that's a good idea."

"Really. You don't think sex with me is a good idea."

"That's not what I said."

"Then what did you say?"

"I said tonight is not a good idea. Your heart is hurt, and you've been downing a ton of champagne, and I'm not the kind of guy who takes advantage of that."

Well, damn.

"Fine."

She closed her eyes and thought about how much fun that could have been.

Fun. She needed some damn fun. And a really good revenge fling. And who better to do that with than Jason?

She lifted her gaze to him. "Then let's just get out of here."

"Where do you want to go?"

"Anywhere but here. I just need . . . some breathing space."

He nodded. "Sure. But we need to let people know you're leaving so they don't think you've just disappeared."

"Okay."

They headed out of the vineyard. Jason picked up her shoes on the way out and she slipped them back on. She found her mother as they made their way back to the barn.

"Erin. Are you all right?"

"I'm fine, Mom. But I need to get away from here."

Her mother took Erin's hands in hers. "I understand, my sweet girl. Go do whatever you need to do."

"I'm sorry about the party, Mom. I thought I could handle it."

Her mom smiled. "The party will be fine without you. Take care of yourself."

When Mom pulled her into her arms, Erin nearly

sobbed in relief. She'd been so much trouble. This whole wedding-slash-non-wedding thing hadn't exactly turned out the way she'd envisioned. She thought she could handle being here, thought she could be the queen of the night—show everyone how unaffected she was about Owen dumping her. Instead, she just wanted to get out. She knew her mother would understand her need to flee the scene.

She turned to Jason. "I'm going to go upstairs and change clothes. It'll only take me a minute."

"I'll bring my truck up front."

She nodded and dashed into the house and upstairs to her bedroom, took off the dress and slipped into a pair of jeans and a button-down shirt. She pulled her hair into a high ponytail, then slipped into a pair of flats. By the time she went downstairs and out the door, Jason was waiting there outside his truck.

Her savior. She slid into the seat and he closed the door.

When he got into the driver's side, he turned to her. "Where to, Cinderella?"

She grinned. "Your place?"

He shook his head and put the truck in gear. "Okay."

Time for some fun.

CHAPTER

······

four

THIS WAS A really bad idea. Jason kept mentally repeating that to himself over and over again all through the drive to his house. But Erin seemed to be in a good mood. She sang along to the radio, she was wriggling in her seat and she was much livelier than she'd been at the party, so if escaping what would have been her wedding reception had brought some life back to her—at least for tonight—who was he to question it?

He stopped at the fried chicken place to grab a big bucket of chicken and all the accessories, along with two large iced teas. He was determined to get some food into her.

He pulled into his driveway, a cacophony of barking coming from the front gate.

"Oh, Puddy!" Erin unbuckled her seat belt and hopped out of his truck, so Jason punched the button for the garage door. Before he even had the engine turned off, Erin was through the door and into the house.

Jason shook his head. He got out and locked the truck, then went inside.

"You've grown so much since the last time I saw you. You're such a sweet boy. I love you so much, Puds. So, so much."

He rounded the corner of the hallway to see that Erin had let Puddy in and was on the floor, her legs crossed, and Puddy, who was not as tiny at six months old as he was the last time Erin had seen him, was sprawled on his back on Erin's lap while she rubbed his belly. His white-tipped paws were up in the air and moving furiously while she patted him.

She looked over at Jason. "He's freaking adorable, Jason."

"Thanks. He thinks so, too."

She laughed. Puddy rolled off her lap and came over to Jason. He set the food on the kitchen counter and bent down to rub his hands along Puddy's back. The dog's tail whipped back and forth, then he went over to his water bowl in the kitchen to take several sloppy drinks before running off to his dog bed to pick up his stuffed toy and settle down to go to sleep.

Jason walked over to Erin and held out his hand. She took it and he hauled her to her feet.

"Now we eat," he said.

"Okay. The chicken does smell good."

He was relieved to hear she had an appetite.

He spread the food out on the kitchen island and got plates and utensils out. He piled chicken and mashed potatoes and coleslaw and a biscuit on his plate. He was surprised to see that Erin had a similar setup on hers.

"What?" she asked. "I'm hungry. I haven't eaten all day."

"Hey, I've got no complaints. Let's eat."

They took the food over to the eating area in the kitchen, a small round table that seated about four people, plenty of room for the two of them.

He dug in, and so did Erin. She had put away quite a few glasses of champagne, so he was happy to see her eating her fair share of the food. And if she hadn't eaten much of anything today, it was no wonder she'd been so affected by the alcohol. He'd nibbled a bit on the appetizers, but since he'd hung out with her, he missed the main course dinner, which was too bad because it had looked amazing.

Still, sharing fried chicken in the privacy of his home with Erin wasn't a bad thing, either, and if it got her away from memories of what would have been her wedding reception, that was even better.

After finishing the biscuit that she'd loaded with honey, she licked her fingers. He couldn't help but respond with a tightening in his stomach, watching her tongue swirl around the tips of her fingers, and imagine what her sweet pink mouth and tongue could do wrapped enthusiastically around the head of his cock.

Back the fuck off from that fantasy, dude. Because it's not happening.

He sucked in a breath and got up to clear the table.

"That was so good," she said, clearly oblivious to his state of discomfort, as she should be. "I was starving."

"Yeah? I'm glad you ate."

"Me, too. I was a little tipsy."

"More than a little, I think."

"Uh-oh. What did I do?"

"Nothing embarrassing. I could just tell that you needed to lay off the liquor and get some food."

"Oh, good. Because I haven't done naked table dancing since college."

He frowned. "Wait. What? I missed naked table dancing? We both went to the same college, Erin."

"You graduated two years ahead of me."

"And then I stayed for vet school, so I was around the entire time." He'd polished off his tea, so he filled a glass with ice water and came back to the table. "So when did naked table dancing happen?"

"It wasn't exactly naked. Or fully naked. And it wasn't on campus. It was at the lake. I'm surprised you didn't see the pictures."

His eyes widened. "There are pics?"

"Well, they tried. But Honor and Brenna both threatened to kill people, so they came down pretty fast."

He leaned back in the chair. "Okay. Now I need to hear the entire story."

"It was a bachelorette party for Rachel Novinski, one of my sorority sisters. And let's just say that tequila and I are not besties. And there were shots. Lots and lots of shots. And then dares and music and suddenly my top is off and everyone's laughing and I'm dancing and someone took a picture and fortunately it was dark so you can't really see my boobs all that well, but there you have it."

She took her phone out of her back pocket, scrolled to an album, and handed the phone to him, which surprised the hell out of him.

Yeah, it was dark, and taken from a distance, but he had damn good eyesight, and there was Erin, on top of the bar, her arms over her head, and damn she had beautiful breasts and dark nipples and goddamn he wanted to see her naked more than he wanted to breathe.

He also wanted to punch Owen more than he wanted anything else in his life. Owen could be having his wedding night with this funny, smart, beautiful and sexy woman right now. Instead, he was . . .

Stupid. Boneheaded. An utter dumbass.

Jason looked up at Erin, who was staring at him in a guileless, innocent way.

He handed the phone back to her. "Nice pic."

She laughed. "Right. I don't know why I haven't deleted it, other than it was a fun night."

"Save the pic. When you're eighty years old and wrinkly and your boobs are hanging to your belly, you can look at that picture and say, 'Hey, look at me. I was hot as fuck.'"

She stared at him. "Is that what I am?"

"Hell yeah you are."

She got up and came over to him, nudged him away from the table, and straddled his lap.

He'd like to think of himself as the kind of guy who'd never take advantage of a woman in a vulnerable state. And Erin was about as vulnerable as anyone right now. She needed validation, to know that she was desirable, that Owen had made a huge mistake. She should already know that, but he understood where her head was right now. And just because she was beautiful and smelled like lemons and she felt perfect sitting on his lap and he'd wanted her since high school didn't mean he was going to do anything about it.

Not tonight, anyway.

"So if I'm so hot, why aren't we having sex?"

He grasped her hips—gently, because what he really wanted to do was dig his fingers into the denim of her jeans and rock her against what was fast becoming a hard anatomical problem for him.

"Because you're hurting, and this isn't what you want."

She arched a brow. "How do you know what I want?"

"I don't. Not really. But tonight, your heart hurts, doesn't it?"

"My heart doesn't even figure into this equation." She pushed off of him and wandered into the living room and plopped down on his sofa. Puddy jumped up next to her and she absently stroked his back.

He took a minute to catch his breath and clean the remnants of their dinner from the table. He put the leftovers in the fridge, then wet a towel to wipe down the table and counter. When he made his way back to the living room, Erin was lying on the sofa. He got closer and realized she was asleep, Puddy curled up against her.

Probably for the best. He had planned to talk to her, try to reason with her and make her see that sex wasn't what she needed tonight.

He pulled her shoes off and she curled her knees up. He took a blanket off the back of the sofa and covered her.

"You keep watch over her, Puds. Come get me if she needs anything."

His dog would cuddle her all night.

He turned off the light and headed down the hall to his bedroom.

CHAPTER
......
five

W HEN ERIN WOKE, she realized three things.

One, she smelled coffee, and she needed a cup desperately.

Two, she was not in her own bed.

And, three, she was nestled up against someone very warm. She peeked one eye open to see Jason's dog Puddy snuggling against her chest.

Okay, that part was forgivable. She hadn't forced herself on Jason. Not that she could remember, anyway. And if she had, she would hope that she'd be naked in Jason's bed and not fully clothed on his sofa.

She sat up and Puddy jumped off the sofa. And then she caught sight of Jason in the kitchen. She rolled her legs over and stood, realizing her mouth tasted like a dry desert and she had the worst headache of her life.

Jason smiled. "There's two acetaminophen on the table and a glass of water. I put an extra toothbrush and some toothpaste in the guest bathroom."

"Bless you," she said, making her way to the table to down the water and the tablets. After downing those, she headed into the bathroom next to take care of business and brush the aftereffects of the overabundance of last night's champagne from her teeth. She felt much better, other than her hair looking like an absolute train wreck. At least she had a ponytail holder, so she finger-combed her hair into some semblance of order and wound it into a messy bun. Her shirt was wrinkled and she'd really like a shower, but this would have to do for now. The most important thing at the moment was coffee.

She headed out toward the kitchen, where Puddy was busily shoving his face into a bowl of food.

"He stayed on the sofa with you all night," Jason said.

"No wonder I slept like the dead. He's very cuddly."

"Yeah. Even in my huge bed he thinks he owns seventy-five percent of it."

She smiled and looked down at the pup. "But he's so cute."

"Which is why I let him get away with it sometimes. How do you take your coffee?"

"Just a touch of cream, if you have it."

"I do." He'd already brewed her a cup, so he pushed the cream toward her. She put a dollop in and lifted the mug to her lips for a sip, followed by another, then leaned against the kitchen island in utter bliss.

"Mmm. I needed this. Thank you. And sorry for passing out in your living room."

"Not a problem. You were tired."

"I don't even remember falling asleep. Or much of anything last night, really. I must have been blitzed."

"You did have a lot of champagne."

"Hmm. What else did I do?"

"No naked table dancing, if that's what you're afraid of."

Bits and pieces of last night came floating back to her,

kind of like puzzle pieces that didn't quite fit yet. "Naked . . . Oh, God, I told you about that, didn't I?"

"Yup. And showed me the picture."

She wished a black hole would swallow her up right at this moment. "That's just awesome. Remind me to never have champagne again. What else did I do?"

He leaned against the counter and sipped his coffee, a perfect specimen of the male species with his low-slung relaxed jeans and a T-shirt that hugged his nicely sculpted chest and shoulders.

"You also propositioned me for sex. Twice. Maybe three times?"

She winced. "I did?"

"Yeah."

"And you turned me down?" Hopefully.

"I did."

"I don't know whether to be grateful or insulted."

"Trust me, I didn't want to turn you down."

"You didn't?"

"Come on, Erin. I'm an average guy and you're a beautiful woman. Hell no I didn't want to turn you down. But you were drunk and vulnerable. And I don't take advantage."

Jason was anything but average. "Thank you. I appreciate that. I would have felt awful if we had sex."

"Uh, thanks?"

She laughed. "Not that way. I mean, if we're going to do it, I want to be fully aware so I can enjoy every second of it."

"Good to know."

She could not believe she was having this conversation with a guy she'd known her whole life. She and Jason had been friends for as long as she could remember.

She'd punched him in the face when they were kids. He was her buddy, her confidant. Owen's best friend. To think of him in that way was . . .

Not exactly unthinkable, really. As they stood there in his kitchen, she realized how gorgeous he was. Tall and muscular with dark bedroom eyes and a strong jaw and amazing forearms and long legs.

She'd been thrown off the horse, metaphorically speaking. Getting back on was the best thing she could do for herself right now. Easing the pain of rejection by having a revenge fling would make her feel better. And who better to do that with than with Owen's best friend? Wouldn't that dig the knife in perfectly?

"So let's just say that I wanted to have a no-strings fling. Would you be game?"

"No."

Okay, that was an abrupt answer. She pursed her lips and studied him. "Why? Because you're Owen's best friend and concerned about his feelings?"

"His feelings? Trust me, I'm as angry with Owen as you are right now. He's my friend, but I'm pissed at what he did to you, Erin. But fucking me isn't going to make you feel better."

"It might. And I want to do it with someone I trust. Someone I know won't hurt me."

He pushed off the counter and came over to her, stopping just inches away from her. "You'd risk losing our lifelong friendship for what? So you can ease some ache that isn't going to get any better by having sex?"

He had a point. She valued her friendship with Jason and wouldn't want to do anything to lose that. But at the same time, she wanted to hurt Owen. And doing Jason? That would hurt her ex-fiancé in a major way.

"I'd be using you," she said.

"Yes."

"Does that hurt your feelings?"

He paused before answering, and she wondered why.

"No. But I'm more concerned about your feelings. Your heart. Haven't you been hurt enough?"

"This won't hurt me, Jason. Because my heart won't be involved."

"Right. Because you don't care about me."

She laid her hand on his chest, feeing the rock-hard muscle there, along with the rapid beating of his heart. "I do care about you. I've always cared about you. Just . . . not that way, if you know what I mean."

"Yeah, I know what you mean." He took her hand and wrapped both of his around it. His fingers felt warm and powerful surrounding hers, and she realized how much she needed to feel . . . wanted.

He put her hand down. "I'll think about it. In the meantime, I should drive you home."

She nodded, trying not to show the disappointment she felt. "Sure."

He didn't say much on the drive back to the house, then dropped her off in front. She slid out of the truck.

"Thanks for taking care of me last night."

"No problem," he said.

She lingered, her hand on the open truck door, not knowing what to say, but not wanting to say good-bye just yet.

"So . . . you'll think about it and let me know?"

"Yeah. I'll think about it. See you later, Erin."

"Okay. Bye."

She shut the door and walked up the steps, realizing he was waiting there until she went inside. With a sigh, she opened the door and walked in, then peeked through the glass to watch him drive away.

Okay, so she'd planted the seed. With a little push, she knew she could get him there. Not that she was irresistible or anything, but she and Jason were lifelong friends. He'd come around in time. And if he didn't, well, that'd be okay, too.

She just wanted some fun. She deserved that, didn't she?

She went up to her room, grateful not to find her wedding dress hanging prominently on her closet door anymore. After sending up a mental thank-you to her mom or sisters for removing the dress, she stripped and climbed into the shower, scrubbing away last night's makeup and hangover. When she got out, she combed out her hair and changed into a clean pair of leggings and a T-shirt, then dried her hair and went downstairs.

It was nearly lunchtime, which was good because she was starving.

"You're home," Brenna said, coming up to hug her. "Where did you go last night?"

"Jason's house."

Honor came up behind her and put an arm around her. "Are you all right?"

"I'm fine. A little tired and worn out, but I'm good."

"She stayed with Jason last night," Brenna said.

Honor's brows rose.

"I stayed at Jason's house last night," Erin corrected. "I did not sleep with him. Unfortunately."

Brenna frowned. "Unfortunately?"

"Yes. I'm trying to plan a revenge fling, and Jason is being uncooperative."

They made their way into the dining room, where her

mother and father were already seated. Erin turned to her sisters. "We'll discuss this after lunch."

The last thing she wanted was to have a conversation about sex—or her wanting sex—with her parents in the room.

Her mom hugged her. "You look rested."

"I passed out on Jason's couch. With his dog. Puddy and I slept there all night."

Her dad laughed. "Puddy is a fine pit bull puppy."

"Well, he cuddles like a champion, that's for sure."

Her mother patted her cheek. "I'm glad you got some rest. Still, there are dark circles under your eyes."

Nothing like brutal honesty from your mom. "Probably from all the stress and crying, which I'm now over."

"Are you?" her mom asked.

"Yes. Now we put Owen and all the wedding nonsense behind us, and we move forward."

Her dad made a harrumphing noise. "Until that boy shows his face in town again, and then he and I will have a conversation."

Erin sighed. "Dad, please."

"He needs a talking-to. Or a swift kick in the ass."

"No, he needs to be ignored. By all of us. For the rest of his life."

"Let it go for now," Erin's mother said.

She wanted to argue, but then Louise, their cook, brought out lunch, and food took precedence. She dove in and ate, glad to have her appetite back after days of not wanting to eat. She stuffed herself with salad and ham and vegetables until she could barely move. When she was finished, she went outside to walk it off, relieved to have another day off to allow herself some breathing space before she had to go back to work tomorrow.

Her sisters came up on either side of her.

"Okay, so about Jason," Brenna said.

"Yes," Honor said. "We were just getting to the good part when Mom and Dad came in."

She knew her sisters weren't going to let that go.

"There is no good part. We ate fried chicken, then I propositioned him. He said no."

"Why did he say no?" Brenna asked.

"This morning he told me that we've been friends since we were kids, and he doesn't want to do anything to ruin that."

"Aww," Honor said. "That's sweet."

"And honorable," Brenna said.

"Yeah, whatever." Erin would have rather had great revenge sex last night.

They walked along the side of the house toward the backyard, heading toward the gazebo. It had always been their sanctuary, a place where no business was conducted and no guests were allowed. Erin often took her lunch break out here, especially in the spring, when it was finally warm outside and the flowers were up and the grass was green again.

She took a seat on one of the cushioned benches. Honor and Brenna sat across from her.

"So you propositioned him and he turned you down," Honor said. "That surprises me."

Erin frowned. "Why?"

"He's a guy," Brenna said. "You'd think he'd jump on the opportunity for sex."

"Oh. I guess. It doesn't matter anyway. I'm going to change his mind."

"Good lord, Erin, why?" Honor asked.

She lifted her chin. "Because I intend to have my revenge on Owen. And what better way to do that than with Jason?"

"So you're going to use Jason to get back at Owen?" Brenna asked.

"It's hardly using him if we both get sex out of it. And it's not like I'm declaring my love for him or anything. It'll just be a fun fling. Then we'll go back to being friends."

Honor cast a worried gaze at her. "I don't know, Erin. I don't think flings with friends work that way."

"Well, I'm sure as hell not going to grab some random at a bar and screw him."

"Of course not," Brenna said. "Maybe you should . . . rethink this whole revenge-fling idea entirely."

She shook her head. "Nope. My former fiancé is enjoying our honeymoon in Aruba by himself at the moment. At least I think he's by himself. For all I know he could be with another woman."

"I doubt that," Honor said.

"I don't doubt anything at this point," Erin said. "Clearly I don't know a damn thing about Owen like I thought I did. Anyway, I should be entitled to a little fun, too, don't you think?"

"Kind of hard to argue with that one," Honor said, looking over at Brenna.

Brenna shrugged. "I don't even know what to say. When I got a divorce, I moved back here, started jogging around the property, lost ten pounds and bought new clothes. That was revenge enough for me."

"And you were miserable the entire time," Erin said, cocking her head to the side to prove her point. "You should have gotten on another horse immediately. And by horse, I mean another man."

"I know what you meant. And getting anywhere near another man was the last thing I wanted at the time."

"Come to think of it, it's been two years, Brenna. Have you even dated anyone seriously since Mitchell?"

"Not that I've noticed," Honor said.

"I've dated. And I've been busy. The vineyard keeps me occupied."

"The vineyard doesn't give you orgasms," Erin said.

Honor sputtered out a laugh. Brenna glared at her.

"I can take care of my own orgasms, thank you," Brenna said.

"Not the same thing at all and you know it. And it's more than the orgasms I'm after."

"You want everyone in town to know you've moved on, that you've got a guy and you're having the time of your life and not thinking about Owen at all."

She looked over at Honor and nodded. "Exactly."

"I can understand that. You're hurt and you don't want people to feel sorry for you. I think it's more that people are hurting for you."

"I don't want that, either. I just want to go back to the way things were—without Owen, of course."

She sighed. She had to go to the condo and get her stuff, then figure out how to get out of the lease. No, she'd let Owen figure that out. He caused this mess, he could deal with the condo. Or live in the condo by himself. She really didn't care what he did.

All she wanted was to have some fun. Why was that too much to ask?

"You know what I think?" Brenna asked.

"No, but I'm sure you'll tell me."

"I think you should do whatever makes you happy. If you want to have a fling, go have a damn fling. Go have wild monkey sex. Burn bright, little sister. You damn well deserve it after what Owen did to you."

Erin blinked. This was so not like her normally reserved oldest sister. "Seriously."

"Yes. I know I'm always the one to advise caution, but

you should grab some happiness for yourself, especially right now. I did it all wrong after Mitchell and I divorced. And all I've been doing is hiding out ever since."

Honor cracked a smile. "Now you're talking, Brenna."

"So does that mean you're going to get out there and start dating again?" Erin asked, hopeful that her sister would do something other than run the vineyard with Dad.

"I have dated some, just not a lot. And I don't know. We'll see. I'm more interested in you getting back on your feet again."

Erin stood and looked down at her feet. "Look at me. Back on my feet. Back to you, Brenna."

"Funny." Brenna stood. "I'm doing just fine. I have the vineyard, the garden, my friends, my other projects. I stay plenty busy."

Brenna always had a project going on. She loved the vineyard, but she also loved planting vegetables with Mom, and there were fresh flowers in the house because the Bellini property had loads of flowers thanks to Brenna's green thumb. And there was always something new and exciting to read in the library thanks to Brenna's frequent trips to the bookstore in the city. And their family lineage on both the Bellini and Connor sides had been traced back to the eighteenth century thanks to Brenna's detailed work on genealogy.

But what Erin wanted for Brenna was to put the pain of her divorce aside and find someone worthy of her love. She had so much of it to give.

"Those are things," Honor said. "Projects to occupy your time. We both want you to be happy."

Brenna held out her hands. "I am happy. And we aren't talking about me. We're talking about Erin."

"I'm fine," Erin said. "And I'll take my love life— correction—sex life, into my own hands."

Honor wrinkled her nose. "You might want to re-phrase that."

Realizing what it sounded like, Erin said, "Good point. I'll go after what I want and I'll get it."

"Atta girl," Brenna said. "As for me, I'll take every-thing you both said under advisement."

Which meant Brenna would consider being Brenna. But she hoped her sister would get out there and start dating again.

In the meantime, Erin had to figure out how to get Jason on board with her plan for hot revenge sex. Because she was going to do this. Do him.

She just had to get him to agree to it.

CHAPTER

......

six

Jason FINISHED MEASURING, then cut the piece of wood he was going to use to fit to the deck he was building in the backyard. He nailed it to the pieces already in place, then measured for the next piece. He went back to the saw and swiped sweat from his face. It was damn hot, but he wanted to get as much of this deck done as he could before the sun went down.

Puddy had a ball in his mouth. He flung the ball up in the air, then did a terrible job of catching it. But since it rolled away, it was a fun game for him. At least his dog was good at amusing himself.

A truck rolled up in the driveway, so Puddy ran to the gate and wagged his tail. Clay Henry stepped out and came to the gate with his Labrador, Homer.

"Okay if we come back?" Clay asked.

"Sure."

He opened the gate and Homer shot in, immediately running amok with Puddy. They took off toward the back part of the property, both of them nearly running over each other.

Jason grinned at that.

"What brings you over this way?" Jason asked.

"I had to get a few things at the feed store, so I thought I'd stop by and see if you wanted to grab some dinner."

"I thought Alice was in town."

"She flew to LA this afternoon. She has a few client meetings set up, so she'll be gone a couple of days."

Jason grabbed a rag from his back pocket and wiped his hands. "Let's go inside and get something cold to drink."

"Sounds good."

After he swiped the sawdust from his jeans, they walked inside and Jason washed his hands at the kitchen sink, then grabbed two beers from the fridge. They took seats at the kitchen table.

"So it's working out okay for the two of you?" Jason asked.

Clay took a pull from his beer, then nodded. "Better than I'd hoped, actually. Alice has her office all set up at the house, and she teleconferences with a lot of her clients. Then she sets up face-to-face meetings once they're interested in signing up with her matchmaking service. So she hasn't been gone as much as I thought she would."

"That's great. I know you like having her around."

"Yeah, I do."

"And she doesn't miss LA? This is a much slower-paced lifestyle."

"She says she likes it better. No traffic, she loves the weather, especially rain, and she loves all the friends she's made."

"I'm really happy for you, Clay."

"Thanks."

They drank their beers in silence for a few minutes, allowing Jason to cool down in the air-conditioning.

"So what are we gonna do about Owen?" Clay asked.

"Hell if I know."

"None of what happened is like him," Clay said. "That's what I don't understand. The Owen I know would never walk out on his fiancée just days before the wedding. Not without a good damn reason."

Jason took a drink and nodded. "Agree. But he's not answering anyone's calls, not even his parents'. So I don't know, Clay. He's got a lot to answer for."

"To Erin, first and foremost."

Clay had that pegged right. "That's for sure. Though I don't think she's in the mood to listen to anything he's going to say."

"Can't say I blame her," Clay said. "At least she has the whole town on her side. I talked to his parents and even they're pissed at him."

Jason had talked to them as well. They were confused, hurt and angry, and even more irritated that their son couldn't be bothered to answer his phone. He was mad about that, too. And also worried about Owen.

"I stopped off at The Screaming Hawk Brewery yesterday," Jason said. "His employees have no idea what's going on. When he left on Wednesday, he told them he'd see them when he got back from the honeymoon. Now, with everything that happened, and not being able to get hold of him, they're wondering if he's okay. They're worried about their boss and their jobs."

Clay frowned. "And now I'm thinking he's an even bigger asshole. He'd better not be lying on some beach dead or I'll kill him."

Jason laughed. "You and me both. He's probably fine, having the time of his life, and we're all worried about him for nothing."

Clay finished off his beer and pushed it away. "Which only makes me angrier. Let's go get a burger."

"Okay." He supposed the back deck project could be put off for another day, because now he was hungry. And irritated at Owen. Plus, he hadn't seen Erin for two days. He should check in on her while he was out and see how she was doing.

Then again, after her suggestion that they become sex friends, maybe some distance was a good thing. Because despite telling her no, he wanted her. Hell, he'd always wanted her. And being the sensible one was going to be really damned hard.

For now, though, the only thing on his mind was having a good meal. Tomorrow, he'd think about talking to Erin and seeing how long his resolve was going to last.

CHAPTER

· · · · · ·

seven

BURYING HERSELF IN wedding budgets and schedules, vineyard profitability forecasts and future planning was exactly what Erin had needed to keep her mind off of herself and her stupid feelings. She had been submerged in work for the past few days, exactly how she liked it.

She'd closed herself in her office every day, and had been diligently working on getting both the vineyard and the wedding business in order. Fortunately, no one had bothered her. Of course she'd had meals with the family, but other than that, she had stayed occupied.

Honor knocked on her office door, which was actually two beautiful white French doors with glass because while she liked privacy to work, she also liked to be able to see outside of her office.

She motioned for Honor to come in.

"I know you've been busy. I don't mean to interrupt, but we have the Hansen/Marsey wedding next weekend and I want to discuss a few items with you."

"Sure. Come on in."

She pulled up the wedding file on her laptop while Honor took a seat in one of the chairs across from her desk. "Okay, what's up?"

Honor looked down at her notes. "Ellen called and said she and Tamira wanted to increase the final guest count by fifty people. And they've added three more cases of the merlot and two more cases of the prosecco."

Erin found the line items and made the changes in the wedding budget so she could adjust the final invoice. "Got it. Anything else?"

She sighed. "Nothing."

They always talked to each other about their respective jobs within the structure of the family business, because sometimes you just had to vent. "What is it, Honor?"

"I don't want to bother you with wedding stuff, Erin."

She rolled her eyes. "I'm not going to crumple every time the word 'wedding' is mentioned, if that's what you're worried about. It's what we do here. It's May. We have a wedding every weekend from now until October. I think I can handle it. Spill."

"Fine. The Taylor/Giani wedding this weekend? The cake decorator's mom has to have surgery and they aren't going to be able to make the cake."

Erin looked up from her laptop. "Oh, crap."

"Yes."

"Is the bride-to-be having a panic attack?"

"She called me in tears and said her wedding was ruined."

Not the first time Erin had heard that about a bride-to-be. The week of the wedding was always the most stressful time, and a time when if something was going to go wrong, it generally would. Erin had firsthand knowledge of that now. She only wished her own wedding disaster had been of the cake variety.

"And you told her you'd call Rietta, right?" Rietta May were their savior, a wonderful friend of the family who had been making cakes for over forty years.

Honor nodded. "We're meeting with her this afternoon. The only problem is that Heather had this elaborate cake design in mind and I'm not sure Rietta can pull it off with such short notice."

"Hey, she'll get a wedding cake that didn't come from the grocery store. She should consider herself fortunate."

"Let's hope she sees it that way."

Erin sighed. "I don't envy you your job, Honor. Dealing with brides is like defusing bombs."

Honor laughed. "It's not that bad. Most of my brides are lovely."

"Uh-huh. If you say so."

"You're just not a people person."

"If by that you mean that I'd tell prospective brides, their pushy mothers and whatever family members who want the world at a discount to kiss my ass, then yes, I'm not a people person."

"Which is why I handle the weddings."

"And I do the budgets. Happily. Alone in my beautiful office."

Honor lifted her lips in a teasing smile. "You mean your ivory tower."

"Hey. I don't live in an ivory tower. I get out. In fact, I have an appointment for a massage in an hour."

"Good for you. After all the stress you've had, you deserve it."

"Damn right I do."

Honor stood. "Okay, thanks for letting me vent. I need to get some things done before I meet Heather at Rietta's bakery."

"You have fun with that."

Honor smiled on her way out. "And you enjoy your massage."

"I intend to."

Erin went back to work, losing herself in her spreadsheets. When she looked up, she realized she'd totally lost track of time and she only had twenty minutes to make it into the city.

She could do this. She exited the program she was working on, grabbed her purse and her keys and tucked her phone in her bag. She sent a quick text message to her mom to let her know she'd be gone for a couple of hours, then dashed outside to get in her car.

She left the property and headed down the road that would lead to the highway.

Honor was right. She needed this massage. She'd gotten the gift certificate as a wedding shower gift, and since it wasn't returnable, decided she might as well use it. After all, Owen was probably sunning himself on the beaches of Aruba, so she might as well have some enjoyment out of what would have been her honeymoon week.

That bastard.

She could feel the tension in her shoulders. Oh, yeah, she definitely needed someone to work the rage out of her back muscles.

Something dark skirted in front of her car and she slammed on the brakes, skidding to a halt.

What the hell was that? It was too small to be a deer, but too big to be a squirrel. Also, it stopped on the side of the road.

Oh, crap, she hadn't felt a thud under her tires, but still, she hoped she hadn't hit it, whatever it was. No, she would have felt it if she'd hit it, but it wasn't moving.

Dammit. She put the car in Park and got out, wanting to make sure that whatever it was wasn't injured.

She approached slowly so as not to spook it.

"Hey, little thing. Are you okay?" she asked, using her softest voice.

As she got closer, she could see it was a dog. Not a dog. A puppy. A furry brown and dirty, matted little puppy. She crouched down to see it was trembling. And it was easy to see there was something wrong with its leg.

"Oh, you poor baby. Are you okay?"

The little thing wasn't even trying to get away from her, but looked up at her with sad, soulful brown eyes that made her tear up.

"You're hurt, baby. Let me help you."

She scooped the puppy—she looked and it was a her—up and cradled her close. "Don't you worry, little girl. Erin is going to take care of you."

So much for her massage appointment. But this little pup needed help, and that took priority. She got back in the car, grabbed a blanket from the back seat and laid the pup on the blanket on her lap. She settled right in, no longer shaking.

Okay. She had to take the pup to Jason.

He'd know what to do.

"I KNOW BUSTER loves sausages, Mrs. Klein. But the fact is, your dachshund is fat."

His client, a very lovely woman in her seventies, offered him a concerned look. "He eats meals with me. Since Al died, he's been my only companion. With the children spread out in different states, I just wanted to feel like I had someone to share my life, you know?"

"I understand. And you can still do that. We'll write out a plan for how much of his dog food you can split into three meals a day. But only give him dog food. Table scraps are bad for his pancreas, some foods are toxic to animals, and overfeeding him will ultimately shorten his life."

Mrs. Klein winced. "I thought I was giving him love, and instead I'm hurting him."

He saw the tears well in her eyes and wished he hadn't been the one to put them there, but here at his clinic he had to be Dr. Jason Callum, veterinarian, and that meant his primary concern was for the animals in his care.

"Do you take walks?"

She nodded. "Around the neighborhood. It's so lovely this time of year. My friends and I like to see all the flowers."

"Take Buster with you. He can use the exercise and it'll help get his weight off faster."

Her face brightened as she smiled. "Oh, he'll enjoy that. I'll be sure to do that every day."

As he walked out of the exam room with Mrs. Klein and Buster, he put an arm around her. "I know you love him. You and Buster can do this."

She looked down at her waddling dog. "Of course we can, can't we, Buster?"

He looked over at Casey, his tech. "Set Mrs. Klein up on the low-cal dog food and a three-time-a-day feeding schedule for his weight, including when and how to offer some allowable treats."

She nodded and walked away with Mrs. Klein.

Jason went back into the hallway and stopped to review some lab reports that had just come in. He was particularly interested in one for a ten-year-old mastiff he'd seen a couple of days ago who presented with a sizable lump on his belly. They'd removed the lump and taken a biopsy. From the looks of the sample it hadn't appeared to be just fibrous or fatty tissue, so they'd sent it off to the lab.

He was relieved to read the report and discover the cells weren't cancerous. Jose and Teresa would be relieved to know their dog was going to be okay.

Joe, one of his techs, came over to the desk. "We have an emergency in room five, Dr. Callum. And the woman specifically asked to see you."

He worked with two other vets, so typically whoever wasn't busy with a patient or in surgery would take any incoming emergencies. But if someone asked for a certain veterinarian they also tried to accommodate the request.

"Be right there." He left the rest of the reports in his inbox and washed his hands, then made his way to the exam room, surprised to find Erin in there holding on to a mess of a puppy that couldn't be more than six months old.

"Hey, Erin."

She stood. "I was driving down our main road and this little girl dashed away from my car. I stopped to check on her. I think something's wrong with her leg."

"Okay. Let's take a look." His tech Joe had come in with him, so Joe set up a towel on the exam table and took the pup from Erin's arms to place her on the table.

Erin stood up there with them.

"I didn't hit her, Jason."

At her worried look, Jason offered up a smile. "I didn't think you did."

He felt around the pup's body, looking for swelling or fractures anywhere else. He didn't find anything that felt out of place, fortunately. He took out his stethoscope and listened to her heartbeat, as well as other parts of her, hoping he wouldn't hear anything out of sorts. Everything sounded good, too. Her three uninjured legs were fine, so he concentrated on her front left paw.

The puppy cried when he tried to straighten her leg, and Jason could tell from feel that there was something off.

He looked up at Joe. "Let's get an x-ray."

Joe nodded, scooped the pup up in his arms and carried her out the door.

Erin chewed on her bottom lip and cocked her head to the side. "Do you think she's going to be okay?"

"Other than the leg, she seems fine. A little undernourished, which isn't a surprise considering where you found her. People dump unwanted animals on country roads all the time."

Erin frowned. "Those people are assholes."

"Yeah, they are."

"She's so sweet, Jason. She just laid in my lap the entire way here, snuggling close to me like she didn't have anyone to love her."

He saw her eyes shimmer with tears.

Shit. He stepped in and put his arms around her. She laid her head on his chest, her hands pressed against him, and all he wanted to do was make this all right for her.

He took a step back and looked down into her incredibly sad green eyes.

"We'll fix her, Erin."

"I know you will."

"I'm gonna go take a look at those x-rays. Take a seat, take a breath and I'll be back soon."

She nodded and he escaped the room and leaned against the door so he could take a breath, too.

Something about being so close to Erin always made him feel so . . .

Hell. He didn't know how he felt, but she messed him up in a way he couldn't explain.

He went over and read the x-rays, grimacing as he

examined them closely. He'd thought maybe it was a sprain, but it was more complicated than that.

He walked back into the exam room. Joe had brought the pup back in so Erin was cradling her against her chest. She looked up.

"What's the verdict?"

"She has a fracture of the radius and ulna."

"Okay. How do we fix it?"

"I'll have to do surgery and realign the break, then put in some screws and plates to make sure the bones don't move."

"Oh. Will she be okay?"

"She'll be fine. It won't hinder her mobility, though whoever fosters her during her recovery will have to limit her mobility some while she recovers."

Erin cuddled the pup closer. "Someone will foster her?"

"I'm assuming she was dumped on the side of the road, Erin. We'll have to find a foster organization to take her in. Then, when her cast comes off, she'll go up for adoption."

She looked down at the pup. "What if I wanted to keep her?"

"You want to foster her?"

"No. I want to keep her. Adopt her. Make her part of my family forever."

Oh, crap. He was already in dangerous territory with Erin as it was. And now she wanted to keep this dog?

"You can definitely do that, but she'll require some extra care. You sure you're up for that?"

"I'm absolutely up for it. You tell me what I need to do and I'll take care of it."

"Okay. First, she probably needs a name."

"Agatha."

He laughed. "That was quick."

"Come on, look at her face. Doesn't she look like an Agatha?"

He looked at the pup, who had fallen asleep cradled in Erin's arms. "Sure. We'll note it on her chart. Agatha Bellini."

Erin grinned. "Perfect. Hey, what do you think her breed is?"

"Let me see her." He went over and Erin handed the puppy over to Jason. The puppy yawned and opened its eyes. It had distinctive coloring and fur, but he couldn't be certain of all of its origins. Some were clear though.

"For sure it's part Goldendoodle."

"What's that?"

"Golden retriever and poodle. It's a very popular mixed breed. But there's something else mixed with it and I can't say for certain what that is. She sure is cute, though."

"Exactly. So why would anyone dump her? She's adorable. A little filthy and she smells, but she's adorable."

"No clue why some people are dicks. But you're right. She's very cute. We'll get her cleaned up before we give her back to you, and we'll give her all the vaccinations she needs to have at this age."

She smiled, and her face lit up. "Thank you. I know you'll take good care of her."

"I'll do the surgery this afternoon, and I'll call you once it's done."

"When can I take her home?"

"Probably tomorrow."

"Okay. I'll get things ready for her." She stood. "Oh, food and toys and things. I've never had a dog, Jason. I don't know anything."

"I can help you with that. Want me to take you shopping tonight?"

"That would be great, thanks."

He nodded. "No problem. I'll text you once I get home."

"Sure. I'll let you get to work."

She started to turn, then went over to him and flung her arms around him. "Thank you."

He couldn't help but wrap his arms around her again, absorbing the feel of her body pressed to his. "You're welcome. I've . . . got to go."

He took a quick step back, needing the distance from her to gather his bearings.

"Oh, right. You go work. I'll wait to hear from you. See you later, Jason."

She looked nervous, but there was a small twinkle of joy in her eyes.

The puppy put that there. Not him.

And he needed to remember that.

CHAPTER

· · · · · ·

eight

Erin told her parents about the incident with the puppy that day, and also that she'd be bringing it home with her, bracing herself for the potential blowup.

Surprisingly, it didn't happen. Her mother—who was not an animal lover—told her she would be fully responsible for the pup, and her father's eyes twinkled as he nodded in agreement. After that, the subject was closed.

That had gone better than she'd expected.

Maybe her parents figured she'd had enough crushing disappointment and they were giving her a break. She certainly hadn't intended to use being left at the altar as a way to finagle puppy acceptance out of her parents, but hey, whatever worked, right?

Besides, she wouldn't be staying with them forever. She was going to move out, get her own place and carve out some independence. After all, she was supposed to be moving into the condo next week.

After the honeymoon that she didn't get to have.

I hope you choke on a piña colada, Owen. You bastard.

She wondered what Owen was doing right now. Swimming in that amazing blue water? Sunning himself on the beach? Did he take someone with him?

Was that why he had left her? Did he have another someone, and he hadn't had the guts to tell her about it?

Wouldn't that just add salt to the wound? It would be bad enough having to live in the same vicinity as him when he got back. But knowing he had a girlfriend? That he'd left her for another woman? She'd never live that down.

"You look like you might kill someone."

She'd come back home to finish working on a financial project, figuring keeping herself busy would help pass the time while Agatha was in surgery. Instead, she was sitting at her desk fuming about Owen.

She looked up at Brenna. "Owen."

"Oh." Brenna came in and sat in the chair, then frowned. "He didn't contact you, did he?"

"Of course not. That would be kind. No, I'm just making up 'what if' scenarios in my head and driving myself crazy in the process."

"Don't do that, Erin. There's no sense in trying to figure out why he did it until he explains it himself."

She snorted. "Right. Like he's going to show up all tanned from his trip and this will be his first stop when he gets off the plane."

"He might," Honor said, coming into the room to take the other chair next to Brenna. "He's always been an honorable guy."

"Correction," Erin said. "He *was* an honorable man. Until he ran right before the wedding."

"Why are we even talking about him?" Brenna asked. "I want to know about the new puppy."

"Mom told you?" Erin asked.

"Yes."

"Wait," Honor said, looking from Brenna to Erin. "What puppy?"

Erin filled them in on what had happened when she left the house for her massage appointment, and how she took Agatha into Jason's clinic.

"Aww," Honor said. "When does she get to come home?"

"I don't know. Jason said probably tomorrow."

Her phone buzzed and her heart thudded when she saw it was the clinic. She pushed the button.

"Jason?"

"Miss Bellini, it's Joe from the Well Pet Clinic."

"Oh, hi, Joe. Is Agatha all right?"

"She's fine. We're prepping your pup for surgery and Dr. Callum wanted me to ask you if you also wanted us to spay Agatha while we had her under. She's old enough, and he thought it would spare her from having to have another surgery later on."

"Oh. Yes, of course do that if he doesn't think it'll be too hard on her."

"It won't be. We'll let you know as soon as we're finished with the surgery."

"Thanks, Joe."

She hung up and looked at her sisters. "They're getting ready to start the surgery. They're also going to spay Agatha while they're fixing her leg."

"Good idea," Honor said. "That way she won't have to have a second surgery."

"That's what Joe said."

Brenna cocked her head to the side. "You're nervous."

"Of course I am. You should have seen her, Bren. She was dirty and matted and shivering in my arms."

"And now you're going to be a mommy." Brenna's lips lifted. "Hope you're up to the challenge."

Erin lifted her chin. "Of course I am. You think I can't handle having a dog?"

"When have you ever wanted a dog?" Brenna asked. "Or a cat? Or any kind of animal, for that matter. I wanted to get a hamster when we were kids and you screamed about that until Mom said no."

"Hamsters smell."

Brenna rolled her eyes. "Oh, and dogs don't get dirty or stink?"

Honor slanted a sympathetic look at her. "She's got you on that one, Erin."

"Fine. I apologize for the hamster thing. And I promise to keep the puppy as clean as I can."

"Hey, I don't care," Brenna said with a slight shrug of her shoulder. "She's your responsibility. I just think it's ironic since you're the last one of us that ever wanted a pet."

As irritating as Erin found her oldest sister, she was telling the truth. Erin had never been an animal person. Yet something about Agatha's pitiful cries as she lay there in the ditch had called to her in an emotional way that had never hit her before.

"You're right. When we were kids, I never wanted a pet. I mean, yesterday I could say I still didn't want one. But that was yesterday, and as we know, things can change in a heartbeat. Now I do, and I promise to do my best to give her the best life I can."

Brenna opened her mouth to say something, then shut it.

"That's all you can ask for," Honor said. "I know you'll give her all the love you have in you, Erin."

After her sisters left, she finished the project she'd been working on, then organized her files, cleaned her desk, set up her planner for next week and by then she still hadn't heard back from Jason, which only made her stress level shoot up to stratospheric levels.

She needed to talk to someone. She decided to get out and take a walk. She headed outside, breathing in the fresh spring air as she walked along the side yard and toward the vineyards.

She never took part in the vineyard business—not the actual growing of the grapes, anyway. That was Brenna and Dad's job. But she loved coming out here when she needed a break. She'd stroll along to watch the tiny grapes growing on the vine. To her, it signaled growth and renewal, and a wonder at what these grapes could become.

She made her way down the line, checking out some of the riper grapes, nearly ready for picking. She wished she could grab one and taste it, but she knew better.

What she really needed was a nice glass of wine, but she wanted to stay clearheaded, so she went into the clarification room, where she found her dad and Brenna working on a batch of red grapes.

"How's it going?" she asked.

"Good," her father said. "What brings you out here?"

"Just . . . wandering."

"She's waiting to hear from Jason about her new puppy," Brenna said. "He's in surgery right now fixing the pup's broken leg."

"Ah," her father said. "Puppy will be fine. Jason is a good doctor."

"I know he is, Dad. So, what are you working on?"

"Checking this batch of pinot noir," her dad explained. "It's been in fermentation for a month."

"It should be ready to move to clarification soon."

Her father nodded.

Her phone buzzed. She grabbed it and stepped outside.

"Hello?"

"Hey, Erin. It's Jason."

Her stomach tightened. "Hi, Jason. How's Agatha?"

"She came through surgery great. Plates and pins aligned the leg perfectly, and the spay was routine, with no complications."

She sagged against the outside wall in relief. "That's great. So great. Thank you."

"Not a problem. Since she had a double surgery she was under anesthesia a little longer, so she's really groggy right now. We'll keep her overnight to maintain her fluids and keep a close watch on her. You can pick her up tomorrow afternoon."

That would give her time to make things ready for her pup. And for Agatha to recover with people who knew how to take care of her. "Okay, sure."

"Someone on the staff will come in every few hours to check on her. If anything changes with her condition, they'll contact you."

"Thank you."

"Do you still want me to go out to the store to help you pick out things she'll need?"

"You don't have to do that. I'm sure I can figure it out."

"I don't mind. I'm kind of hungry. Maybe we could grab something to eat first?"

"Only if you let me buy you dinner for taking care of Agatha."

He laughed. "Taking care of animals is my job, Erin. It's what I love to do."

Of course it was. Jason was dedicated. Ever since they were kids he'd loved animals. He always said he'd become a veterinarian one day, and he'd never once wavered from his commitment.

"I'm still buying dinner," she said.

"Sold. What are you in the mood for?"

She hadn't even thought about food, in fact wasn't even hungry. "I . . . don't know. You choose something."

"Okay. Tacos. How about that new place everyone's talking about?"

"The one on Memorial? The Asian/Mexican fusion?"

"Yeah."

"Sounds good to me," she said.

"I can meet you there in about forty-five minutes. I have to wrap up a few things here, then dash home and take a quick shower."

"I'll see you then."

She hung up, and walked back to the house. Relieved now that she knew Agatha was going to be all right, she was looking forward to shopping for everything her puppy would need to start her new life.

And she knew Jason would be able to help her with that.

Now that she had relaxed, she could have a glass of wine with dinner and enjoy some great company.

JASON WALKED INTO the restaurant, expecting dark, and was surprised by all the twinkling fairy lights. He'd heard good things about the place, and the smells that hit him made him hopeful.

It had been a long day and he'd barely been able to choke down a turkey sandwich for lunch, which had been hours ago. He was so ready to eat. Fortunately, Erin was punctual, as always, so she was waiting for him inside. She was wearing a brightly colored short-sleeved dress and sandals, her long hair pulled up, giving him a nice view of her neck.

She lifted up to kiss his cheek. "Thanks for saving my puppy's life, and for taking me shopping tonight."

He smiled at her. "You're welcome." Her lips pressed soft against his skin and she smelled like a vanilla ice cream cone. He wanted to linger near her, kiss her back, let her know he felt something for her. But he was still hesitant about intimacy with Erin, about how that would change the dynamic of their friendship. He wanted to give her what she wanted, but he was afraid the cost would be too high—their friendship.

"I like this place," she said. "It's bright and cheery."

"Yeah, it seems nice. I hope the food is good."

"Me, too." She opened up the menu, then wrinkled her nose. "Wine list is super sparse. They only carry a chardonnay and a merlot, and very off brands."

"Maybe they haven't hooked up with a liquor distributor yet."

"Which means they need someone to supply excellent wine to them. Like Red Moss Vineyards wines."

He nodded. "It would be a great tie-in. New local business, supplying wine from a local vineyard."

"Right?" She perused the menu. "I'd like a glass of the chardonnay. And if I'm not back shortly, I'll take the vegan taco, and the pork and crab steamed buns."

"Got it."

"Thanks." She slid off the barstool and grabbed one of her business cards from her purse. "I'm off to talk to the manager."

He smiled as she walked away. The one thing he'd always admired about Erin was that she wasn't shy about pushing the winery or the wedding business. Which she shouldn't be. It was part of her job and he could tell she loved it.

Their server came back so he ordered a beer for himself and Erin's glass of wine, checked text and e-mail messages that he'd ignored all day and replied to a few.

They had a fourth-year veterinary student starting a rotation next week at the clinic, and since Jason was the youngest of the doctors, it was going to be his responsibility to work with her.

It wasn't all that long ago that he was doing his internships at various clinics. It had been his most stressful and yet exciting year, being so damn close to graduating, but not yet a full-fledged doctor. Still, he'd learned a ton under the vets he'd worked with that year, so he intended to do his best with the students who interned under him.

He flipped through his messages. Still nothing from Owen. Damn. He hoped Owen's parents were okay. He made a mental note to call them tomorrow to see how they were doing. He knew they'd let him know if they'd heard anything.

Erin surprised him by sliding back into her seat.

"Done already?"

"Yes. I talked to the manager, who's also the owner of the restaurant. Actually, it's a husband and wife enterprise and they're both here. Dinner is busy for them, but they're very interested in stocking wines from a local vineyard, so I have an appointment with them tomorrow at nine."

"That's excellent. I hope it works out for you."

She took a sip of her wine, then nodded. "Me, too. They're a small enterprise, but they said they know several of the restaurants in the area who might also be interested in stocking our wines. So if this works out, we might also be able to pick up additional business."

Their server stopped by, so they ordered their food. He ordered pork buns and some oyster soup, along with fish tacos.

After their server left, he took a long pull of his beer.

"You must be hungry," Erin said.

"I had a busy day with no damn time to eat. I'm starving."

"I'm sorry. I probably added to your busy day."

"All my days are like that, Erin. Emergencies come in and I deal with it. Today was no different from any other day."

She swirled the wine around in her glass, then took a sip and set the glass on the table. "Do you love it?"

"The job? Hell yeah I love it. It's everything I always thought it was going to be. Except longer hours on the days I'm on call."

"Are you on call tonight?"

"No. Which is why I wanted to go into practice with other doctors. While I always wanted to be a veterinarian, I didn't want to work twenty-four-seven. I also wanted to have a life."

"I can't blame you for that. But still, you do work hard."

"I like to stay busy. So do you."

"I do. Busy makes me happy. Especially right now."

He fiddled with the label on his beer. "So you don't have to think about Owen?"

"Yes."

"You know eventually he'll come back."

"Will he? He might stay in Aruba, set up a brewery there."

His lips lifted. "You hope. But then you wouldn't get closure."

She polished off her wine, then waved the empty glass at her server for a refill. "Closure is for losers. And I've already been one of those. I don't intend to ever speak to him again. So I hope he finds his miserably-ever-after in Aruba. Or wherever. As long as it's not near me."

When their server returned with another glass of wine

for Erin, Jason handed his empty beer to her. "I'll have a water."

He turned his attention back to Erin. "You'll have to talk to him eventually."

"No, I won't. The Owen chapter of my life is closed."

"Yeah? And what's the next chapter?"

She traced a nail down his forearm. "Jason."

He laughed. "We're just having dinner, Erin. And then shopping. Your next chapter is Agatha."

"Why are you so resistant to having a little fun?"

"I'm not resistant to fun. I'm resistant to hurting you."

She lifted her chin. "You couldn't possibly hurt me. Because my heart's not in this."

"Your seduction game is a little off. You're not exactly sweeping me off my feet here."

She laughed. "Come on, you know what I mean. We're friends, right?"

"Yeah."

"We've known each other forever. You're hot. I'm hot. So why can't we merge our hotness and blow off some steam?"

She made it sound so easy. And Jason was certainly interested. But he knew it wouldn't be that simple. Not for him, anyway. Not when he'd wanted Erin for years.

Then again, maybe it would be nothing more than having what he'd always wanted. He'd indulge in the fantasy, get it out of his system, and then they could go back to being friends again, no harm no foul.

Easy, right?

Maybe. Maybe not.

Was his lifelong friendship with Erin worth the risk?

Now, that, he didn't have an answer to.

CHAPTER

· · · · · ·

nine

DINNER WAS GREAT. The wine? Eh. Not so great. The chardonnay was weak and lacked flavor. She knew Mr. and Mrs. Dae—and their customers—were going to be so much happier once they started serving Red Moss Vineyards wines.

She left her car in the restaurant parking lot, and they took Jason's truck to the pet supply store.

There was nothing better than having a veterinarian by her side while they walked the aisles and she filled her cart with puppy food and treats and a collar and a leash and toys—oh, God, that was so fun, all the toys.

"I don't think she needs all these toys, Erin."

She gave him a look. "Side of the road with a broken leg, Jason. Of course she needs all these toys."

He shook his head. "You're going to spoil her."

"My stuffed teddy bear had twelve outfits. Was there any doubt?"

"I guess not." He shook his head and they made their way down the next aisle.

By the time they got to the checkout, her cart was full.

Jason looked down at the cart, then up at her.

"What?" she asked. "She needs everything."

"Not all those things. Not the tutu and four teddy bear chew toys and all those snacks. You're going to make her fat."

"She needs training treats. And I'm going to walk her every day. She will not be fat."

"Uh-huh. We'll see."

"Yes, you will see. Agatha is going to be amazing."

"With you as her mama, I have no doubt."

She handed the clerk her credit card, then smiled up at Jason. "That's the sweetest thing you've ever said to me."

Her smile could light up a city. He needed to make sure she did a lot more of that. And if that meant dressing up her dog and buying her twenty-seven toys, then that's the way it would be.

One thing was certain. Agatha wouldn't be neglected, because it was obvious Erin was going to pour all her love into that puppy.

He carried the bags out to his truck and they climbed in.

"We should go somewhere for a drink."

"I have surgery at seven in the morning, Erin. I can't do a lot of drinking before an early surgery day."

She leaned across the seat and laid her hand on his thigh. "How about dancing, then?"

He could tell she had some excess energy she needed to let off. "Fine."

He drove to a dance club a few miles away and parked.

"I haven't been here in years," she said. "Let's go kick off our shoes, metaphorically speaking."

He didn't mention that this was where Owen had first asked her out. He'd been there that night. He wondered if she'd say anything, or balk about the club. Since she didn't, he figured maybe she didn't remember.

They went inside. The club was still dark and atmospheric, but the dance floor was lit, both in brightness and the number of people on the floor.

"Do you want something to drin—"

She grabbed his hand. "Let's go dance."

Okay, so no drink. But Erin was laughing as she got to the floor, and who was he to complain about dancing next to a woman whose hips could move like that?

He let Erin take the lead and she sure as hell was enjoying herself. One song turned into two, then three, and by then sweat was pouring down his back. But if she could take it, so could he.

Fortunately, she finally moved in closer. "I need a drink."

Thank God. Sure, he could handle it, but he'd already put in a full day at work, almost entirely on his feet. And he was thirsty as hell.

They wound their way through the crowd to the bar. Erin ordered a glass of wine and Jason got a beer and a water. He downed the water first to hydrate, then sipped the beer.

"That was so fun," Erin said. "I haven't danced like that in a long time."

"Me, either."

She pressed her finger against his chest. "Then you're dating all the wrong women. And Owen and I hadn't gone dancing in . . ."

He waited, but she'd drifted off.

"In when? When was the last time?"

She took a swallow of wine, then shrugged. "I don't remember. I guess we got busy and forgot to go out."

"Forgot to go dancing, you mean."

"And other things. I need some air."

He followed her outside. There was a back patio with

tables and chairs where people could sit. Erin found them a table, so he took a seat in the chair next to her.

She tilted her head back. "The stars are pretty tonight."

"Yeah." He wasn't going to push her to talk about Owen. If she wanted to discuss him, he'd be there for her as a sounding board, but he sure as hell didn't want to talk about her ex-fiancé right now.

She straightened and picked up the glass. "You know he asked me out here. For our first date."

"Yeah, I know. I was there."

She turned to him. "You were? I don't remember that."

Ouch. "It was you and Brenna and her husband, Honor and some guy she was dating, Clay, Owen and me. We'd just gone to see a movie. I don't remember which movie. But we all came here after."

Her eyes widened. "Oh, that's right. Now I remember. We all went to see *Captain America: Civil War*, then went out to eat and came here for drinking and dancing. We argued about Cap versus Iron Man and who was on whose side."

"I was team Iron Man and you were team Cap."

She shook her head. "And you were wrong, as usual."

"I am never wrong. You were blinded by Captain America's ass."

She shrugged. "It's a very fine ass."

"You are never going to get me to agree with that."

She laughed. "Whatever. Owen picked Cap. And then he asked me out."

"So you went out with him because he agreed with you about Cap's ass."

"No, dumbass. Because I liked him. But it didn't hurt that he was on the side of right."

Jason rolled his eyes. "So if I'd asked you out first, you would have said no because I chose Iron Man?"

"Of course. Iron Man was wrong."

He wasn't sure she was serious or not. He was hoping she was teasing about the Iron Man thing. "Good to know."

"And because we've been friends since we were kids."

"So were you and Owen."

"That's . . . different."

"I see. But now you want to have sex with me."

"Also different."

"How?"

She opened her mouth, then shut it. "I don't know. It was different then. Owen and I had been circling each other for a while before he asked me out. We were both interested. He knew I wanted to go out with him, so when he asked, I jumped. Obviously it was a bad choice."

He heard the pain in her voice and wanted to take it away.

He finished off his beer.

"Like you choosing Cap."

She laughed again. "Asshole. Let's dance."

This time he led her inside and they dove right into a hard rocking beat. When the song ended, something smooth and slow played. He looked at Erin and she shrugged and moved into him, so he took her hand, wrapped his arm around her back and tugged her close, feeling the beat of her heart against his chest.

It was just a slow dance, but she laid her head on his shoulder and strands of her hair teased his chin and she was rubbing her hand over his arm and dammit, he'd wanted her for a lifetime. And all she wanted from him was a revenge fuck so when Owen got back she could tell him she'd boned his best friend.

So not only would he lose Erin, he'd lose Owen, too.

He wanted Erin in his bed, but not that way.

• • • • • •

ERIN WAS HAVING such a good time. A great time, actually. She'd lost herself in music and dancing and the feel of Jason's rock-hard body against hers. For a moment, she'd even forgotten about Owen, and that hadn't happened in . . .

Actually, never. She had Jason to thank for that. Or maybe just the feel of him, the fresh soapy scent of him, the way he smiled at her, the way he made her laugh.

Now, if she played her cards right, maybe he'd ask her to go home with him tonight.

He pulled away. "I need to get home."

Or maybe not. Now she was confused, because he'd been giving off some definite signals tonight. And the way his body reacted to the two of them dancing close had been "I want you in my bed." Not "I want to get away from you."

She shot him a confused look, but nodded. "Okay, sure."

If there was one thing she realized she did not understand at all, it was men.

They got in his truck and he drove her back to the restaurant. Jason was being uncharacteristically quiet. Was he tired? Probably. Was he mad? Had she said or done something to upset him? Normally he talked to her.

And now she was worried, which was stupid. He was probably tired.

He pulled up next to her car and got out, opened her door and carried the bags from the pet store to her car. After he put the bags in her trunk, she turned to him.

"Are you feeling all right?" she asked.

"Yeah, I'm fine. Just have a full schedule tomorrow, so I need some sleep."

She touched his arm. "Thanks for taking me shopping. And dancing."

She teased her fingers along his skin, surprised at her own sexual reaction to touching him.

Whoa.

Sure, she wanted to have sex with him, but this sudden lightning chemistry between them was new. And very exciting. And something she wanted to explore further. Starting with a hot kiss in the parking lot. She took a step forward.

And he took a step back.

"Jason, what's wrong?"

He stuck his hands in his pockets. "I don't know. I can't be what you need me to be, Erin."

She frowned. "And what is it that you think I need you to be?"

"You know what. You want some revenge fling so you can get back at Owen. And that guy isn't me."

"Wow. Okay. You do realize I want more from you than just some one-off fuck, right?"

He dragged his fingers through his hair. "I don't know what you want."

She sighed, realizing she might have given him the wrong impression. "I don't know what I want, either, Jason. Some fun. Kissing. Touching. Maybe some sex. I don't know. But couldn't we explore it together?"

He palmed the hood of her car, his body caging hers. The delicious heat of him surrounded her and she wished they weren't outside in the parking lot. What she wanted was more of him, all of him, unclothed, all of that delicious heat moving against her, inside of her.

"When we're together, Erin? Naked, sweaty, our bodies touching and me kissing and tasting you? It's going to be when your head is clear and you aren't talking about or thinking about Owen. When you're ready for that, you let me know."

He opened her car door for her and she slid inside. She looked up at him, suddenly wishing his mouth was on hers more than she'd ever wanted anything in her life.

He smiled at her, and her heart did a series of jumbled flip-flops, her stomach tumbling along with it.

And then he closed the car door.

Damn. What had that been all about?

Well, she knew what it had been all about.

Desire. Raging, hardcore, *I want you right now* desire.

For Jason.

Not just for revenge. But just for her. Her own wants, her own needs.

And she wanted him right now.

Unfortunately, he'd already walked away, gotten into his truck, and was waiting for her to leave.

Also unfortunate? She was turned on, hot as blazes, damp and so ready for sex she might explode right there in the car. She shot a look over at him, but he wasn't paying attention.

Come on, Jason. I'm sending sexual vibes your way. Look at me.

She tapped the steering wheel, waiting.

And . . . nothing.

Clearly, she was no sexual psychic.

She should just give it up for tonight, give Jason some space, because she'd already taken up enough of his time today.

But she wasn't finished with him yet. In fact, things were just heating up between them.

CHAPTER

......

ten

S HE'D HAD AGATHA for five days. Five relentless days
of Agatha running amok in her office, chewing on her
laptop cord, eating one of her favorite shoes—that one
had been painful. And the running. So much running,
when Erin had been given specific instructions not to let
the pup run. She'd called Jason and told him the pup
would not listen to her. He had laughed. Laughed at her.

Jerk.

Laughing was not useful advice. He said to keep her
contained in a small area, then laughed again when he'd
told her he had to go.

Asshole.

And then the whole housebreaking thing? How many
trips outside to pee could one pup make during a twenty-
four-hour period?

And the crying at night. Agatha did all right in her
crate, but Erin felt kind of bad about abandoning her,
when all she really wanted to do was cuddle her. Though
she knew crate training was the right thing to do for her,
especially while she was trying to housebreak her.

The whole thing was frustrating. And she was so damn tired she wanted to lie on the ground and cry.

But right now she was walking with Agatha, who bounded ahead like the happiest dog ever, oblivious to Erin's plight. The cast on Agatha's leg didn't seem to hinder her ability to maneuver at all, which was both a good and a bad thing.

At least they had the property. Agatha liked being around people so she never wandered too far, fortunately. After the first few days Erin already knew where her puppy was headed.

"*Buongiorno*, Agatha," her dad said as Agatha found her father in the vineyards and limped over to him, her tail wagging furiously. "How's the beautiful girl today? Would you like a treat?"

Her father had absconded with one of the bags of treats Erin had bought and kept some in his pocket at all times, giving one to Agatha every time he saw her.

"You're going to spoil her, Dad."

"Puppies should be spoiled. Like babies."

Erin rolled her eyes, but watched as her dad spent some time with Agatha, using treats to teach the pup how to sit. Agatha was a free spirit and conveniently ignored anything Erin asked her to do. For treats, apparently, she could sit on command. Erin made a mental note about that one.

"She likes you."

Her dad laughed. "She likes treats. And people who pay attention to her."

"I pay plenty of attention to her. I'm walking her right now."

"Your mind is scattered and puppies need your full attention. She knows it, which is why she gets into trouble. You need to sit on the floor and wrestle with her, tire her out some so she won't be so rambunctious. And carry treats with you for training. She'll follow you everywhere."

"Okay, Dad. Thanks."

Her father handed her the treat bag. "Try it."

"Sure. Come on, Agatha."

The pup had planted her butt on the ground and stared up lovingly at her dad.

"Agatha, come."

"Rattle the treat bag," her dad suggested.

Erin lifted the bag and shook it. It worked. Agatha bounded over to Erin, and when Erin took off, Agatha stayed in step with her.

"You will never be a success in life if you're motivated by food, Agatha. You need to find your purpose."

Agatha looked up at her with a happy puppy smile as if to say, *Yeah, my purpose in life is getting what's in that bag you're holding.*

She rounded the side of the house toward the front, surprised to see Jason's truck pulling up. When he got out, Agatha dashed over to him.

Jason crouched down and rubbed all over Agatha's furry body.

"Hey, Agatha. You're looking very cute today. Are you out for a walk?"

Erin caught up. "She's taking me for a walk."

"Maybe too much freedom for her," Jason said, examining her cast. "This might be a good time to start leash training her."

The last thing she wanted was more advice from the men in her life, but since Jason was a veterinarian and knew better than she did, especially about Agatha's injury, she supposed she had no choice but to listen to him. "Okay. I'll go get her leash."

"I'll hang out here with her and help you, if that's okay."

She looked down at him. "You don't have to do that."

"Hey, I came here to check on her. And you. So I don't mind if you don't."

She definitely didn't mind him spending time with her and Agatha. "Sure. I'll be right back."

She went inside and fumbled through the bags of things she'd bought at the store, grabbing the harness and leash that she had yet to figure out how to use. For someone who prided herself on being able to master anything, she'd been a mess about taking care of Agatha's needs. Sure, she'd fed her and taken her on walks around the property, and she had her crate set up in her bedroom, but other than that, she was kind of useless.

She went back outside and handed the items to Jason, who cocked a brow at her.

"These still have the tags on."

"I was going to figure them out soon."

"Uh-huh." He dug into the back pocket of his jeans and pulled out his pocket knife, sliced the tags off both the harness and the leash, then handed the tags to her.

"Come here, baby," he said to Agatha, his voice softening and making Erin melt in the process.

She wondered if that was his bedroom voice, or if that was deeper, more demanding. Would his hands be gentle, or rough as he explored her body?

And why was she suddenly so damn hot? She blew out an exasperated breath.

"What's wrong?" he asked as he stood, holding the leash in his hand.

"Nothing. I'm just . . . frustrated."

"About?"

Because a very hot man was standing only a few inches away from her. Among other things. "I guess because I should be doing all these things for Agatha and

I've never had a dog and I have no idea what I'm doing. Why did I think I could raise a puppy, Jason? She cries all night in her crate, and runs around all day and I'm worried about her little leg and I feel like I'm doing everything wrong."

He put his arm around her, which did not help matters at all.

"It's okay. Puppies are hard. She'll get used to her crate. Where do you have it set up?"

"In my bedroom."

"That's good. She can see you and hear you, and that'll comfort her. You don't let her out of it at night, do you?"

"No. But I'm tempted."

"Don't be. She'll adjust. Make sure she has a soft toy for comfort. Take her out for a walk before bed to tire her out, and then be firm with your training. It just takes a few days. Eventually she'll learn to see her crate as her safe space where she goes when she wants to sleep and when she needs comfort."

She sighed. "If you say so."

"I do. And eventually, once she's fully housebroken, you'll be able to leave the crate door open at night and she'll still want to sleep in there."

She tilted her head back to look at him, unable to believe the truth of that. "Seriously."

"I would never lie to you."

Which was the truth. As long as she'd known Jason, he had never once lied to her. "Okay. I believe you."

"Now let's work on the leash training."

The one thing she had learned about Agatha in the few short days she'd had her was that her puppy was stubborn. Jason was gentle, but firm, and had way more patience than Erin did. Eventually he coaxed Agatha into walking on the leash. Treats definitely helped, and Erin began to see the light. They took a walk around the perimeter of the house, Jason showing her the pace she should set with the pup for her leg.

"Until the cast comes off," Jason said, "no free-range running. If she's outside, she needs to be on the leash."

"Got it."

"Good. Now you try it."

"It's all right for her to walk some more?"

"Walking's good for her. It's the running that isn't right now."

"Okay."

He handed the leash over to her and she took the lead. Agatha had no problem walking with her, and now that Erin wasn't chasing her all over the property, she relaxed into it.

This was so much better, both for her and for her puppy. "I don't know why I didn't think of the leash and harness before."

"Probably because you bought eighty-seven things for her at the store that night and maybe you forgot?"

She laughed. "Maybe."

"And because you have other things on your mind in addition to raising a new puppy?"

"That's no excuse. Agatha has to come first."

"See?" He smiled at her. "You're going to be great with her."

They headed back toward the vineyards, Agatha sniffing every part and parcel of the ground.

"The grapes are looking good," Jason said.

"They're coming along. Brenna and Dad are happy with this year's crop. And the wine being bottled is fabulous this season."

"Don't suppose you want to take me into the bottling room for a taste, do you?"

She laughed. "I'll tell you what. You fix me dinner, and I'll bring over one of the new bottles."

"Deal. I make a great steak."

"We have a fabulous cab that'll go great with said steak."

"Is tonight too soon? You can bring Agatha. She and Puddy can play."

"Are you sure it's okay for her to wrestle around with Puddy?"

"They'll be fine as long as we're there to watch over them. Plus, some socialization with other dogs will be good for her."

"How about her shots? Is it okay for her to be around other dogs?"

"She's fine. We ran blood work on her and she looks good, and now she's current on all her vaccinations."

She was relieved to hear that. "Then, yes, tonight sounds great."

They walked their way around to the front of the house and it appeared that Agatha was tiring, which was good because Erin had a lot of work left to do.

"I've gotta go. I just stopped by on my way back from a ranch call."

"Okay. Thanks for hanging out and showing me the way with Agatha."

"It was my pleasure." He looked down at her, his eyes dark and full of meaning.

Erin thought maybe he was about to lean in and kiss her, but they were out front and people were wandering by. Still . . . that look.

He stepped back. "See you tonight, Erin. About seven thirty?"

"Perfect. I'll see you then."

He climbed into his truck and pulled away. Erin

looked down at Agatha, who lay at her feet, more calm than she'd ever seen her.

Jason was magic with dogs. She wasn't at all surprised, since the man had magical qualities. Maybe tonight she'd get to explore more of them.

"Agatha, we have a date tonight."

The pup was already asleep.

CHAPTER
......
eleven

AFTER WORK, JASON stopped at his favorite meat market to pick up some prime cuts of filet, then hit the grocery store for the rest of the stuff he'd need for dinner that night.

Since Puddy had been at the clinic with him today, the dog wagged his tail, happy to be back home. He jumped out of the truck and ran straight inside, lapped up an entire bowl of water, then went to the back door. Jason let him out and went to the truck to get the groceries, put them away, then looked around, realizing he'd left a mess here that needed cleaning up.

He picked up clothes and dog toys, then vacuumed and cleaned the counters and the bathrooms. The floors also needed mopping, but he didn't have time since he needed to take a shower, and that took priority over a dirty floor.

After his shower, he put on jeans and a T-shirt, then went into the kitchen and downed a glass of ice water. He'd had a full day and most of that was spent outside with horses and cattle. He and the other doctors in the practice traded off outside calls versus clinic appointments. Today had been his day for outside calls. One of the reasons he loved being a small- and large-animal vet was the opportunity to get out of the clinic setting and broaden his practice. He liked helping out the larger animals as well as the smaller ones, and it gave him a chance to roam the countryside. But dealing with farm and ranch calls also made for a longer day, which meant he barely had time to finish cleaning up before Erin was at the door.

He opened it, smiling at how cute she looked in her dress and sandals. Agatha's tail whipped furiously back and forth.

"She had a nap, and she's so ready to play now," Erin said. "I don't know whether to apologize to you for that, or be happy that she's so enthusiastic."

He laughed. "Come on in. Puddy's out back."

She handed him a bag. "I brought three bottles."

He arched a brow. "Planning on a long night?"

She walked in and followed him into the kitchen. "Maybe. We could have in-depth conversations about our childhoods or something."

"We spent most of our childhoods together. I doubt there's anything about you I don't already know."

"Hey, I kept some secrets from you."

He pulled the bottles from the bag and laid them on the counter. "First boy you kissed was Steve Gregarian in sixth grade. He shoved his tongue in your mouth and you hated it."

She gaped at him. "I can't believe you remember that. Though I seem to recall you telling me about Beth Francis and one night on the football field in seventh grade."

He grinned. "Oh, right, Beth. She was a wild thing."

"And now she's been married three times and has four kids."

"Told you she was a wild thing." His lips curved in a knowing smile.

She shook her head.

He took Agatha's leash. "Come on, Agatha. Let's introduce you to Puddy."

Erin followed him out the back door, where Puddy was already wiggling with excitement.

Jason opened the door and there was a tangle of wagging tails and sniffing and excited barks. Fortunately, Puddy and Agatha were about the same age, and Puddy instinctively seemed to know that Agatha was a little handicapped by her cast and her cone, so his play was gentle.

Although Agatha didn't think of herself as anything but Puddy's equal, so she nipped and played and tried to run.

Jason took over the leash and walked around the yard with Agatha, giving her enough lead so she could wrestle around with Puddy, but when Puddy tried to take off in a run, he used verbal commands to bring his dog back, keeping both pups in a fairly close circle.

When the dogs were tired out they came inside. Jason closed off all the doors leading into the other rooms, which left only the kitchen and living area. Erin removed Agatha's leash, and both pups got a long drink of water then went to lie down on the blanket that Jason had for Puddy in the living room.

Within a few minutes, they were curled up together, both of them happily chewing on a couple of soft toys.

"Oh, that's sweet," Erin said. "Agatha has a new best friend."

"She did good." Jason moved into the kitchen to wash his hands.

Erin came in there with him, washing her hands as well. "She obviously loves having a companion."

"So maybe you need two dogs."

She laughed. "She's all I can handle right now."

"She makes you happy. You're smiling again. You needed that."

She hadn't realized that, but he was right. Despite how overwhelming bringing Agatha into her life had been this past week, the puppy had also taken her mind off everything that had happened with Owen. She hadn't had time to think about him . . . or herself. And that had been a huge relief.

"You're right. She is just what I needed. Thank you for that."

"It was her, not me. She was yours from the minute you rescued her."

She looked over to see Agatha and Puddy playing tug-of-war with a long knotted rope. Seeing her puppy engaged and happy made her heart swell. "Yeah, she sure was."

"Good."

"Okay, so what are we cooking?" she asked.

"Steaks on the grill. Roasted potatoes. Grilled corn salad."

"Fire up that grill, then. I'll start the potatoes."

"Sounds good. They're in the pantry. Make yourself at home."

He grabbed a beer and headed outside while she put the potatoes on to boil. She opened one of the bottles of the wine she'd brought and grabbed a glass from the cabinet, then perused his fridge. It was nicely stocked, so she decided a watermelon salsa also sounded good. While the wine breathed, she chopped watermelon, jalapeño, mango, onion and cucumber, tossing it all into a bowl she found in one of the cabinets.

Jason came in to grab the corn, then eyed the bowl on the counter.

"You're making a fruit salad?"

She shook her head. "Watermelon salsa."

"I knew there was a reason I wanted you to have dinner with me."

"Other than my sweet disposition and charming personality?"

He snorted out a laugh as he walked back outside.

"Jerk," she said to herself, but then she glanced outside and noticed both dogs were looking up at him with pure love. Sure, because he had the steak, but she had to admit, he was quite the man. Tall, rugged, with nice lean muscle, and he was good with animals? So gentle and sweet but also . . . oh, so damn hot. She just knew he'd be dynamite in the sack.

Girl, you are so smitten.

She blinked. She was not smitten. She just got dumped. She just wanted a hot revenge fling with Jason. Who wouldn't? The man oozed masculinity and ultimate hotness.

She finished chopping the basil and added it to the bowl, marveling at her own wayward thoughts.

"Smitten" meant there were emotional things involved. Heart things. And she was in no place to even think heart things. Her heart lay broken at the altar of her non-wedding, and it would be a long damn time before she could duct-tape the pieces together and even think about falling in love again.

No, what she wanted from Jason was smoking-hot sex and nothing more.

If she classified Jason into the "sex only" category, she could handle this.

Smitten? Emotion? Nope. She was not going to go there. Not with him. Not with anyone.

Not for a very long time.

If ever.

But she glanced out the door again, and there he was, teaching her puppy how to obey commands. Agatha's little wiggly butt plopped firmly on the ground as Jason leaned over and smiled at her, and then he gave her an overabundance of affection, causing the pup's entire body to vibrate with absolute adoration.

Well, hell. Who wouldn't be affected by a sight like that?

Jason popped open the door and since she'd already been ogling him, he didn't need to catch her attention. "Would you mind bringing me the salt and pepper? It's in the door of the small pantry."

"Sure."

She found them and brought them to him.

He graced her with a warm smile. "Thanks, beautiful."

Zing. Bang. Boing. "You're welcome."

She closed the door, trying very hard not to be affected by him calling her "beautiful." He'd always called her that whenever he saw her. It was a throwaway term of endearment and meant absolutely nothing.

Except now the word felt like a caress all over her extremely sensitive skin. Which was ridiculous and probably meant she needed to get laid.

She was just raw and hurt and once she got her revenge, she'd feel more in control of her own destiny and feelings and every damn word Jason uttered wouldn't feel so . . .

Special.

Whatever. She tucked her raw feelings inside and finished the salsa, putting it into the fridge. She took a couple long swallows of the wine, which was delicious, of course. Not too dry, not sweet, but oaky, leaving a buttery vanilla flavor on her tongue. It was a perfect vintage.

She was so proud of her family. They made damn good wine. From the time she was a child, she'd watched the vineyard and its products grow in popularity. They'd added the wedding venue fifteen years ago, just when Erin was hitting adolescence, and she'd been dreamy-eyed and starstruck seeing brides and grooms profess their love for each other at the place she called home. She used to hide out on the side of the house to watch the bridesmaids and the bride walk down the aisle. They were always so pretty, the brides so happy.

Erin and her sisters used to sneak peeks at the receptions, peering into the barn windows when they were supposed to be in bed, watching the bridal party and their families and guests dance late into the night. While Brenna and Honor gushed over how in love the bride and groom seemed to be, Erin always wanted to see how many bottles of Red Moss Vineyards wine got consumed and tally up how many guests were present, her mind calculating the profits.

Huh. She took another swallow of wine. Maybe she lacked a romantic side. Though that couldn't be true. Owen had fallen in love with her. He'd asked her to marry him.

He *had* loved her, right? Of course he had. And she was totally fun. She wasn't all numbers and business. Once she walked out of her office at the end of the day, she shut all that down and she could really let loose. That was the part of her that Owen had fallen in love with.

There was nothing at all wrong with the business side of her.

She had no idea why she was even questioning herself.

She'd been ready to get married. The fault was all Owen's, who she was *not* going to think about tonight.

She set the table and dumped the water out of the potatoes and patted them dry. She sliced them in half, put them in a pan, seasoned them and added butter, then turned on the stove to get them nicely browned.

Jason came in with the corn and the steak. He sliced the niblets off each ear. While she worked on the potatoes, he set to work on making the corn salad. The dogs curled up on the pallet on the floor and went right to sleep.

"They were very busy outside fighting each other for a stick, so I think they'll nap for a while."

"It was nice of you to play with Agatha."

"She's a great puppy, Erin. And she's fast with learning commands. I don't think you'll have any trouble with her."

"You'll have to teach me how to teach her."

He crooked a smile at her while he dried his hands on the kitchen towel. "I'll be happy to."

Once the potatoes and corn salad were ready, Erin took the watermelon salsa out of the fridge, added a little garlic salt and tossed it. They set the food on the table and started eating.

"How was your day today?" she asked.

"Good. Nothing traumatic, mostly routine stuff, so that made for a noneventful day."

She slid a bite of steak into her mouth, loving the burst of flavor. After she swallowed, she said, "And you like noneventful days?"

"Not every day. That would be boring. But it's better for the animals we treat if nothing bad happens."

"Of course."

"But I do get the opportunity to work on some pretty

detailed surgeries. Our senior vet, Carl Sunderland, is one of the best veterinary orthopedic surgeons in the state. I've learned a lot working with him. And this watermelon salsa has a kick. I really like it."

She smiled. "Thanks. So tell me what some of your favorite things to do at work are."

"I like going out on the farm and ranch calls. I don't like to be idle."

That didn't surprise her. "When Owen and I were inside playing video games, you were always outside. You were always on the go. You wanted to be out riding bikes or at the playground, or shooting hoops."

He nodded. "Yeah. Being cooped up inside was like punishment. The only way I like it even now is if I'm working on something complex, like a detailed surgery. I can get inside my head and work it out, like a puzzle."

Her eyes widened and she set her fork down on the plate. "Remember the puzzles we used to do? You and me and my sisters and Owen and Clay?"

"Oh, yeah. We'd set it on the table in my parents' dining room and spend hours putting those things together."

"Sometimes days. And then we'd get to the end and realize we were missing a couple of pieces."

"Yeah. Piece of shit puzzles."

She laughed. "Still so fun. How's your mom doing these days? I haven't seen her around town."

"She's doing okay. Has her good days and bad days. It's been hard for her since Dad died, but she has her friends and they drag her out of the house as much as they can. And I try to go over there a couple of times a week to have dinner with her, mow the lawn and stuff. I think selling the store has been the hardest for her. She saw that as Dad's identity and without that, she's been lost."

"I can't even imagine. But I'm glad you're there for her." Erin couldn't fathom how tough it must be for Nora Callum. She'd spent her entire life being Ben Callum's wife and work partner at the hardware store. Then when Ben died unexpectedly of a heart attack three years ago, her entire world crumpled. She'd lost the love of her life, then the store that had been their everyday existence.

"Is there anything that interests her, that can keep her occupied?"

"She's getting involved with some of the Cherokee Nation tribal stuff. Helping some of the kids, going to the meetings, that kind of thing."

"Oh, that's good."

"Yeah. I remember when I participated in Johnson-O'Malley programs when I was in school. I'd go to the meetings, learn about the culture of the nations, do arts and crafts, and there was always someone from one of the tribal nations there. Mom wants to get involved in that."

"That would be wonderful for her."

He nodded. "I think it would. She's also been doing some research into the family history, especially on her side—the Cherokee side. She's been delving deep recently, doing some online and library research and gathering photographs."

"I'm fascinated. I'd love to know more about that."

"Yeah, me, too. I know who my grandparents and great-grandparents were, on both my parents' side. Beyond that, I don't know much."

"I'm sure it's a rich history. Genealogy is so important, especially with your Native American heritage. Brenna does that for our family, tracking both Irish and Italian sides of the Connors and the Bellinis. I'm sure your lineage is fascinating."

"That's very true. I hadn't thought much about it until

Mom brought it up. But since I don't have siblings, and no kids—"

"Yet."

He laughed. "Okay, fine. Since I don't have kids—yet—I should probably pay more attention to who came before so we can do this whole lineage thing."

"You might have famous people in your background. Chiefs. Leaders."

"Entirely possible. Or not."

She shrugged. "You never know. I'll be interested in what your mom comes up with."

"I'll just be happy if it makes her happy."

She finished off her glass of wine. "You want her to love living life again."

He nodded. "Yeah."

"It sounds like she's getting her feet wet, one step at a time. Grief doesn't have a timeline, Jason. Everyone goes through it at a different pace. You just have to let her get used to living her life without your dad in it."

"I know."

"Your mom and dad were in love for all those years. I've never known two people who loved each other more. They were like my parents. They spent every day together from the moment they met. So when your dad died, it was like a piece of her went with him."

He reached out and touched his fingertips to hers. "You're very insightful."

She shrugged. "I understand hurt and loss. I've seen it before."

"You talking about you and Owen?"

"No. I'm not even thinking of him in this kind of scenario. We didn't spend our lives together. My hurt over him is a different kind of hurt. And I don't want to talk about him tonight."

"Okay. Sorry I brought him up."

"It's all right." She got up to take their plates into the kitchen.

Jason went in there with her and they worked side by side cleaning up. After, she refilled her wineglass and they went outside. He lit torches and he showed Erin how to do some simple commands with Agatha using training treats. Okay, so with some directed attention, training her dog wouldn't be all that hard. Agatha was a quick learner. Or, at least she liked the snacks. She had "sit" and "stay" mastered with no problem before Agatha got bored and went off to play with Puddy. Now that she'd had a great deal of exercise, she was a lot calmer and Erin didn't have to worry about her running.

She took a seat and picked up her glass of wine.

"How's the renovation going?" she asked.

"Pretty good. Got the deck finished, so that's one to check off the list. Kitchen's done, as you can see. I've torn out the master bath and am working on putting new floors in the master bedroom, so that's a mess right now, which means I'm sleeping in one of the spare bedrooms."

"But it's a great house, Jason, in a perfect location. And with a little elbow grease you can make it just the way you want it. You've already done a fantastic job on the kitchen."

"Thanks. That's the idea." He took a swallow of beer. "Want to give me some suggestions on the master bath?"

"I'd love to."

She followed him inside and down the hall. She'd been over—with Owen—when Jason first bought the house a year ago. It was a nice big one-story with four bedrooms and two and a half baths, but it was outdated and needed some work. He'd already done a major overhaul of the kitchen, modernizing everything from the floors to the appliances and adding a kitchen island, new cabinets and a fabulous backsplash. He had great taste in flooring and paint colors, which he'd carried into the living room.

But the master bedroom and bathroom were nothing but a barren wasteland at the moment. Still, both were spacious, which meant they were a blank canvas. The bedroom had arched ceilings and there was a copious amount of space in the bath.

"What do you think of me adding a walk-in closet here?" he asked, pointing to a spot in the left corner.

She studied the location and nodded. "Plenty of space there. You'd end up with a huge walk-in, and you'd still have an extra-large bedroom. I love how tall these ceilings are."

"Yeah, me, too." He took her hand and walked her around the boxes and tools and into the bath.

"I want to do a huge shower against the wall, then double sinks and mirrors with a closet there."

She listened while he lined out his plan for the master bath. "No tub?"

"You think I need one? I don't take baths."

"But someday your future Mrs. Callum might like them. And you need a tub for resale. And for babies and kids."

"When I redo the guest bath I'm planning to put a nice soaker tub in there. If it were you and this was your house, would you be okay not having a tub in the master, but only in the guest bath?"

She shrugged. "I don't take a bath every day, just now and then. As long as there's a tub somewhere in the house, I'd be happy."

"Good enough. I'll leave the plans as they are, then. Now tell me what you think about this floor tile."

She laughed, as if her opinion mattered. This wasn't her house and never would be, but she appreciated that he asked for a woman's point of view.

She liked the options he'd chosen for the vanity and the floor tile, as well as all the hardware.

"You have a good eye for everything," she said, then scrolled through his phone and pointed at some mirror options she'd pulled up. "I like these better than the ones you chose. The other ones are too fancy and they'll collect more dust."

He looked, then nodded. "I like these, too. Thanks."

"Hey, I'm happy to spend your money. Feel free to take me shopping with you anytime."

He lifted his gaze to hers. "I might hold you to that."

"I won't say no."

He took a step forward. "What if I asked to kiss you right now? Would you say no?"

Her heart fluttered and her pulse began to race. "No. I mean, I wouldn't say no if you asked."

He traced his thumb across her bottom lip. "I'm asking."

She shuddered in a breath. The bathroom, which just a few seconds ago seemed huge, suddenly felt like it was closing in on her. "I'm saying yes."

With one step forward his body touched hers. He cupped the back of her neck, and their lips met.

The kiss made her feel like a volcano had erupted inside of her, all hot and molten, melting her to the floor. She grabbed his arm to hold on to him, afraid if she didn't she might fall. She leaned in and he wrapped an arm around her to draw her closer.

His body was all hard muscle and he smelled of wood smoke and delicious male. She licked at his tongue and he deepened the kiss until her head spun.

She'd been kissed in many places in her lifetime. In the high school gym, outside a restaurant, at the lake, in front of a bonfire in college. But never in a bare, unrenovated bathroom.

As far as kisses went, this one was definitely top three on her all-time list of hot-damn, hair-raising, toe-curling kisses. Jason put everything into this kiss, smoothing his hands down her sides, rolling over her lower back and resting them just above her butt. She appreciated that he was respectful enough not to grab a handful of her ass, but oh, she wanted him to. So she reached behind her and lowered his hands.

He groaned, pulled his mouth from hers. "You're killing me."

She licked her lips. "Not my intention."

He also didn't remove his hands, and the way he touched her, drawing her against his erection, made her body weep with need.

"How about we go to your bedroom?" she asked.

"The one that's just concrete floor?"

"Okay, fine. The place where you have a bed."

"It's a mess."

"I don't care. I want to get naked with you."

"I think you need some time, Erin."

His slight hesitation was like a cold splash of water. "Time for what?"

"To get over Owen. To think about what you really want."

He laid his forehead against hers, and this was where she knew for sure she was about to get rejected.

Again.

She laid her palms against his chest, then . . .

Pushed. Hard.

"How dare you presume to know how I feel?"

His look of shock and concern didn't fool her. "Erin. I didn't mean—"

"What? You didn't mean to hurt me? You're only thinking of what's best for me? How about letting me decide what's best? How about treating me with a little dignity and respect and letting me choose what I want to do with my body?"

He took a step forward, reached for her.

She stepped back.

He laid his hand down at his side. "It's not your body I'm worried about, Erin. It's your heart."

Said heart squeezed in pain. She shoved that pain deep inside, locked it up where it couldn't hurt her. Where he couldn't hurt her.

Now she was the one to step forward, so she could poke her finger at his chest. "My heart is just fine. And none of your business. And I get to choose what I want to do with my body. Clear?"

"Yeah."

"Good."

She started to walk out, then stopped and pivoted. "Why start this when you had no intention of finishing it?"

He cocked his head to the side. "What?"

"That kiss. Touching me. Only to put the brakes on and tell me you're concerned about my heart? Don't play games with me, Jason. I don't like it."

She turned and walked out of the room. She gathered up Agatha, grabbed her purse and keys and walked out the door.

Agatha curled up in the back seat and went back to sleep. Erin gripped the steering wheel to calm her shaky hands, alternating between righteous anger and hurting so much she had to constantly fight back tears.

Anger was better. It kept her from crying.

What was it with men who thought they knew what was best for her, anyway?

She knew what was best for her. She knew her own mind, her own body, and damn them all for getting in the way of that.

She was better off on her own.

CHAPTER

······

twelve

JASON DOVE INTO work over the next several days, burying himself in surgeries and ranch calls so he wouldn't have to think about the colossal fuckup he'd made with Erin.

She was right about everything she'd said. He'd started something with her he hadn't been prepared to finish. But she'd looked so beautiful there in the bathroom, and impulse made him want to kiss her. Then he'd made decisions for her that he'd had no right to make. His intentions might have been honorable, but he should have asked her how she felt instead of putting a stop to things thinking he knew what was best for her.

Because it was obvious he didn't know shit. And all he'd done was driven their friendship—their relationship—several steps back.

He was no better than Owen.

He finished entering procedure notes into a patient's file.

"Jason. I've got two emergencies coming in. Can you take one?"

He looked up at Carl Sunderland and nodded. "Yeah, I can take one."

His vet tech set up the operating room for the emergency surgery, and he concentrated on what needed to be done for the abdominal obstruction case.

The surgery was delicate and complex, and his focus had to be on saving this two-year-old boxer's life.

The problem with dogs—many dogs—was their utter love for chewing and swallowing things they weren't supposed to. In Radar's case? His owner's sock, which had gotten stuck and festered into a rotten infection in his gut. Jason removed it and irrigated his belly, checking for any other obstructions. Fortunately, nothing else impeded Radar's digestive tract, so Jason and his team closed him up. He gave the dog some strong antibiotics to fight off infection, and was confident Radar would recover.

After calling Radar's humans and giving them an update, Jason did some office calls, finished up his daily reports and checked his messages. He was finally finished, and he'd made it through one grueling day. While rooting through his messages he saw there was one from his friend Clay Henry, who asked him to stop by after work if he had a minute.

Huh. He wondered if there was something wrong with Clay's Labrador, Homer, or maybe one of his horses. Then again, Clay would just put in a ranch call if there was an issue with the horses or cattle, so that probably wasn't it.

Maybe he just wanted a visit.

He stopped at home and took a quick shower to wash off the grime from the day, then changed into jeans and a T-shirt before driving over to Clay's ranch. Since he didn't know whether or not Homer was sick, he didn't want to risk bringing Puddy with him, so he left him at home with his food and toys. He parked and rang the bell. Homer barked, which was a good sign.

Clay opened the door, a bottle of beer in his hand. "Hey, I thought maybe you'd call me."

"Your note said to stop by."

"Oh, sure. Come on in."

Jason followed Clay in.

"I was just having a beer. Want one?"

"Definitely."

Clay pulled a bottle out of the fridge and handed it to Jason.

"Rough day?" Clay asked.

"Busy one. How about yours?"

"About average."

Since Homer had come over to greet him, Jason knelt to pet him. "Is Homer all right?"

"He's fine. I just thought you might want to have a beer and dinner with us."

Jason lifted his head and looked at Clay. "Us? Is Alice back in town?"

"Yeah. She got back a couple of days ago."

He looked around. "Where is she?"

"In her office. She's on a Skype call with a client. Since she's on LA time, her day ends later than mine."

Homer ran off, so Jason stood and grabbed his beer, taking a long swallow before answering. "I don't want to interrupt your reunion with your girlfriend."

Clay laughed. "We've had plenty of reunion time since she's been back. Don't worry about it."

"If you're sure."

"About the reunion time?" He quirked a smile. "Definitely sure."

Jason rolled his eyes. "Not what I was talking about. And I don't want to know that part."

He slanted a knowing smile at Jason. "You're not interrupting us. I already told Alice I was inviting you over. She was all for it, so quit worrying. You can help me get the burgers ready."

"Oh, well, if you're talking burgers, then I'm definitely staying for dinner."

"Thought you might."

While Clay was in the process of getting the meat ready, Alice came down the hall.

"Hi, Jason."

She came over to give him a hug.

"Hey, Alice. How's everything going?"

"It's going great."

"How was the trip to LA?"

"Very productive. I picked up two new clients, and possibly another one based on my very productive teleconference today."

"That's great news." He didn't really understand how her matchmaking business worked, but according to Clay, she was damn good at it, with a high percentage of success. "Lots of happily-ever-afters in more couples' futures, then?"

She gave him a genuine smile. "You know it."

"Burgers are ready to go on the grill, babe," Clay said.

"Okay. I just need to clean up my work area, then I'll start working on the sides."

Clay came over and slid his arm around her. "I said I had dinner handled."

"And I told you I'd help if I finished work in time. I'm finished, so go put burgers on the grill. I'll pour myself a glass of wine, then start on the sides."

"Yes, ma'am." Clay bent and brushed his lips across hers, then grabbed the tray holding the burgers, looking over at Jason. "You heard the lady. Let's go."

Jason followed Clay outside, Homer right on their heels.

While Clay put the burgers on, Jason took the ball Homer had dropped at his feet and tossed it across the yard.

Homer ran and grabbed it, then brought it back, let it fall out of his mouth and waited, his tail thumping madly until Jason picked it up and threw it again. And again.

Homer was a very good dog.

"How come you didn't bring Puddy with you?" Clay asked.

Jason tossed the ball, then turned to Clay. "I wasn't sure from your message if there was something wrong with Homer, and I didn't want to stress him out by bringing Puds with me."

"If Homer was sick I'd have brought him into the clinic. And next time I'll be clearer in my messages."

"Yeah, do that."

Alice opened the back door. "Corn on the cob, green beans or a salad?"

Clay looked over at Jason, who shrugged and said, "Yeah."

Alice laughed and shook her head. "Neither of you are helpful. I'll decide."

After Alice went inside, Jason noticed some spray-painted area around the yard. "Plans?"

"Yeah." Clay closed the grill. "We're building a patio and outdoor kitchen, a shaded porch and an outdoor entertainment area."

"Oh. So big plans."

"Yeah. We have the space for it. I figure if we enclose the porch with drop-down screens, it'll be great for grilling and football in the fall."

Jason nodded. "Always think big, my friend."

Clay laughed. "I try. I don't want to have to redo this in five years. Not when there will be little ones running around by then."

Jason plopped down in the chair and took a swig of his beer. "You do have big plans."

"I'm going to marry that woman and have babies with her."

"Does she know that?"

"She does. I mean, I haven't formally proposed yet, but yeah, she's in on the grand plan."

"Maybe you should get to the formally proposing part."

"That's in the works. Her parents are coming to town next week to visit over Memorial Day weekend. I'm going to do it then. I figured having her family here along with my family would make it more meaningful."

"That's nice."

The door popped open. "What's nice?"

Shit. Jason had to think fast. "How well Homer was doing on his training. That dog can really chase after a ball."

Alice came out and took a seat next to him, looking cool and beautiful in her long flowery sundress. Homer ambled over and dropped the slimy ball in her lap. Unruffled, Alice picked up the ball and threw it. "He's so smart, and, yes, he does love his ball. And his fluffy toys. And things to chew on. Plus, he only chews the things he's supposed to."

"She's just happy he doesn't chew up her shoes," Clay said.

Alice nodded. "That is a bonus."

"Clay told me you two are building an outdoor oasis."

She rolled her eyes. "His idea. I suggested a patio. I go away for a few days and come home to painted lines in the backyard and blueprints for an entire outdoor kitchen and an enclosed sunroom with an entertainment area and drop-down screens and what have you."

"Yeah, but you didn't complain about it when I showed you the plans, did you?" Clay asked as he took the burgers off the grill.

She lifted her chin. "I believe I mentioned it was all too much."

"She came around after I told her how much our future children were going to love it."

"He agreed we'd put a pool in next year."

Jason nodded. "You definitely need to add the pool. With a slide. And a playset, too."

She laughed. "We should probably have children first. Or maybe get married before the kids come along. Though if the first little one should pop up as a surprise, I won't complain. I'm so ready to have babies."

She got up and went into the house. Jason shot Clay a look, and Clay's lips lifted.

He envied his friend. He was one lucky man.

When the food was ready, they went inside, sat at the table and dug in. The burgers were great, and Alice had made a salad plus green beans, along with a nice fruit salad, too, and there was bread. By the time he'd cleaned his plate he was stuffed and very happy.

Alice had opened a bottle of a damn fine Red Moss Vineyards cabernet that was tart and smooth and had gone well with the burgers. It had also made him miss Erin.

Clay poured more wine for Alice. She swirled the liquid around in her glass.

"I'll have to tell Erin how good this cabernet is," Alice said. "What did you think of it, Jason?"

"Yeah, it's good."

"You should tell her, too," Alice said. "I know how much the Bellinis love feedback on the wine."

"I don't think she wants to hear anything from me right now."

"Uh-oh." Alice gave him a concerned look. "What's going on?"

"Let's just say she's not currently speaking to me and leave it at that."

Alice frowned and laid her glass on the table. "Okay, buddy. Spill."

He shook his head. "Kind of personal stuff, Alice."

"Personal . . . Are you two dating?" She looked from Jason to Clay. Clay shrugged.

"Don't look at me. I don't know a thing."

So she looked back at Jason.

"I don't know. It's not really dating. She wanted to use me for a revenge fling after Owen dumped her. And I've been resistant to that and she's kind of pissed at me about it."

"I see." Alice took another sip of wine. "Probably because she feels like you're rejecting her just like Owen did."

"I'm not rejecting her. I . . . ." He wasn't about to get into a discussion about his feelings for Erin. "I don't know. I screwed up, did something stupid, said some things I shouldn't have said, and she stormed out of my house a couple of days ago."

"And then what happened?" Alice asked.

"Nothing. I haven't talked to her since then."

Clay shook his head. "Man, you are so dumb."

He looked at Clay. "What?"

"You. Dumbass. Go talk to her. Fix it."

"I thought I'd give her time to calm down."

Alice laughed. "We don't calm down, idiot. We just

keep thinking about what you said, which makes us even more angry. Clay is right. Go see her and fix what you broke."

He scrunched his nose, trying to figure out how to prove them wrong. But the more he thought about it, the more he realized they were right. He had to talk to Erin, and the sooner the better.

Because she'd been damn angry that night. And now that a few days had gone by? She'd had a lot of time to think about what he'd said. She was probably really pissed now.

CHAPTER
······
thirteen

IF WE MOVE this here," Erin said, looking over the master schedule with her sisters, "couldn't we fit the Richardson/Evans wedding in on that Friday?"

Honor's brows wrinkled as she studied the schedule. "I think so, which would actually work out perfectly because it'll free up the third Saturday in July for the McKesson/Bainbridge wedding."

Brenna looked up at her. "Wait. Aren't they next June?"

Honor shrugged. "They want to move up."

"By almost a year?" Erin asked.

"Yes." Honor stared at her sisters. "Is that a problem?"

Erin rubbed the side of her temple. "Any change in the schedule is a problem. Swapping dates on two already scheduled weddings? That's a double problem. What about caterers and cakes and music and guests and all that?"

"I'll handle it," Honor said. "Don't I always handle it?"

The one thing Erin didn't like was a change in the schedule. She needed balance and order in her life—especially her work life. When a wedding went on the schedule, it tended to stay there. Change meant an upset in her plan, reordering things. She stared at her spreadsheet, her calendar, her planner, and thought of everything that would have to be redone. It made her twitchy.

"Erin," Honor said, her gaze gentle. "I've got this. Trust me."

"I assume we're not also adding to the guest list?" Brenna asked.

"Guest lists aren't changing at all, so the wine orders will remain the same."

Brenna shrugged. "Then it sounds fine to me, and I'm happy we can accommodate everyone. I'm out. Just send me an e-mail so I can change it on my schedule."

"Will do," Honor said, still keeping her attention focused on Erin.

"All right," Erin said, holding up her hands. "We'll make it work." They were in the business of making brides happy. And if changing wedding dates fit into their schedules? That's what they'd do.

Honor grinned. "Awesome. Thanks. After I confirm everything with both groups, I'll e-mail you the details, because I know you like to have everything in writing."

"You do that."

Honor got up, then paused. "Are you all right?"

"I'm fine. Why?"

"You seem . . . tense. More tense than normal."

"I am not tense. I'm busy. We're entering our busiest season of the year."

"Of course. But, I know this is also tough for you right now. If you need someone to talk to, I'm always here for you."

There were so many things on her mind right now she wouldn't even know where to begin. And one of those things was Jason, who was a good friend of the Bellini family. She wasn't sure she wanted to open that particular can with one of her sisters. "I'm good. But thanks for asking, Honor."

"Anytime."

After Honor left, Erin plugged in the tentative changes on her calendar, making sure she made notes about the shuffling in wedding dates. She'd wait for the e-mail to come through from Honor before she made official additions and changes in her planner and calendar.

As the wedding coordinator, she knew Honor would handle all the rearranging with the caterers and cake decorators and everyone else. It was Erin's responsibility to make sure dates stayed clear and budgets stayed on track. So once the dates were firm, she'd assess everything and figure it all out to see if any changes needed to be made, and work with her sisters to come up with a final budget for each wedding.

She pushed back from her desk, needing a break. Some fresh air would help to clear her head. She looked at her phone. It was after six and she'd eaten lunch with the family at one. Some food would probably help. Maybe after she took a walk she'd see about dinner.

She stepped outside, stopping in her tracks when she saw Jason climbing out of his truck.

It had been days since she'd stormed out of his house in a fit. She thought maybe he'd call her or come over. Instead, she'd gotten nothing, so she'd assumed he'd thought she wasn't worth the effort.

Kind of like Owen thought she wasn't worth the effort.

She narrowed her gaze at him. "What are you doing here?"

He walked up the steps. "I came to tell you I was sorry . . . for several things. First, for starting something and then putting a stop to it. That was stupid. And second, for assuming I knew what was best for you. Clearly I don't. And last, for not coming after you that night and apologizing right away, which is what I should have done. Instead, I thought maybe giving you some time . . . Well, anyway, that was wrong, too. I'm sorry, Erin. I acted like an ass and I'm here to beg for your forgiveness."

She was all set to get a good mad going, and then he had to go and come up with the perfect apology right off the bat. Damn him for ruining that for her. "I was planning to yell at you for acting like a misogynistic dick."

"I did do that. And you can still be mad and yell at me all you want."

And then he had to go and be sweet and allow her to kick his ass anyway. Damn him again. She stepped forward, inhaling the scent of freshly showered male. The man could almost make her swoon. "You presumed."

"I did."

He wasn't going to take another step, so she did, planting her palm on his chest. "That was wrong."

"It was."

Lord, his eyes were beautiful dark chocolate, so filled with soulful honesty. He wasn't looking down or away, instead directly at her, owning up to the mistake he'd made. That was a man she could fall—

No, she didn't intend to fall. But she could forgive. "Don't do it again."

"I won't."

And his mouth . . .

Despite being so pissed at him for all those days, she couldn't forget what it felt like to be kissed by him. She wanted it again.

"One more thing," she said.

He nodded. "Go ahead."

"I'm starving and I need a margarita."

Finally, he smiled. "Can I take you out for drinks and dinner?"

Her lips curved. "I'd like that. Let me grab my purse."

"I'll wait right here for you."

She went inside and saw Honor, so she told her she was having dinner with Jason.

"And Agatha is out in the vineyards with Dad. Could you let him know I'll be out for a bit, so he'll keep an eye on the pup?"

"I'll do that. Dinner with Jason, huh?" Honor asked with a knowing smile on her face.

"It's just dinner, Honor."

"Sure it is, honey," Honor said as she turned, then stopped. "Oh. I'm having dinner with a new guy, by the way."

"Yeah? Who's the guy?"

"Randall Black."

Erin frowned. "The band guy?"

"He's a musician. And he's very nice."

Erin thought he was one of those singers who thought he was a bigger name than he really was. The guy did weddings, but thought of himself as some kind of superstar rock god.

Randall was anything but.

"You have a good time, honey," Erin said. "Be careful with Randall."

"You have fun out to dinner with Jason," Honor said. "And I'll do the same."

Deciding now was not the time to argue with her sister, she went into her office to grab her purse, then stopped in the bathroom to check her face. She was dressed casual today, in capris and a button-down short-sleeve white cotton shirt, with her hair up in a messy bun. But she had makeup on, so she decided she didn't need any fixing up.

Besides, it was just margaritas and dinner. She didn't need much sprucing up for that anyway.

She walked outside and, true to his word, Jason was leaning against the side of his truck, one hand casually tucked in his front pocket, one leg hooked in front of the other, looking like a tree she wanted to climb.

She sighed in appreciation.

"Ready?" he asked.

"Definitely ready."

They caught up on their weeks during dinner, Jason filling her in on his surgeries and some of the animals he'd seen, while Erin told him about some of the wedding swaps.

He took a bite of his food, then a swallow of beer. "Does that happen a lot?"

"No, fortunately. Most people stick to the dates they choose. This is kind of an anomaly."

"You'll make it work. If anyone can juggle weddings, you and your sisters can."

"Thank you. I appreciate the vote of confidence."

"You've always had good organizational skills. Remember when we built the fort out behind the vineyards?"

She laughed. "I haven't thought about that in years. It was all of us girls, then you and Owen and Clay. How old were we then? About nine or ten?"

"I think so. And we spent weeks building that thing."

"Yeah. And we borrowed—and I use the word 'borrowed' loosely—old pieces of wood from behind the barn."

"The guys liberated tools from home, plus nails. We'd spend every day—"

"All day," she added.

He laughed. "Yeah, all day working on it."

"And Louise would bring lunch out to us, and we'd sit on the ground eating sandwiches and talk about how we were going to decorate on the inside."

"No, you and Honor and Brenna would talk decorating. Clay and Owen and I would discuss various ways we'd defend it."

"I beg to differ. I discussed having enough windows to overlook all defense points. Brenna was the one who wanted curtains."

"Oh, right. And then Owen wanted to boot you off our team because you were a girl, and the two of you argued sexism for at least an hour."

She grinned. "I believe I made my point clear. That was a fun day."

His lips curved. "Not for Owen it wasn't. If I remember right, as punishment, you made him go into the house with Honor to help her search for the plastic dishes and the curtains."

"He was so miserable."

"And you loved every minute of it."

Thinking about Owen's misery—even past misery—made her happy at the moment. "I did. I believe that was the day he became a feminist."

Jason laughed. "He definitely believed in equal rights for women all his adult life. You obviously made him see the light."

She leaned back in her chair and sipped her water. "See? If men and women could just build a fort in their backyards more often, there'd be less arguing over equal rights."

"You think that's the way to solve arguments?"

She shrugged. "It's a start. Maybe a tree house could be the answer as well. Neutral ground, have a tea party."

"Put up some curtains."

"Develop common ground for enemy vantage points."

He laughed. "I can see the benefits."

"Defeating common enemies can bring about world peace. Or at least end an argument. Though nothing could beat our first fort."

Jason nodded. "That one was the best."

Erin could clearly visualize exactly what their fort had looked like—a serious disaster. But oh, how they'd loved the finished product. To their child imaginations, it was a castle. And they'd played in there the entire summer. Though they never had put drapes up in it. Their mother had balked when she'd found Brenna rooting through the linen closet, and had absolutely denied Brenna's request for fort drapes.

Well, they couldn't have everything. But they had managed to sneak out some rugs and pillows. And Louise always made them a big pitcher of lemonade, perfect for hot summer days.

"I guess I'll have to build a fort or a tree house in my backyard. Next time you and I have a disagreement, we'll take it to the fort."

She looked up at him. "Or maybe we could keep our arguments to a minimum?"

"You're ruining my fun, Erin. I was looking forward to building that tree house. You know I have that great big oak tree out back. It's perfect for a tree house."

She shook her head. "Fine. Build the tree house. I think you're just a big old kid at heart and you want that tree house for yourself."

He looked at her with that kind of direct, heated look that made her toes curl. "You could do all kinds of fun things in a tree house."

She arched a brow. "Like?"

"I don't know. Picnics. Read books. Defend yourself from invading zombies."

"And here I thought you were going to say something entirely different."

"Like what? Hot sex in a tree house?"

Her body flamed. "Yes."

"You know I think about that. Not tree house sex. But sex. With you. All the damn time."

She sighed, her body aching at the thought of being with him. "Then why the pull back the other night?"

"Because I'm at war with myself. I want you, Erin. I think you know that. But I don't want to do anything to screw up our friendship."

"And you think sex will do that."

"It might."

"And it might not."

"I'm not sure I'm willing to risk that just for some revenge fling."

His words stung. "So we won't have a revenge fling."

He looked confused. "Now you don't want to have sex."

"I do. I just don't want it to be about revenge, if that makes sense. I just want it to be about you and me, and what we want with each other."

He waited a beat before answering. "Okay."

"Look, just think about it. And I'll think about it. And we'll press pause on this whole thing for a minute. Take a breath, you know?"

He nodded. "Sure. So what do you want to do tonight?"

She exhaled, happy that they were back on solid ground again. She'd hated having that distance between them. Now it felt good between them again. Better than good, actually.

"How about a movie?" she asked. "There's that new romantic comedy that just came out."

He grimaced. "Sounds great."

Jason hated romantic movies. He was a horror-movie guy all the way.

He might have apologized, and they might have made some headway in their relationship, but that didn't mean she wouldn't make him suffer a little.

CHAPTER
······
fourteen

Even though Honor was the Bellini Weddings official planner, all the sisters typically pitched in to help on wedding days. Honor generally handled overall wedding planner duties, Brenna dealt with wine and the caterers, and Erin assisted Honor and otherwise went wherever she was needed.

This morning they all had a hearty breakfast, as was typical on wedding days.

"I forgot to ask you how your date went with Randall the other night?" Erin asked as she finished up her omelet.

"Oh, well, he's very nice."

"Code for they have nothing in common, Randall's a horny bastard and he probably tried to grope her midway through dinner," Brenna said.

"Brenna," their mother said.

"What? It's the truth, isn't it?"

Honor scooped eggs onto her fork and didn't answer.

Brenna gave a smug smile. "Thought so. Why do you always pick such losers, Honor?"

"That's not true. He seemed very nice."

"Oh, right. That's why he's always hitting on the bridesmaids at the weddings."

"What? I've never noticed that."

Brenna rolled her eyes.

Honor looked at Erin, who nodded. "He does."

"Really? I didn't know. Why didn't you tell me?"

"Because I thought you already knew that. Everyone knows it."

Honor sighed. "Okay, so maybe he wasn't such a good choice in dating material."

Brenna snorted.

"Hey, at least I am dating, which is better than hiding in the house all the time, Brenna."

Brenna lifted her chin. "I'll have you know I have a date this coming Friday."

Honor gave her a suspicious look. "With whom?"

"Travis McIntosh."

"Who the bloody hell is Travis McIntosh?"

Erin's gaze shifted to Finn, who normally stayed quiet during meals. Right now he was glaring at Brenna.

That was a fascinating development.

Brenna gave Finn a curious stare. "He's a guy I met at the library when I was doing genealogy research. He's doing research for his masters in communications."

"How interesting," Erin said.

"Oh, good," Honor said. "I'm happy to hear you're dating again."

Finn responded with a grunt, took his plate and got up from the table and went into the kitchen.

"What's up with him?" Brenna asked.

Erin and Honor exchanged glances and half smiles.

"No idea," Honor said.

They finished breakfast and Erin went upstairs to get

ready for the day. Today was Ellen Hansen and Tamira Marsey's wedding, and the early June day had dawned bright and sunny and absolutely perfect.

Since they had two brides marrying each other today, and Honor typically handled the brides, Honor was taking care of Ellen, and she asked Erin to look after Tamira. They had turned the groom's dressing room into a bride-to-be's paradise, complete with flowers and comfy cushioned chairs for family and attendants.

Armed with a tray of lemon-flavored water, orange juice and cookies, Erin knocked on the door to her bride's suite. Stefanie, Tamira's mother, opened the door.

"I thought you could all use some drinks and cookies," Erin said.

Stefanie smiled broadly. "Come in, Erin. We were just about to help Tamira get into her dress."

Tamira, a vision with her auburn hair curled and pulled up, one curl cascading over her shoulder, looked longingly over at the tray Erin had set on the table. "I was so nervous I couldn't eat breakfast. Now I want a cookie so damn bad I could scream. But the corset in this dress is so tight if I eat anything I might explode."

"I'll wager you have room in that dress for one cookie," Erin said. "And if you pass out at the altar it'll be all over social media before you can say 'I do.'"

Tamira nodded. "Point taken." She grabbed a cookie and nibbled. Then devoured. And ate another. Erin handed her a glass of orange juice and she took several sips.

Satisfied that her bride wouldn't face-plant at the altar, Erin stepped out and went to check on said altar. Flowers were set, the chair count was right and the grounds looked impeccable. She saw Agatha out of the corner of her eye going for a walk with her dad, so she sidestepped to catch up with them.

"Thank you for taking Agatha with you today, Dad," she said, bending down to give her some love.

Her puppy was doing great. She'd taken well to her harness and leash, and her dad seemed to have all the patience in the world in working with her. Erin felt bad that she'd been so busy the past few days, but they'd had a rush of brides come in to do tours and plan weddings for next summer and Honor had been inundated, so Erin was helping pick up the slack. Then they'd had several sit-down meetings with families and brides and grooms to go over budgets and planning, and Erin was always involved in those. Which meant Agatha had to be somewhere else because not everyone wanted an exuberant puppy in a wedding conference.

Fortunately, the entire family had fallen madly in love with Agatha, so whenever Erin couldn't be with her, someone was always happy to take over. She spent a lot of time with her dad or with Finn, since she loved being outside. Even the vineyard workers seemed happy to love on her or take her for walks. The one thing she never had to worry about was Agatha being neglected.

She ruffled Agatha's fur, then went back inside the main house to grab her planner, checking off items that had been taken care of for the wedding.

Guests had started to arrive, and they had people to help direct the guests to their seats at the vineyard.

Erin found Honor on the walkway between the bride and groom areas.

"How's Tamira?" Honor asked.

"Hungry. I took care of that. How's Ellen?"

"Calm as can be, surprisingly. She just wants to marry her girl."

Erin smiled. Wedding days always warmed her heart in ways she couldn't describe.

Honor laid her hand on Erin's arm. "You okay?"

"Of course I am. Why wouldn't I be?"

"It's a wedding day. You know."

"Oh. I'm fine, honey. We've done weddings here for as long as I can remember. This isn't my wedding day. It's someone else's. And, no, it doesn't bother me in the least."

"I'm so glad. Okay, I've gotta run. I'll text you when my bride is ready."

Since they had two brides today, they were going to do things a little differently. Ellen would walk down the aisle first, and then wait for Tamira to come down.

Erin was happy that both of the brides' parents were present for the wedding, though not all of their family members had approved or would be attending. Even in this day and age, there were still some people who objected to gay weddings.

Erin shrugged. It was their loss. Love was love and those who decided not to attend would miss out on a major happily-ever-after today.

Honor texted, so Erin went to Tamira's room to let her bride know they were ready. She had two bridesmaids with her, and her man of honor, her best friend from college.

The music started, and Erin led Tamira to the waiting area. The bridesmaids and the maid and man of honor had already walked down and were in place. After Erin got the text from Honor that Ellen had made her way down the aisle, she walked Tamira to the entrance to the vineyard.

Tamira took a deep breath, slipped her arm in her dad's, and made her way down the aisle.

As was typical, all three sisters stayed back and watched the ceremony, out of the way, but close enough in case someone needed them.

It was beautiful, and when the two brides enjoyed

their romantic kiss to seal the deal, everyone clapped. Erin and Brenna dashed away to make sure the barn was all set up for the reception, while Honor stayed behind to coordinate the bridal party and family photographs.

The afternoon wore on with drinks and lunch and photos and dancing. Everyone seemed to have a wonderful time. Erin didn't even have a chance to check her phone until after the reception ended at eight that night.

She had a text from Jason.

Free after the wedding stuff?

He'd asked her out for today. She'd told him they had a wedding that would likely not end until evening, and that she'd need to be involved.

She texted him back. Reception just ended. My feet hurt.

He replied right away. Come over. I'll rub your feet. Or any other parts that need rubbing.

Her lips curved and she typed a reply.

Okay.

Fortunately, they had a cleanup crew, so her services were done for the day. On her way back to the house, her phone buzzed. It was Jason again.

And bring Agatha with you.

Her face hurt from smiling so widely.
Damn that man.

CHAPTER

......

fifteen

JASON DIDN'T WANT to light candles or spread roses around the house or anything that would make Erin think he was assuming anything about tonight. But he did want her to know he was thinking about her comfort. He made some snacks, chilled wine and, just in case, put fresh sheets on the bed in the room where he was sleeping. He also cleaned the house so it would smell good.

After their conversation the other night, he didn't know where she stood, but he needed her to know he was open to the possibilities.

He was tired of tiptoeing around his need for her. It was time to man up and let her see how he felt. And if she wanted the same thing, great. If she didn't, they'd go back to being friends. But this nothing zone was driving him crazy.

Puddy followed him around while he put some touches in the living room. He'd stopped and bought a bouquet of fresh-cut flowers while he was in town today, so he laid those on the coffee table in the living room. His dog thought those were a gift for him and kept trying to nibble at them.

"Dude, not yours."

Puddy seemed offended by that, but after a couple of stern looks from Jason, the pup wandered off to wrestle with one of his toys.

He took a shower and changed into a clean pair of jeans and a T-shirt, then came out to the living room to find Puddy with a mouthful of flowers and stems.

"Dammit, Puddy," he muttered. "I told you those weren't for you."

He could have sworn Puddy smiled at him. He shook his head.

The doorbell rang, so he cast a glare at his misbehaving dog and went to answer the door.

Erin took his breath away. She wore a yellow sundress. Her raven hair spilled in waves over her shoulders.

"Hey," he said when he finally found his voice. "You look gorgeous."

"Thanks. You took a shower." She stepped closer and ran her fingers through his hair. He sucked in a breath at the feel of her fingers sliding along his scalp.

"I worked on the house today, so I had sawdust in my hair. Plus, I was sweaty."

She lifted up on her toes, leaned in and pressed her nose against his neck. "Mmm. You smell good."

He wanted to wrap his arm around her and kiss her right there on his doorstep. She'd probably let him. But he wanted to take things slow, let her decide the tempo this time. "Thanks. Come on in."

Since she had Agatha with her, who was straining at the leash to get at Puddy, she walked in and let Agatha off the leash. The two dogs ran down the hall and disappeared.

She looked down at the petals and stems on the living room floor. "What happened?"

He knelt down and picked up the mess. "My attempt to have flowers for you. Puddy had other ideas for them while I was showering. Sorry."

She laughed and squatted down, picked up one semi-intact daisy and brought it to her nose. "Pretty. Thank you."

"I tried. Next time I'll make sure any flowers I bring to you aren't left at dog level."

She stood. "Oh, there'll be a next time?"

"Hell yes there will be. A woman like you deserves flowers every day." He took one of the flowers he'd managed to salvage and tucked it behind her ear, enjoying the slight flush to her cheeks.

"I don't know what to make of you, Jason. I'm used to you teasing me. You've done that our entire lives. But this is a new side to you."

"Oh, you mean you don't know everything about me after all?" He went into the kitchen to get the wine, opened a bottle and poured two glasses.

"I guess not."

"That's good." He handed her a glass, then took the snacks he'd made out of the refrigerator and laid those out on the island, too. "I'd hate to think I was boring and predictable."

She took a sip of the wine, then picked up a mushroom and bacon bite and popped it into her mouth.

"You are anything but predictable, Jason. Did you make these?"

"Yeah." He took a bite as well.

"And these, too?" She tasted the apple-gouda pigs in a blanket, then smiled. "They're amazing."

He shrugged. "Just some easy-to-make appetizers. Not exactly rocket science."

"But you baked things. Tasty things. I'm impressed."

"I like to make interesting things. You can cook, too, if I remember right."

"Yes, I can. And I'm stealing both of these recipes for my next party."

He arched a brow. "You're having a party?"

"Yes. As soon as I find a place to live."

"What about the condo you and Owen got together?"

"I talked to the leasing manager the other day, told her the story about Owen dumping me at the altar. She was horrified and immediately let me out of the lease."

"Seriously?"

"Yes. She just went through a not-so-fun divorce, so I think I hit her emotional buttons. We won't get our deposit back, but at this point I'm happy to get out from under a long-term lease on a condo, or having to argue it out with Owen over which one of us has to live there. It was a place we chose together, and I don't want any part of it."

"I understand. You need a fresh start. Now you can take your time looking for your own place. Or just stay at the house for a while until you get your bearings."

She shrugged. "Maybe. I had planned to be out of there, to be living an independent life. A married life."

"I know." He wasn't sure how in depth she wanted to talk about Owen, so, again, he was going to let her take the lead on this. He was open to letting her vent about it. No matter how he felt about her, she was first and foremost his friend, and she'd been hurt. It was going to take her a while to get over it.

But instead she dove into the snacks and drank two glasses of wine and told him all about the day's wedding, which sounded like it went well.

They had moved over to the sofa to drink their wine. The dogs were playing together on Puddy's blanket on the floor.

"I'm glad you had a good day," he said.

"I did, actually. Seeing two people who obviously really care for each other made me realize that's what I deserve. I want someone who loves me unconditionally, who's going to be there for me no matter what."

"You do deserve that."

"But I'm not looking for that right now."

"What are you looking for right now?"

She laid her head against his shoulder and looked up at him. "Honestly? Just some breathing room, some space to gather my bearings and get back to normal life again. I don't want people tiptoeing around me thinking I'm going to burst into tears at any moment. I'm made of stronger stuff, you know?"

"Yeah, I do know that."

"I'm hurt, for sure. And I'll probably be hurt for a long time. Maybe forever. But I don't spend every waking moment thinking about Owen. He doesn't occupy space in my head or in my heart. What he did to me was devastating. I had a few days where I cried hard about it, and now I've moved past it. I go to work every day, and we have weddings at the vineyard every weekend, and when I see a bride I don't fall apart envisioning the wedding I didn't get to have. Owen and I weren't meant to be, and now it's time I get on with my life."

He admired Erin for her resilience. A lot of women would still be crying over how they'd been treated, making everyone feel sorry for them. Not her. She was mad, and she deserved to be mad. But she wasn't going to let that one incident in her life define her.

"You should have everything you want, Erin. Whatever you want."

"I want you, Jason. I don't need promises or a relationship. I don't want to look too far into the future. I just
want to live in the moment."

He wanted so much more, but he could give her what
she needed right now. He pulled her onto his lap and
cupped his palm on her neck, drawing her face to his.
When their lips met, it was an explosion of heat and passion that this time wouldn't be extinguished. Not by him,
anyway.

And from the way Erin gripped his shoulders, her
nails digging into his skin, he didn't think she wanted to
stop, either.

As they kissed, she rolled her hips across him, against
him, and he reached for her to draw her closer, her dress
riding up higher on her thighs. He let his fingers map a
trail across the satiny soft flesh of her skin, sliding his
hands under her dress.

Erin moaned against his lips, which made him lift his
hips against her.

She straightened. "We should be naked so we can rub
all our fun parts together."

He slid his hands up under her dress, teasing her inner
thighs. "You definitely have some fun parts I want to play
with."

She slid off of his lap, stood and tugged on his hand.
"Let's go."

He appreciated her enthusiasm. He stood and led her
down the hall, wishing his master bedroom was finished
so he could lay her on a new, bigger bed. Instead he could
only offer the small bedroom he currently occupied. He
opened the door and led her inside.

"Sorry about this," he said. "The master bedroom is still a work in progress."

"Trust me. The last thing I'm worried about right now is the size of your bedroom." She palmed his erection through his jeans. "This, though? Extremely interesting."

He sucked in a breath when she unzipped his jeans then tugged on his T-shirt. He drew the shirt over his head and tossed it aside.

Erin ran her hands over his chest and shoulders. "You have an amazing body. Look at all this chisel."

He laughed, then reached behind her to unzip her dress. "And you have curves that I've been dying to get my hands on for—"

She looked up at him, curiosity making her head tilt.

He didn't want her to know for how long. "For a while." He took the straps and pulled them down her arms, the top of her dress falling to her waist.

"No bra," he said, admiring the fullness of her breasts. "I like that."

"It's efficient. Plus, it's hot outside."

"It's hot in here, too."

He tugged the dress down, holding her hand so she could step out of it. He took the dress and draped it over the arm of the nearby chair, since her dress was much nicer than his clothes. Then he looked up at her.

She was wearing yellow lace underwear, a tiny scrap with just bands holding it to her hips.

Damn sexy woman. Curvy in all the right places, with hips and a waist and legs. Oh, her legs. He knelt to smooth his hands over her ankles, lingered at her toned calves, then behind her knees, making her laugh.

He looked up at her. "Ticklish there?"

"Maybe."

He grinned, then spread her legs and continued to map his way up her body with his hands, learning her beautiful thighs, her hips, reaching around to cup the globes of her ass.

How many times over the years had he admired her butt, had he fantasized being able to grab a handful of this sweet ass? Now he was here, on his knees in front of this amazing goddess, with his hands on each cheek, her sweet sex right in front of his face.

He reached for the straps of her underwear and drew them down, leaving her beautifully bare.

He stood, and she tugged his jeans to draw her closer to him. "I'm naked. You, on the other hand, still have some clothes on. Fix that."

"You got it." He dropped his jeans and boxer briefs, letting her see just how much he wanted her. And when her gaze roamed over his body, his cock grew steely hard.

He drew her into his arms and showed her how much he wanted her, taking her mouth in a hot kiss that made her tongue search for his. And when she sucked his tongue into her mouth, he groaned in response. He slid his fingers into her hair, all that softness spilling over his hand.

She smelled like his favorite cookie, a sweet vanilla scent that climbed into his senses, making him want to lick her all over. He moved his mouth from her lips to her jaw, down to her neck, feeling her body tremble in response. He ran his fingers down her back, memorizing every vertebra, every curve of her body.

He walked her backward, laying her down on the bed. He climbed next to her, taking this time to touch her, to kiss her collarbone, then her breasts, cupping the weight of one in his hand, molding and playing with her and then putting his mouth over the nipple.

Erin arched her back, gasping as he sucked.

God, she tasted good. He flattened his tongue across one nipple, then the other, teasing back and forth until her entire body shuddered.

This is what he wanted—to see her shatter, to watch this normally put-together woman totally come apart against his mouth.

He kissed the side of her breast, then moved down her rib cage, sliding down her body to kiss her belly, then her hip bone, teasing her with his teeth.

"Jason."

His name was uttered as a low moan, and he liked the way she said it. Like a plea.

He knew exactly what she needed.

A nest of raven curls covered the top of her sex. He touched her there with his fingers first, testing her readiness. She pressed against his hand, her body hot and damp.

Oh, yeah.

He placed his mouth over her, tasting the salty softness of her, then used his tongue and lips to tease and taste her until she writhed against him, making sounds that told him she liked what he was doing. So he kept doing it until she rolled against his face, her body shuddering around him as her orgasm hit her fast. He slowed, letting her come down a little, then brought her back up again, taking it slow and easy. And this time, she fell easy, but it was still just as sweet.

She made a satisfied sound, then lifted her head.

"Come up here with me."

He crawled up her body and lay next to her. She swept her fingers across his bottom lip.

"Anyone ever tell you that you're very good at that?"

His lips curved. "Anyone ever tell you how damn good you taste?"

She inhaled deeply, then let it out. "I needed that release. Thanks."

"You're welcome."

She rolled to her side and reached out to circle her fingertip over one of his nipples, then traced her fingers over his abs, down to his lower stomach, and wrapped her warm hand around his cock.

He hissed out a breath as she stroked him, all the while her gaze stayed focused on his face. And if he let her keep doing that, he was going to lose it.

He rolled her over and planted his mouth on hers, climbing half on her so his cock rested against her thigh.

She lifted her lips from his. "You're teasing me."

"How?"

"With your damn cock. I want it inside me."

He smiled. "I can make that happen."

"Then do it. Now. Not that I have a complaint about you rubbing against me. Because I like that part. I like all your parts, actually. One of your parts specifically. That needs to be in me. Did I mention now?"

She was making him crazy.

He rolled off of her and ripped open the drawer of his nightstand, fumbling around for the box of condoms he kept there. It took him a few seconds to find it, but he pulled out the box and grabbed a condom. He had it on in record time.

Erin was propped up on her side, her head resting on her hand as she watched him.

"That took forever. Now I'm out of the mood."

He arched a brow. "Seriously?"

"No, of course not." She laughed and held her arms out for him.

He blew out a breath. "Dammit, Erin. I was prepared to do math to get my hard-on to go away."

"Now, why would we want to waste a glorious hard cock like that on math? Get over here."

She really was trying to kill him. But as he looked at her, her beautiful raven hair spread out like midnight waves across his pillow, her knees raised and her legs spread in blatant invitation, he figured if he died now he'd be happy.

Okay, not completely happy because he hadn't had her yet. So maybe dying could wait just a little longer.

He climbed between her legs and settled his body on top of hers, then slid inside of her, feeling all of her heat surrounding him. And when he kissed her, she wrapped her arms around him and locked her legs around his back, pulling him in deeper. Fully settled, he stilled and closed his eyes, absorbing the way her body convulsed around him in warmth.

"Mmm," she said. "Now this is good."

Yup. She was definitely going to kill him.

But then she lifted, and he met her with a thrust, and it was on, because this was what he'd waited a lifetime for and never thought he'd have. To have his face buried in her neck and inhale her fragrance, to feel her nails raking down his arms as he moved within her, and to hear those hot-as-fuck moaning sounds she made? It was all a rush, a high he didn't want to come down from.

Their bodies were slick with sweat, sliding against each other as the pace quickened. He felt her restlessness peak as she tightened around him. He swept his hand under her butt and lifted her pelvis so he could grind against her.

"Oh," she said. "Oh, Jason, yes. Right there."

She spun out of control, convulsing around his cock as waves of climax made her cry out. She bit his shoulder and shuddered and he lost it right there, tilting his head back as he groaned, his orgasm like lightning bolts shooting through his body.

He rolled over to his side and took Erin with him, not wanting to let her go. He kissed her, their breaths mingling hot as passion still lingered between them. He left her to dispose of the condom, then went into the kitchen to grab two glasses of water. When he came back she had propped herself into a sitting position.

"Water?" he asked.

"Yes, thank you."

He handed her a glass and stood at the side of the bed while he took several long gulps, then put the glass on the nightstand. Erin took a few sips and handed her glass to him. He climbed onto the bed next to her and she laid her head on his chest, murmuring satisfied sounds as she did.

He couldn't help but smile at that.

She smoothed her hand down his chest and abs. "That was magnificent."

"Yeah. Sure was."

She tilted her head back to look at him. "I hope you don't expect this to be a one-and-done thing. I expect to use you repeatedly."

He snorted out a laugh. "Use me? You intend to use me? I'm hurt, Erin."

"No, you're not. Your cock is already at half-mast and jumping for joy at the thought of heading back into action."

"Okay, fine. But I hope you'll at least take me out to dinner on occasion."

She shrugged. "I'll think about it."

He could fall in love with this woman. Hell, he was already half there.

And that was a dangerous thought, because she just wanted sex and he knew it.

"So?" she asked. "You ready?"

"To service you, m'lady? Your wish is my command."

She climbed onto his lap and straddled him, gracing him with a wicked smile. "You always say the right things, Jason."

CHAPTER

......

sixteen

ERIN WOKE EARLY. She never needed an alarm anyway. They had an appointment with a bride and groom at ten thirty, so she had to get back to the house to shower and get ready.

But rolling over and seeing Jason's naked back was the nicest way to wake up this morning. She wanted to linger, to run her hands over his skin and kiss him and make love to him again. And maybe again.

They'd barely managed four hours sleep last night. Jason was a very generous lover, with amazingly talented hands and a mouth that could do incredible things. Not to mention a cock that got so hard and could go and go and go. She came so many times she knew she was going to be sore today.

She'd smile about that all day long. If a girl was going to have a hot fling, she should do it up right. Though she supposed a fling should be with someone random, and Jason wasn't random at all. After they were done doing whatever it was they were doing, he was still going to be in her life.

So maybe this was a friend fling instead. She trusted Jason. And when this was over, they could go on being friends.

Simple, right?

He rolled over and gave her a very hot, sleepy smile. "Want some coffee?"

"I'd love some coffee."

He got out of bed and gave her the opportunity to ogle his extremely fine naked body. Her own body reacted viscerally with a rush of desire.

Down, girl. You have to get to work.

With a reluctant sigh, she left the bed, used the bathroom and got dressed.

"Coffee's on," Jason said as he met her in the hall. "And both the dogs are outside."

"Thanks."

He stopped and pressed her up against the wall, his hands all over her body as he kissed her and made her hot and needy and regretting the morning meeting. Because if she had her way they'd be back in his bed right now. And judging from the erection rubbing between her legs, that's what he wanted, too.

She laid her hands on his chest. "I have a meeting this morning."

He took a step back. "Dammit."

"My thoughts exactly."

"I'll be back in a minute."

"Okay."

She went into the kitchen and poured herself a cup of coffee, opened the fridge and was happy to find cream in there. She added cream and inhaled the first few sips.

Her phone buzzed so she picked it up. It was Honor reminding her of the meeting this morning. She rolled her eyes. Like she'd forget. Jason's phone was right next to hers so she heard it buzz. Her eyes widened when she saw Owen's name light up on his phone. She couldn't help but glance at the message.

Hey, Jason. Is Erin okay?

Her stomach dropped. She looked over at her phone, scrolling through her messages. One from her mom; one from her friend Alice; and one from Brenna.

Nothing from Owen. Owen, her ex-fiancé who'd left her two days before their wedding.

He hadn't texted her. She assumed he was back in town and he hadn't texted or called her to see how she was.

But he'd texted Jason asking about her.

That son of a bitch. That coward. How dare he?

Fury boiled inside of her. She slipped on her shoes, grabbed her purse and her keys and opened the door. Agatha and Puddy came in so she put on Agatha's leash.

"Whoa," Jason said as he came into the kitchen. "You're leaving?"

"Yes. I've . . . gotta go."

"So fast? I was going to make us breakfast."

She couldn't even find the words to tell him how upset she was right now. "I've gotta go, Jason."

"What's wrong?"

She was already at the door, but he followed. "Check your phone. You'll figure it out."

"What?"

"I glanced at the message on your phone when it buzzed. I just can't deal with that right now. I'll talk to you later."

She was out the door before he could say anything else, tears pricking her eyes as she got Agatha into the car and started it up.

No. She would not cry another tear over that bastard.

She turned onto the main road, focusing her attention on driving.

Of course Owen would have texted Jason instead of her. He couldn't even face her to break up with her in person. Why did she think he would do that now, even with something as simple as a text?

Was he back in town? It had been over two weeks since their non-wedding. He was likely back and had been back. Had he come to talk to her, to explain his change of heart? No. He hadn't. Maybe he never would. He probably intended to leave her wondering forever what the hell had happened to make him change his mind.

She turned onto the highway, shoving Owen out of her mind. She would not think about him. Not now, not ever. It was over. Why did she even care that he texted Jason?

Because his text had been about her, asking if she was okay.

No, she was not okay, dammit.

The display on her car brought up a call. It was Jason. She ignored it, knowing he wanted to talk to her about the message from Owen.

She couldn't do it. Not now. Later, after she'd calmed down. Because she was most definitely not calm right now.

She pulled off the highway and made a turn, her stomach still in knots, her emotions a mess. She still had Jason's scent on her, could still feel his touch and the warmth of his body against hers. And with one text, all the deliciousness had been wiped away.

They'd had such a perfect night together. And Owen had ruined it.

Damn that bastard.

• • • • • •

JASON DRAGGED HIS fingers through his hair as he paced the kitchen and stared at the message from Owen. He couldn't imagine what must be going through Erin's mind, knowing she'd seen that.

Obviously, Owen hadn't called or texted Erin. That had to be what had upset her.

And why the hell was Owen asking *him* how Erin was doing? If he wanted to know he should find out for himself by going directly to Erin.

He was still so damn mad at his best friend that he wanted to kick his ass. He grabbed his phone and typed out an angry reply, then immediately deleted it.

"Shit." He tossed the phone back on the kitchen island.

He was torn, felt stuck in the middle between his two best friends, one of whom he'd slept with last night.

He needed to hear Owen out, figure out why Owen had done what he had. But doing so felt like a betrayal of Erin.

He didn't know what to do.

So, instead, he went to grab a cup of coffee. The rest of it he'd figure out later.

CHAPTER

. . . . . .

seventeen

WAIT. SO HE texted Jason but not you?"

Erin nodded, taking two very long sips of her margarita, so happy that Alice Weatherford had called her today and asked if they could have dinner. She needed a night out with someone she could be honest with and sort her feelings out with, and Alice was the perfect friend for that.

"But why?" Alice dug a chip into the guacamole.

"I have no idea."

"Did you ask Jason if he'd been in contact with Owen?"

"I didn't. I was so shocked and pissed off I ran out of there like my hair was on fire."

"And this was after the night of hot sex?"

"Yes. And now I've let an entire week go by without talking to him. I was so embarrassed after what happened that every time I picked the phone up to call or text him, I just couldn't do it. And now he probably thinks I'm not worth the trouble."

Alice tilted her head and gave her a sympathetic look. "Oh, honey."

"I know. It was stupid. But just seeing Owen's name come up on Jason's phone made me . . . I don't know. Temporarily lose my mind, I guess."

"And you haven't talked to Jason at all this week?"

"No. He called and texted several times. I just felt so idiotic after running out of his house I didn't know what to say."

Alice tilted her head. "You have to talk to him. If nothing else, to find out what Owen had to say."

"I don't care what Owen has to say. I do care that I probably hurt Jason's feelings. We had such a good night, Alice. And I ruined it by bailing."

"I doubt you ruined anything." Alice took a sip of her drink. "But you should still talk to him."

"I will." As soon as she developed some courage. She ate some chips and dip, then polished off her margarita, signaling her server for a refill. "Anyway, enough about me. Tell me what's going on with you. How was your trip to LA?"

"It was good. I picked up a new client and I've already got him set up to meet someone."

"That's fabulous."

"Thanks. I think the two of them have so much in common. They'll make a great match."

"When's the date?"

"Saturday night. He's a musician and she's a graphic artist."

Their server brought her margarita, and she ordered more chips and salsa along with guacamole. Erin turned her attention back to Alice. "Okay, so they're both creative types. That gives them something in common."

"Exactly. They both work very hard, sometimes too hard. Neither of them have taken enough time to work on their personal lives. So I think the idea of both of them looking for someone at this time is kind of like . . ."

"Kismet?" Erin asked.

Alice smiled. "Yes. I mean, even on paper I could feel it. It's like I know they're going to hit it off right away, that their match is going to be like lightning in a bottle."

"I see that Clay has convinced you of that chemistry thing you used to object to."

She offered up a serene smile. "Don't tell him he was right. I'll never live it down."

Erin shrugged. "I saw the chemistry between the two of you from the first day you met."

"He proposed last weekend."

Erin's heart did an excited flip. "Wait. What? Oh my God, Alice. He did? Why didn't you tell me that first thing?"

Alice's face blushed a peachy pink. "I don't know. I'm still getting used to the idea of being engaged."

Erin grabbed Alice's left hand. "I didn't see a ring. No ring?"

"No. He wants us to pick it out together. He said he'd never presume and choose one that he liked when he knows I'd want to shop."

"Aww. What a man. He's so right about that. Tell me everything."

"My parents were in town, so we all had dinner at his folks' place. I thought it was just going to be a nice dinner, with our parents getting to know each other. And then after dinner and before dessert, we were all sitting in the living room, and he gets up and starts talking about how he knew almost instantly that I was the one woman he wanted in his life forever, and how he loved me, and how he'd move heaven and earth to be with me."

"Which he did."

"He so did. And then he got down on one knee and asked me if I'd do him the honor of marrying him. It was very traditional and romantic and I cried and threw myself into his arms and said yes."

Erin's eyes filled with tears. "That is the sweetest, most romantic proposal I've ever heard, Alice."

"It was really lovely. My mom told me later that Clay had pulled her and my dad aside before dinner to ask for their blessing."

Erin laid her hand over her heart. "He really is your cowboy."

"I never in a million years thought this LA city girl would fall head over heels in love with an Oklahoma rancher. And yet here we are. I live here, and now we're getting married."

"You know I'll help you plan the wedding, no matter where it is."

"Oh, we want to get married at the vineyard, Erin. Clay and I have already talked about it. My parents are in love with the idea."

Erin's heart picked up its pace. "Seriously? We'd love that. You know Honor and Brenna will go crazy."

"I wanted to tell you first before I do it all official-like and book an appointment. And I was kind of hesitant to tell you."

Erin frowned. "Why?"

"I didn't want to throw an engagement in your face after what you've gone through."

"Don't be ridiculous. I'm fine. A little pissed off at the moment, which has nothing to do with you. In no way would I ever want you to downplay your own happiness on my behalf." She slid out of her chair and pulled Alice out of hers so she could give her friend a hug.

Alice squeezed her back, then the two of them sat back down and consumed more margaritas in celebration.

"Now, tell me your wedding plans," Erin said. "Have you made any yet? I know you have because you're a planner like me."

Alice slanted a wry smile at her. "Actually, if it were up to Clay we'd elope. Like tomorrow. He mentioned Paris."

Erin knew Clay. He was practical as hell. But with Alice? Completely smitten and madly in love. "That boy wants to marry you."

"In the worst way. I just love him so much."

"So what date are you looking at?"

"Next spring. Which I know is crazy because it's less than a year away and you're probably all booked up."

"It's tight, but let me pull up the schedule." She grabbed her phone.

"Of course you have it in your phone."

Erin looked up from her phone and grinned. "Of course I do. You never know when I might run into a prospective bride."

"See? This is why we plan."

Erin pulled up next year's calendar. "What month?"

"May? I'd do April, too."

She looked at the month of May first, checking each weekend, surprised to see they had a Saturday open, then remembering one of their couples had pushed their date recently and they hadn't filled that spot yet. She looked up at Alice and smiled. "We have the third Saturday in May."

Alice's eyes widened. "Seriously? Put us down for that date."

"Don't you want to check your calendar and ask Clay?"

"No. He'll be fine with it. Put us down for the date before someone else grabs it."

Erin entered Alice's and Clay's names in the schedule, then saved it. "Done."

Alice gave her an enthusiastic grin. "I'm *so* excited. I'm texting Clay the date right now."

"And while you do that, I'll text Brenna and Honor. If it's okay that I tell them the news."

Alice was busy texting, but nodded. "Of course."

She sent a group text to her sisters, letting them know Alice and Clay's engagement news, along with the wedding date that she'd entered into the master system. It didn't take long before they responded.

First, from Honor: Engaged! This is so exciting. And wedding here at the vineyard? Can't wait to start planning!

Followed by another text from Honor: Wait. Where are you? I'm coming to help celebrate.

She gave Honor their location.

Honor replied again: Brenna's with me. She squealed. We're both coming.

Erin looked up at Alice. "My sisters are thrilled for you. And they're both joining us."

Alice nearly vibrated with joy. "Who knew tonight was going to be such a celebration?"

"Clearly we need more margaritas."

"Yes. More margaritas."

Erin signaled their server.

CHAPTER

......

eighteen

JASON FINISHED MOWING and trimming the yard just before dark, then started laying the tile in the bathroom. He liked the style and the way the pattern looked on the floor. It was an oversized bathroom and would take a while, especially since he had to tile the shower, too, but in another couple of weeks he'd have the master bedroom and bath finished.

After he took a long lukewarm shower, he changed into shorts and a sleeveless shirt. He fixed a tall glass of ice water, then stared into the fridge, trying to figure out what he was going to fix for dinner. It was humid as hell outside since a storm was coming, so he didn't feel like firing up the grill. He decided to make a turkey and avocado sandwich instead along with some carrots and hummus.

He took his drink and food into the living room and turned on the TV, found a baseball game and settled in. Puddy came over with his favorite chew bunny in his mouth, did three circles on the floor by Jason's feet and went to sleep.

Jason polished off the sandwich, then dove into the

hummus with his carrots. It tasted good. When the doorbell rang, he frowned, picked up his plate and went to the
door. Who the hell would be here this late? He took a
peek and raised his brows.

Erin.

He opened the door and found her leaning against the
door frame.

"Hey," she said, "you up?"

His lips curved at the slight slur to her words. "Obviously. You drunk?"

"Maybe a little. But not so much that I don't know
what I'm doing or saying. Are we clear on that?"

"Perfectly."

"Good. Can I come in?"

"Sure." He made room for her. She stopped to give
Puddy some love, then dropped her purse on the table.

"Did you just eat?" she asked, looking down at the
plate in his hand.

"Yeah. I mowed, then worked on the master bath."

She nodded. "You're always working, always doing
something. You stay busy."

He didn't think that needed an answer. "You didn't
drive over here, did you?"

"No. Clay dropped me off. He came to pick up Alice,
who had too much to drink. We were celebrating. Did
you know they got engaged?"

"I heard that today. Pretty great, huh?"

"Yes. It's very exciting. Anyway, Clay offered to drive
me home. I suggested here would be better since we need
to talk."

"Okay." He put his plate on the island. "Would you
like some . . . water?"

She wrinkled her nose. "I'd rather have a margarita. I
had a few of those at the restaurant."

Clearly.

"I just want to make it clear, though, that I'm not drunk. I'm clearheaded enough to have a conversation. To make decisions. To know what I'm doing."

"Okay. How about some water anyway?"

She shrugged, then kicked off her shoes. "Fine."

While he fixed her glass, she made her way to the sofa and plopped down on it. He wondered if she'd still be awake when he got there. She was, sitting straight up, her legs crossed over each other. She was seemingly riveted to the baseball game.

So she did have her shit together. Fine.

He handed her the glass.

"Thanks," she said, taking a few sips then setting it on the table. "About the other day, when I ran out on you. I saw the text from Owen and I reacted. I was mad. Not at you. I just needed to get out. I'm so sorry for the way I behaved, for not answering your calls and texts. Obviously, I'm still kind of a mess about him."

Not exactly what he wanted to hear. But it made sense. They'd been about to get married. It wasn't like her feelings for Owen were just going to disappear after a few weeks.

"It's okay. But you know you don't have to run whenever his name comes up. You can talk to me about how you feel."

"I feel pissed off. I'm mad that he texted you and not me. Is that the first time?"

"The first time I've heard from him? Yeah."

"Did you reply?"

"No. I don't know what to say to him without telling him to go fuck himself. And if he wants to know how you're doing, he should ask you."

That made her smile. "Thank you."

He picked up her hand. "Owen and I have been best friends since we were kids. You and I, we've been friends since we were kids, too. And now? We're something else. So now I don't know what the hell to do. But what he did to you was shitty, so I'm on your side, no matter what my relationship with Owen is. And that's just the way it has to be right now."

She let out a breath, feeling as uncomfortable as Jason likely felt. "I never meant to put you in the middle, to make you feel like you have to choose between your friendship with Owen and your friendship with me. And I didn't set out to do that when I . . . when we . . ."

He rubbed her arm. "I know that. And it's not your place to worry about it. Owen and me? We'll work out our own shit. That has nothing to do with you. You and Owen? That's between the two of you and none of my business."

"There's nothing between Owen and me. He lost the right to have any relationship with me when he walked out on me. It's over, Jason. I need to make that clear to you."

He wanted to believe that, but he didn't. There were way too many unresolved issues between Erin and Owen. And until they truly ended things, Jason knew he couldn't have a future with her. But the one thing he was afraid of was ruining the great friendship he had with Erin. The problem was, every step they took forward into having some kind of a relationship could potentially risk putting an end to their friendship.

Was he willing to risk that? Was he willing to have *his* heart broken?

He didn't have an answer. All he knew was that she needed him right now. And he wouldn't walk away from her.

He pulled her against him. "You don't have to do anything about Owen right now. You know that, right?"

"I guess I didn't. Until now. I just saw his name and thought . . . Oh, God. I have to talk to him now, don't I?"

"No, you don't. He doesn't get to make that call. You don't have to see him or talk to him until you decide the time is right."

He felt her body relax against his. She turned and molded against him. "You know what I'd like to do right now?"

"What?"

"Watch a baseball game and be with you."

He smiled and rubbed her back. "That sounds like a great plan."

She was asleep before the end of the inning. He stayed with her—holding her in his arms—for two more innings, then he carried her into the bedroom and laid her on his bed. She helped him get her clothes off, then she rolled over on her side and went right back to sleep.

He texted Brenna to let her know where Erin was so no one at the Bellini house would worry, then he let Puddy outside to run around for a bit while he cleaned up the kitchen. He brought the dog in, turned off the lights and went into the bathroom to brush his teeth. He stripped and climbed into bed next to Erin, sliding his body alongside hers. She rubbed her butt against his crotch and snuggled in against him, making him instantly, painfully hard.

She might have passed out right away, but it was going to take him a long time to fall asleep tonight.

CHAPTER

······

nineteen

ERIN SLOWLY OPENED her eyes, trying to gather her bearings.

First, she wasn't in her bed. Second, she had a slight headache. Third, she was wrapped up like a cocoon with a solid, warm body behind her.

Right. Jason. She'd demanded Clay drive her over to Jason's house last night so she could apologize for running out on him. They'd talked. Then she'd fallen asleep while curled up in his arms on the sofa. And woken up the same way, apparently, except now she was naked, with a deliciously hot naked man behind her.

She scooted against him, and he made a muffled noise that sounded like a mixture of a groan and a moan. But his cock was hard, and his hand came up to cup her breast. And when his thumb brushed across her nipple, she drew in a sharp breath. She didn't need words to express her pleasure at his movements, she just let her body do the talking by writhing against him.

His body knew exactly how to respond, hard and

exciting and sliding between her thighs in a delicious tease of thrust and parry that left her damp and trembling.

He moved away, but she heard the tearing of a package, and then he was right back there, against her, his cock probing as he reached his hand around to find her clit and make her ready.

She was more than ready. So when he slid inside of her, she was the one making moaning sounds. And then it was all breaths and Jason kissing her neck, heavy breathing and moans and the two of them moving slowly against each other until she peaked with a gasp, and Jason shuddered right after.

Now that was the perfect way to begin the day.

They stayed like that for a few minutes and Erin enjoyed the feeling of being in Jason's arms. Until Puddy's face appeared at the side of the bed.

"Hi, Puds," she said, reaching out to rub her hand over him.

"He needs to go out," Jason said. "I'll take care of it."

"Mind if I take a shower?"

"No. Go ahead. I'll make coffee while you do that."

They both got out of bed and Erin went into the hall bathroom and took a quick shower, wishing she had a change of clothes with her. But she didn't, so she had to put on last night's clothes. Then she found her purse and grabbed her hairbrush to comb out the tangles in her hair.

Now she needed some damn coffee. She made her way into the kitchen to find Jason sitting at the island with his cup. He was scrolling through his phone while Puddy had his face in his food bowl.

"Hey," she said, leaning over to press a kiss to the side of his neck.

"Hey. You smell good."

"In yesterday's clothes, unfortunately." She walked over to the coffeemaker to pour herself a cup.

"You could leave a change of clothes here."

Her hand stilled. She turned around. "Are you comfortable with that?"

"Well, yeah. Are you?"

"I guess. I don't know. I mean, we're just fooling around, right?"

His lips curved. "Definitely fooling around."

"Doesn't me leaving clothes here imply something else?"

"I don't even know what you're talking about, Erin. I just figured if you ended up spending the night sometimes, you might want fresh clothes for the next day. It's not a big deal unless you make it one."

He was right. She was reading way too much into it. It wasn't like he'd asked her to move in or anything. She needed to relax and roll with it. This thing with Jason was all about having fun and reclaiming her joy.

"So what's on tap for today?" he asked. "A wedding, I presume?"

Oh, right. It was Saturday. And, fortunately, it was early in the day and the wedding wasn't until tonight. "Yes. An evening event."

"Do you have time for me to make breakfast?"

Her lips curved. "I have time."

"Good."

They ended up making breakfast together, because Erin wasn't the type to sit and watch. They had pancakes and eggs and sausages, which were all delicious. Then they cleaned up and Jason drove her back to the restaurant so she could pick up her car. He opened the truck door for her and helped her out.

"What are your plans for today?" she asked.

"Working on the master bathroom."

"Fun."

He laughed. "Yeah."

He pulled her against him. "Any wedding stuff tomorrow?"

She shook her head. "No. We have a free Sunday."

"Good. How about I take you fishing with me tomorrow?"

Her brows shot up. "Fishing? Do I look like the kind of girl who likes to go fishing?"

"Yes, you do. You'd love to get up before dawn and go fishing with me."

At the moment, his hands roamed up and down her back, and she'd love to do just about anything with him.

"Okay. Let's go fishing before dawn tomorrow. And then after that we'll go shopping. I need some new shoes."

She wished she had her phone out so she could capture the look of horror on his face.

"Shopping. You mean like at the mall?"

"Yes, that's exactly what I mean."

He grimaced. "Okay. Fishing, then shopping. But I've seen your shoe collection, Miss Bellini. And you do not need new shoes."

"I beg to differ. And you agreed to go."

"I did, didn't I?" He bent and brushed his lips across hers, and every time he did that it ignited something warm and sensual throughout her body.

He was a constant surprise to her, and if there was one thing Erin loved, it was surprises.

"I'll text you later," he said.

"Okay."

He released her and took a step back. "Have a good day, Erin."

Oh, she would, because she'd think about that kiss. "You, too, Jason."

She got in her car and watched him in her rearview mirror as she drove off.

CHAPTER

······

twenty

Jason could tell from the moment he picked up Erin that she was not at all thrilled about having to get up before dawn. But he also knew she'd never back down from a challenge. Maybe fishing wasn't really a challenge. He knew from her dad that he'd taken all the girls fishing when they were little, and had taught them how to bait a line. Jason had been fishing with Johnny Bellini, and he'd told him hilarious stories of the girls squealing about worms and lures and wriggling fish. He'd said that's how they'd learned patience. Jason could only imagine how much patience Johnny'd had to have to teach three little girls how to fish.

Maybe someday Jason would have daughters of his own, and he could teach them how to fish. Everyone should learn. It was a great way to capture your own food, something everyone should know how to do.

Erin had fallen back to sleep in the truck on the way to the lake. He'd left her alone, figuring she'd likely been up late last night dealing with the wedding. Plus, she looked pretty with her head propped against her sweat-shirt as she leaned against the window, her long dark lashes resting against her cheeks. If he wasn't driving he'd curl up next to her and grab a little sleep himself.

He'd spent a lot longer working in the bathroom yesterday than he'd planned, but now the tile floor was finished and he could set the vanity. It wouldn't be long now and he'd have an actual working bathroom.

One step at a time. He was looking forward to the day he could stop sleeping in the guest room.

Then he'd invite Erin over to check it out and see if she approved.

She yawned and stretched as she woke, blinking her eyes open to survey the road ahead of them. "How close are we?"

"Nearly there."

"Great. I need to pee."

"There's a place just up ahead. We can get some coffee and breakfast sandwiches, and you can use the restroom there."

He pulled into the shop and parked. They went inside and used the restrooms, then made a beeline for the coffee, grabbed a couple of sandwiches, and Jason bought some bait and a fishing license for Erin since he already had his. They loaded back up in the truck and Jason headed down the road for about a mile, then took a right turn.

"Have you got a favorite fishing spot?" she asked.

"Yeah. I've used it several times. It's remote and quiet, so I don't think anyone else will be there. Plus, the fishing is good in that location."

"So, like a secret spot."

He glanced over at her and smiled. "Kind of, yeah."

He parked at a small spot near the edge of the lake. It was still dark, and he knew his way around this area and didn't really want to set up lights. But Erin wasn't familiar with the area, so he stuck close to her as he unpacked the fishing gear, coolers and chairs. He got Erin positioned at the water's edge and then handed everything off to her, and she set it all up. She did a great job organizing it all, which came as no surprise to him. By the time he grabbed the poles and climbed off the back of the truck, she had the chairs set up, their coffee cups and sandwiches were sitting on top of one of the coolers, and she was already spraying herself down with mosquito repellant.

She handed him the spray and he took care of applying it.

"Do you want me to get your line and pole ready?" he asked.

"No, I can do it."

He smiled, figuring she'd want to prove to him that she was capable. Not that he had any doubts.

He'd grabbed some chicken livers at the bait shop, because it was the best bait for catching catfish, in his opinion. He watched as Erin adeptly wound the liver onto the hook, set her line and dropped her pole into the water.

"You're pretty good at this," he said as he did the same with his line.

She took a seat and grabbed her cup of coffee, popped the top off the lid and took a sip. "I didn't have much choice. My dad was determined to make all of us learn how to fish."

He sat in the chair next to hers and opened up his coffee to take a long swallow. "But did you enjoy it?"

"The first couple of times? No. It was messy and then he taught us to clean the fish we caught and that was even worse. Brenna was the best at it. For some reason fish guts didn't seem to bother her in the least. But after a while I learned that I was the best at actually catching the fish, and when you have two other sisters, everything is a competition."

"I see. And what was Honor the best at?"

"Cooking the fish after we caught it."

He laughed. "Hey, everyone's got their talents."

"The three of us have managed to split them up pretty well." She checked her line. Nothing was happening, so she opened her breakfast sandwich, and Jason decided he'd eat as well.

"This is pretty decent," Erin said. "Eggs, cheese, sausage, and the biscuit is yum."

"Yeah, they do a good job on the food there. They make great lunch sandwiches, too."

"Oh. I've got something, I think." She laid her sandwich and coffee on top of the cooler.

Jason saw the tug as well, so he stood and went over to watch her reel in the line, ready to offer help if she needed it.

She didn't. It may have been a while since she'd been fishing, but she obviously hadn't lost a step. She expertly gave the fish a little line, then gently reeled him in.

It wasn't a huge catfish, but it was a good start. He swept it up in the net, then detached it from the hook and deposited it in the fish cooler.

"Nice job," he said.

She smiled. "Thanks. It feels good to get that first catch under me." She washed her hands, then went back to finish her sandwich.

He liked that she wasn't at all grossed out by handling a fish, that she hadn't once complained—about anything, even though he knew this wasn't her jam, and she seemed totally relaxed, which was what he'd brought her here for.

After they finished eating, they settled into their chairs. Jason stared out over the water.

"How often do you get to fish?" she asked.

"I try to get out at least once or twice a month, depending on what else is going on. But I rotate Saturdays at the clinic with the other veterinarians, and I'm on call the weekend I work, so I don't get out here as often as I'd like to."

"Do you come out here by yourself?"

He nodded. "Mostly. Sometimes Clay will come out with me, and Owen used to until he bought the brew pub, but I like being out here on my own."

"Why?"

"It gives me time to think, to process."

She looked over at him. "Do you have a lot to process?"

"Sometimes. Work stuff, house things, dating."

"Really. Tell me."

"Nothing to talk about right now. Work's going well, the house is moving along, and I'm not dating anyone but you."

She paused and stared at him.

"What?"

"Do you think we're dating?"

Now it was his turn to pause. "What do *you* think we're doing, Erin?"

"I . . ." She didn't finish, just looked out over the water again.

So maybe they did have something to talk about. But then he got a tug on his line and it was his turn to reel in a fish. And his took longer because it was a big one. So by the time he'd struggled with it and pulled it out of the water and they both got it into the net and in the cooler, they were sweating and ready for a cold ice water.

He pulled the water out and handed a bottle to her, then took a long guzzle of his.

"That was a great catch," she said.

"Yeah, it was." And then her line went off, and they were onto another catch, which kept them busy for another fifteen minutes reeling it in. By the time they'd put that one in the cooler they had two nice-sized fish.

"Wow, two good fish in a row," he said.

"I know. That was fun."

"And hey, we were in the middle of a conversation before those fish."

She arched a questioning brow. "We were? About what?"

"You asked if I thought we were dating. And I asked you what you thought we were doing. And then you paused."

"Oh, right." And then she paused again. Only this time she wasn't saved by a fish.

Jason decided to let her talk whenever she was ready, but he wasn't going to say anything until she did. He was content to watch the sun come up over the lake like a big orange fireball, sending streaks of red across the lower horizon and a shimmering glow skimming across the surface of the water.

"I don't know what's happening with us, Jason. You know I'm not looking for a relationship. I just want to have some fun."

"Which we are. At least I am. You're having fun, aren't you?"

Her lips curved. "Yes."

"We're going out and doing things together, right?"

"Yes."

"Are you seeing anyone else?"

She frowned. "Of course not."

"And I'm pretty sure we're having sex."

He watched her sharp inhale, followed by her very satisfied smile. "We sure are."

He grabbed his sunglasses from the front of his baseball cap and slid them on, then looked over at her and shot her a grin. "Then I'd call that dating. It's not a big deal, Erin. No promises are being made here."

"You're right. I just don't want you to think I'm stringing you along."

He laughed. "I don't feel strung. Relax, okay?"

"Okay."

They went quiet and let their lines do the talking in the water, and Jason had time to think. Of course he had feelings for Erin. He'd always had feelings for Erin. But after Owen had stepped in and things had gotten serious between the two of them, Jason had buried those feelings deep. He'd thought they were gone.

They weren't. Now that she and Owen had broken up and the two of them were doing . . . whatever it was they were doing, those feelings had resurfaced. And every minute he spent with Erin made how he felt for her even stronger. But if that wasn't how she felt, he was going to have to give her some space, let things between them develop slowly, and see how it went. He knew she was still raw over the breakup with Owen. What woman wouldn't be after that disaster?

All he wanted to do was be there for her, to show her that he wasn't going to leave her when she needed him, that he was the kind of guy who was always going to be by her side, no matter what.

And if all she wanted from him was some fun and sex, and then she ended up moving on, then . . .

Then what?

Then he'd deal with it.

"Hey, you know what?" she asked.

He turned to look at her. "What?"

"You're right about having this quiet time."

He smiled. "Nice, right?"

"Yes. Though don't you get into your head too much?"

"Not really. I don't think too hard about things I can't do anything about." Which was a good reminder to himself that he couldn't change how Erin felt. That was going to be up to her. So he needed to relax and join Erin in the "have some fun" camp, and let whatever was going to happen between them just happen.

"Good advice."

He looked over at her. "Wanna talk about what you're thinking about?"

"It wasn't Owen, if that's what you were wondering."

"I wasn't, but if you want to talk about him you can."

She inhaled, let it out and got up to check her line, then came back. "I feel like I need to talk to him. At the same time I don't ever want to talk to him again. What could he say to me that would make a difference? He left me. Without talking to me about why he didn't want to get married. It's unforgivable."

"Maybe you need to talk to him so you can hear what he has to say, if only to close that chapter of your life and move forward."

"Hmm. Maybe. But I'm not ready yet."

"Only you know when you will be. Don't let anyone else push you into doing something you're not ready for."

"Thanks for that. I feel like I should woman up and just go talk to him and get it over with."

"Why? Is there some timeline?"

She shrugged. "I don't know. I guess it's this axe hanging over me. I know it's there, following me around."

"I get that. Something left unfinished."

"Yes. I just don't feel like finishing it just yet. Which

is so unlike me, because checking things off my to-do list is what I live for."

He laughed. "I can see that. But this is a big-ticket item, so maybe you just want to carry it over for a while until you're more emotionally prepared to deal with it. Big project and all, you know? Just think of it as something that needs more planning."

She laid her head on his shoulder. "Thank you. I needed that."

"You're welcome."

She lifted her head. "And now I need to pee again."

He hooked his thumb over his left shoulder. "Walk about fifty feet down the road and you'll find restrooms."

"Really. I was sure you were going to tell me there was a roll of toilet paper in the back seat of the truck and I'd need to squat in the trees."

"I do have toilet paper in the truck and you can head to the woods if you're feeling rustic."

She snorted out a laugh. "No, thank you. I'll be right back."

She disappeared and he checked both lines, hanging on to her pole in case she got a bite.

Content that everything was okay, he leaned back in the chair and closed his eyes.

THE WALK TO the restroom and back felt good, so Erin decided to extend it, checking out the lake area. Now that the sun was up and she had her bearings, she could enjoy the view.

Even though it wasn't officially summer yet, the heat was already here. She was glad she'd opted for shorts and a tank top. Too bad they didn't have a boat to enjoy the beauty of the water. The silvery sheen across the lake looked inviting as hell, and the farther she walked, the more she perspired. And the more cars she ran into, causing her to have to skirt to the side of the road.

Deciding she should probably get off the main road before she ended up pushed off by a trailer, she made her way back to the secret spot that Jason had carved out, and walked down the steep hill. Jason was leaning back in the chair, not moving.

Was he asleep? As she approached, he still hadn't made any movement, and she noticed he was one with the chair, his breathing deep and even, his ball cap covering half his face.

It must be nice to be able to settle in like that. She checked the fishing poles and didn't see any activity, but wanted to be sure they hadn't lost the lures, so she pulled the poles out of the water. The lures were secure, so she reset them into the lake. She grabbed another water and took a few deep swallows, helping to cool down her heated body temperature, then moved her chair into a shady spot. She checked her phone and saw a group text from Brenna indicating she had a date tonight and had no idea what to wear.

Erin sent a text back. Where are you going?

Brenna replied right away. Dinner and movies. Where are you, btw?

Erin sent a reply. Fishing.

Honor texted back with several laughing emojis and fish, and a With Jason, I presume?

No, I decided to take up fishing because we had so much fun when we were kids.

Sure we did, was Brenna's response.

Erin sent another text. Oh, and wear capris and a

sleeveless shirt. Or a sundress. Whatever makes you comfortable. And those cute red sandals.

Honor sent another reply: I love those red sandals.

Brenna texted back: Thanks. And I want to hear about the fishing.

Honor replied as well with: Same!

Erin shook her head and sent a reply text: I want to hear about Brenna's date!

Now that she was done with the conversation thread, she tucked her phone into the pocket of her shorts and looked over at Jason. He hadn't shaved this morning and some scruffy beard stubble covered his jaw. With his sunglasses on, the man looked sexy as hell. Not that he didn't always look hot, because he did, even when he was clean shaven. He'd worn board shorts and a sleeveless shirt, giving her the opportunity to admire the chiseled muscle of his biceps, the awesome power of his forearms, and his amazingly talented hands and fingers.

She sucked in a breath remembering how it felt to have his hands roaming over her body, the feel of his fingers sliding over her skin, inside of her, making her come over and over again.

Oh, dear God she should not be having those thoughts when they were out here, unable to do anything about her sudden burst of utter horniness.

"You're staring."

She jumped. "You're awake."

"Yeah. And you're ogling."

"I was not. Okay, I was. And I was having dirty thoughts."

He dragged his sunglasses down. "Yeah?"

"Yes. Which is unfortunate because we can't do anything about it."

"Why not?"

She opened her arms. "We're out here in the open. We don't have any privacy."

He got up and stretched. "Be right back."

He disappeared into the thickness of the woods. Erin shrugged and went back to watching the water, wishing she was out in it instead of sweating on the bank. When Jason returned, she looked up at him.

He dug into his backpack and used some hand sanitizer, then grabbed his water and took several swallows.

"Hot out here," he said.

"I know. I took a walk earlier and I was wishing we had a boat so we could be out on the lake."

"Yeah? Did you bring your swimsuit?"

"It's under my clothes."

He gave her a hot look. "I did say I'd take you shoe shopping. But I have an idea that involves being out on the water. Your call."

"Water. Definitely water." She'd only been teasing him about the shoe shopping anyway.

"Okay." He whipped out his phone and scrolled, then punched a button. "Hey, buddy. You out on the water?" He listened and laughed. "Yeah, I'm on the bank fishing, and me and my lady are hot as hell. Come pick us up by the Johnsons' dock."

Erin just stared as he made arrangements with . . . someone, then hung up and tucked his phone in his shorts.

"Who was that?"

"A friend who has a boat. Let's pack up."

"Seriously? Just like that, and you've got a boat."

His lips curved. "I know people. People who have boats. You wanna go out on the lake or not?"

She definitely wanted to go out on the lake. "Yes."

"Then let's do it."

She liked that he jumped on her suggestion, that he

was the kind of guy who'd give her what she wanted. He listened, and he was game for anything. That meant something to her.

It took them about ten minutes to pull and pack up, then they were on the road. Jason drove them to a parking place near a boat launch.

"Are we bringing the fish?" Erin asked, motioning to the cooler.

"Yeah, we'll bring those along."

Their fish were in coolers, packed with plenty of ice, so they'd stay nice and cold and fresh.

Soon enough a very nice boat pulled up to the shore. There were four people on the boat and she had no idea who any of them were. Fortunately, she was in the business of being sociable around people she didn't know, so she wasn't at all intimidated. She grabbed her tote bag and let one of the guys haul her onto the boat.

"Howdy," the guy said. "I'm Vince."

"Nice to meet you, Vince."

"The gorgeous brunette over there is my girlfriend, Summer."

Summer smiled and came over to greet her, accompanied by a stunning black woman. "Glad to have you aboard. This is my best friend, Daria, and her fiancé, Mike."

Both of the guys were equally fine-looking. Mike was dark and studly and wore glasses, and Vince was lean and muscled in a surfer-boy kind of way.

She shook hands with everyone. "Thanks for letting us come aboard."

"Anything for Jason," Mike said. "You two sweating it out fishing today?"

"Yeah," Jason said. "Caught two nice-sized catfish, though."

"So that means you'll be frying dinner for us tonight?" Vince asked.

"Love to. You game for hanging out, Erin?"

"I have no plans other than being on this boat right now. I appreciate the rescue."

"There's nothing worse than sweating while sitting right at the edge of the water, dying to get in," Summer said. "And we have tubes and a great spot where we can go hang out and you can cool off."

Erin liked these people. They were friendly and accommodating. And when the boat took off, she nearly died from the pleasure of the breeze, the bits of water coming up to relieve her from the oppressive heat and the sheer joy of feeling the waves underneath her as they skimmed across the water.

They anchored near a small cove, out of the way of the traffic from the other boats. Vince, Mike and Jason tied off the tubes to the side of the boat.

"Anyone want some water, lemonade, wine or beer?" Daria asked.

Normally Erin would opt for wine. But it was so hot a cold beer sounded like just what she needed.

Jason grabbed two beers from Vince and handed one off to her. She sat at the back of the boat and watched as Summer and Vince lowered themselves onto the tubes.

"You don't want to get into the water?" Jason asked.

"Oh, I do. I figured we'd let the boat owners go first."

"And you're hot, so let's get out in the water."

From the look on his face and the hand he held out for her, it was clear he wasn't going to take no for an answer. Daria and Mike had just climbed down, so there was no stopping them. After tucking her beer into their drink cooler, she slid out of her shorts and shirt, then kicked off her tennis shoes and followed Jason down the ladder.

The water was icy cold and felt fabulous. They swam over to one of the available tubes and climbed on. Erin pushed her wet hair away from her face.

"This is perfect," she said. "Thank you, all, again."

"You're welcome," Vince said. "Where do you know Jason from?"

"We grew up together. Where did all of you meet him?"

"College," Mike said. "Though Jason was so dumb he had to stay four years longer than the rest of us."

Jason hopped off the tube and shoved Mike off of his. Then Vince joined them and the three of them swam away together.

"Children," Summer said. "They're like small children when they get together."

Erin laughed at the mention of the extra four years of veterinary school Jason had to attend.

"I had to laugh," Daria said, lifting her feet in and out of the water. "I attended an extra three years after my bachelor's degree."

"Yeah, but that was law school," Summer said. "You weren't hanging out with a bunch of animals."

Daria frowned. "Yes, I was. They just had two legs instead of four."

Erin laughed, then asked, "What type of law do you practice, Daria?"

"Civil, mostly. My dad is a lawyer and I followed him into the family business. That's where I met Mike, who's also a lawyer."

"Oh, that's sweet."

"It is," Daria said, shooting Mike a smile even though he couldn't see her. "How about you, Erin?"

"Kind of the same thing, family-business-wise, only not law. My family owns a vineyard and we also hold weddings there."

Daria sat up. "Ooh, don't you have the best job? That sounds so fun and romantic. So you hold weddings at the family vineyard every weekend?"

"Nearly every weekend. We're especially busy during spring, summer and fall. Not so much in the winter, though we get the occasional winter wedding."

"You must love it," Summer said. "I've been to a few vineyard weddings, and they're so beautiful."

"Thank you. I do love it, though one of my sisters does most of the wedding planning. My other sister manages the vineyard with my dad, and I handle the business portion of both the vineyard and the weddings."

"Sounds like a lot to juggle," Daria said.

"It can be, but I thrive on being busy."

"So do I," Summer said. "I'm a surgical scrub nurse, so we're constantly busy."

"Oh, wow. What an amazing job you have."

"Thanks. I do love it. I also love my days off, like today."

"I agree with that," Daria said. "There's nothing like relaxing on a tube, having some drinks and hanging out with your friends. And now we have a new friend."

Erin felt warm and welcomed. She was always so busy, cocooning herself at the vineyard. She made friends easily, though. Part of the job. But she hadn't made a lot of time for that lately. Between work and planning the wedding that never happened, she realized she'd isolated herself.

Not today, though. Today was the first time she'd felt incredibly free, relaxed and unburdened in as long as she could remember.

It felt damn good to let go. And maybe the key to really letting go was to have that conversation with Owen, to close the door on that chapter of her life.

But just the thought of it caused a twinge in her belly,

that sweet, relaxing freedom she'd felt just a moment ago dissipating in the soft summer breeze.

No, the only door she was closing today was on the thought of talking to Owen. She wasn't ready. Not yet. Not when she was finally unwinding and ridding herself of all the hurt and unhappiness.

That conversation could wait. Right now, all she wanted to do was revel in her own personal joy. And this water. And Jason, whose laugh made her look over to see him tilt his head back and let out a guffaw at something Vince said.

Now, there was someone who knew how to live in the moment. He was someone she needed in her life, needed to get closer to. Because his joy was infectious, could make her happier than she'd been in a long, long time.

She wanted a lot more of that.

Of him.

CHAPTER

......

twenty-one

VINCE AND SUMMER and Mike and Daria had rented a lake house for the weekend, and they invited Jason and Erin to hang out with them for dinner that night.

Since Erin seemed to be having a great time, and since they'd caught fish, Jason asked Erin if she was game for that. She offered up an enthusiastic yes, so after they spent another few hours on the water, Vince drove them to the dock and they climbed out, grabbed their truck and drove over to the lake house.

"This place is very nice," Erin said as they climbed out of the truck.

Jason glanced up at the two-story house that over-looked the lake. "Yeah, it's decent."

She laughed. "Decent, huh? Just a shack?"

"Hey, I didn't say that."

"Uh-huh. This place is a dream. Look at all those windows. And the deck overlooking the water. I can't wait to see inside."

He rolled his eyes. "Come on, Cinderella. Let's take you to the ball."

"You're so funny."

Since they'd dried off on the boat ride back, they'd both gotten dressed before they got in the truck. They grabbed their stuff and headed around the side yard to the back.

Music was pumping, and the crew was already out there, along with a few other people. Leave it to Vince to organize a party.

"Your friends are popular," Erin said.

"They do this every weekend in the summer. It's a good time."

"Remind me to start having a good time."

Her sentence was cryptic, so he filed it away to ask her about it later, because Mike waved them over and Erin disappeared into the house.

"Hey, buddy, glad you decided to come," Vince said.

"You're only glad because I'm the best at cleaning and frying fish."

Mike laughed. "That, too. There's beer in the cooler."

"Thanks."

Jason knew his friends. He also knew they were good guys, and he liked their company as much as they liked his. They didn't see each other a lot, but when they did, he knew they could pick up right where they left off. He'd known he could call Vince today, and if he was on the water he'd pick him up and invite him to join them on the boat. That was just the kind of guy Vince was.

It was good to have friends you could count on.

He grabbed a beer from the cooler, then went into the house. He also found Erin, Summer and Daria and a few other people he didn't know. He expected them to be in the living area drinking wine. Instead they were in the kitchen, chatting together while chopping onions and cilantro.

"What are you all up to?" he asked.

"Making some salsa and guacamole for starters," Erin said.

Daria nodded. "We know everyone's hungry. Or at least I am."

Jason nodded. "I'm going to clean the fish."

"There are potatoes in here," Erin said, digging through the pantry. "And there's celery, too. And I saw some eggs in the fridge. If you all would like, I could make potato salad."

"That would be awesome," Summer said. "You sure you want to go through all that trouble?"

Erin smiled at her. "It's no trouble. Plus, the potato salad will go well with the fried fish."

Jason worked silently gutting the fish and getting it cleaned, then sliced it into small pieces while he listened to the women talk. Erin seemed to be in a good mood as she discussed Daria and Mike's wedding plans.

"We're getting married in October, at my family's church in Texas, followed by a big reception at the country club. Over four hundred people."

"That sounds amazing," Erin said.

"It's been a whirlwind. Wedding planning is so stressful. Mike and I are looking forward to it being over with—and to our honeymoon in Maui."

Erin laughed and started peeling potatoes. That's what a lot of couples said as it got closer to the wedding. Daria was right in that planning a wedding caused a lot of stress. She knew that firsthand. There were so many details, and then you had family members and friends adding to it. Erin was a planner, so she'd had everything in order.

Except for that whole runaway groom thing. That she hadn't been able to plan for.

Shaking off that thought, she finished the potatoes and put them in the water to boil, and set a separate pot for the eggs.

"You went after those potatoes with a vengeance. Got murder on your mind?"

Jason had come up behind her and put his arms around her.

"No, that's how I peel and slice."

"Uh-huh. Remind me to steer clear of you when you have a knife in your hand."

He kissed the side of her neck, lingering for a few seconds, which was long enough to banish those non-wedding demons.

She turned to face him. "And how about you? Got that fish ready to fry?"

"Like the master fryer I am."

"Good to know."

Summer handed him a tray. "Here. Take these snacks outside, master fryer."

"Will do."

He took the tray from Summer, laid his beer on it, then leaned over and brushed his lips across Erin's. "Later, master potato-salad maker."

She rolled her eyes and laughed. "Get out."

After he left, she checked on the potatoes. They were boiling, so she'd have to keep a close eye to make sure they didn't overcook.

"Jason's got it bad for you, Erin."

Erin looked over at Daria. "We're just good friends."

"Honey, there's way more than friendship going on."

"Agree," Summer said, pouring more wine into her glass. "I can practically see hearts floating out of his eyes when he looks at you."

"Oh, stop. You cannot."

"There are three looks a man gives a woman," Daria said. "Friendship, lust and love. Trust me, he's looking at you with his love eyes."

Erin shifted her gaze to Summer, who nodded and said, "It's definitely love."

She shook her head, needing to deny what they thought they saw. "He doesn't love me. We're having fun. And sex. And nothing more."

Summer tilted her head. "Is that all you feel for him? Just friendship?"

"I . . . I don't know. A few weeks ago I was supposed to get married."

Daria blinked. "Wait. What? You were getting married?"

"What happened?" Summer asked.

"It's kind of a long story."

"And we've got several bottles of wine," Daria said. "Plus tequila and vodka. Pull up a chair here, honey. I'm ready to hear that story."

"Okay, but let me take care of these potatoes first."

After Erin drained the potatoes and set them out to cool, she poured herself a glass of wine and spilled the details of Owen breaking up with her, and then her decision to have a revenge fling with Jason at her non-wedding that had somehow turned into weeks of fun and games.

"Maybe you think you're just having some fun and sex with Jason," Daria said. "But I see something a lot deeper in how he looks at you."

"I agree," Summer said. "It's in every move he makes with you. The way he talks to you and touches you."

She didn't see it. She knew they were all friends with Jason, so maybe they were just being overprotective. She'd made it clear to Jason that she wasn't looking for a relationship. She needed to protect her heart. But she also needed to protect his. The last thing she wanted to do was hurt him.

Maybe it was time to gently back away from this relationship, to cool things down a bit before it got completely out of control.

She had to think, and she couldn't do it here with this crazy party atmosphere, so she let it go for now, instead diving into the fun, letting herself go with the flow of fun people, great food and a really good night.

They prepped the food, the guys cooked, they had dinner and it was all fantastic. Then they sat outside on the deck and watched the sun set, and just hung out and talked and listened to some amazing music.

And when they said their good nights, she hugged Summer and Daria with the promise they'd get together soon, because she really liked her new friends and wanted to stay in touch.

"Come see me at the vineyard," she said. "We'll do a wine tour."

"I want to come to a wedding," Daria said. "As you can probably imagine, I'm kind of obsessed with weddings right now."

Erin laughed. "I'll see what I can do about sneaking you into one."

"You're the best."

They packed up their stuff and climbed into Jason's truck, then headed back to town.

She yawned.

"Tired?" he asked.

"Very. It was a long day."

"Want to come home with me and snuggle? Or something else?"

She wanted that very much, but then she remembered

the conversation she'd had with Summer and Daria, and her plan for a cooling-off period. "I think I'll just go home."

He waited a beat before answering. "Sure."

He was probably disappointed that she didn't want to spend the night with him. To be honest, so was she. She liked being alone with him. She liked having sex with him. The first thought that popped into her head was climbing into the shower with him, and then moving on from there. She wanted his hands on her. His mouth on her. She wanted to feel him moving inside of her, sparking all of that sweet pleasure that released those endorphins and made her feel so damn good.

But that was what *she* wanted. It was time to think of someone else besides herself.

Like Jason.

And putting the brakes on was the right thing to do.

So he drove her home and opened the door of the truck for her, took out her bag and handed it to her. And when he drew her into his arms and gave her a deep, soulful kiss, she realized he might not be the only one feeling something deep and emotional, because she gripped his arms and held tight for far too long, not wanting to let him go.

And the feeling she was holding so tight to had nothing to do with sex.

Jason was the one who broke the kiss, gazing down at her with a questioning look. "You sure you don't want to go home with me?"

Right now she wasn't sure of anything, least of all her own emotions. "Yeah, I'm pretty wiped out."

Lies. All lies. I want to stay up all night making love to you, talking to you.

Just being with you.

"Okay. I'll talk to you soon." He gave her a short kiss, then got into his truck and drove off.

While she stood there and stared at the retreating truck like some love-forsaken idiot.

Now who was the one who had it bad?

"Good night, Jason," she whispered, then turned and walked up the steps to the house.

CHAPTER

· · · · · ·

twenty-two

MONDAY MORNING MEETINGS with the family could be fast, or unendingly slow, depending on how much business needed to be conducted. Generally, the vineyard business was first because Dad wasn't all that interested in the wedding updates, and he needed to get to work at the winery. Brenna would sit through the entire meeting, but Dad liked to stay updated on the overall thrust of the business, plus give updates on the vines.

Agatha lay at Erin's feet chewing on a rope toy.

"We're thinning the grapes," Dad said. "The good news is, with all the rain we had the growth has been phenomenal. But we have too many clusters per vine, so it's going to take some time to thin them out. Otherwise, everything looks good out in the vineyard. Grapes are healthy."

Brenna took notes on the vineyard report, even though she knew exactly what was going on out there. Erin noted the report as well, and so did Mom since she kept the overall business notes for both companies.

"What does the fall harvest look like?" Erin asked.

Dad grinned. "Bountiful. It's going to be a very good year."

Erin's skin tingled, her heart filled with joy. Some years were lean, some were average. A good year in the vineyards meant happiness for the entire family, especially Dad and Brenna. "That's great news."

She jotted down the note and, once vineyard business was finished, Dad made his escape.

Then they moved on to the wedding business.

"We have a difficult wedding this weekend," Honor said. "The BTB has demanded everything under the sun, some of which we've been unable to accommodate. She's insisted on importing wines from France—"

Brenna gasped, and Honor held up her hand.

"Don't worry," Honor said. "I told her if that's what she wanted she could hold her reception elsewhere. Her mother calmed her down and told her the reason she'd chosen Red Moss Vineyards in the first place was because she loved not only the venue, but our wines. But she's spoiled, an only child, and always gets her way."

Brenna lifted her chin. "I don't care what way she wants it. There will be no imported wines at our vineyard."

Honor nodded. "I made that very clear to her."

Erin rolled her eyes. Some brides-to-be, or BTBs as they referred to them, could be a pain and made their work so much more difficult than necessary. But it was also part of the job. Brides got stressed, families were demanding, and they rolled with it. Because at the end of the day, giving a bride and groom a wedding they'd never forget was their number one goal.

"So, there's more," Honor said.

"What now?" Mom asked.

"The bride wants a red-carpet experience, with limos and spotlights and paparazzi for her grand entrance."

The disgusted look on their mother's face was price-less.

"She does realize she's at a country vineyard and not in Hollywood, doesn't she?" Mom asked.

"I don't think she cares at this point," Honor said. "She wants what she wants and her father is willing to pay to give it to her."

"But are we willing to give it to her?" Brenna asked. "I mean, limo, fine. But spotlights and a herd of photographers? Where are we going to find those at this late date?"

Erin had an idea. "They don't have to be real photographers, do they?"

Honor shook her head. "No. Just the idea of people running up to take her photo like she's famous."

"We know people," Erin said. "We'll get some flash cameras and grab some of our friends to act as the horde of paparazzi."

Brenna leaned back in her chair. "Really. And who are you going to get to give up their Saturday night to do that?"

She thought about it. "I don't know. Finn. Jason. Clay will probably be on board. If Alice is in town she'll think it's totally fun." Then she thought about the new friends she'd made over the weekend. "And a few more people, maybe. Trust me, I can get a crowd that'll wow her."

"Awesome," Honor said with a relieved smile. "I'll take care of renting the spotlights."

"Honor, you'd better make sure we bill them accordingly for this," their mother said. "With profit tacked on for the utter last-minute inconvenience. And the ridiculousness of it all."

"Oh, believe me, I intend to."

Erin was making furious notes about who to contact. Actually, this could turn out to be fun.

"Okay, so that's taken care of and thank you all for your input," Honor said. "Now there's another thing I wanted to bring up."

Erin was still making notes and to-dos on her list while Honor was talking.

"The Phillips/Kanady wedding is in two weeks."

Erin's hand stilled. She'd totally forgotten about Ryan Phillips's wedding. She looked up at Honor.

"Oh, shit."

Brenna's eyes widened. "Oh, shit, Erin."

Owen was a groomsman in Ryan Phillips's wedding. She'd totally spaced and forgotten he would be on site for that wedding. In two weeks. She'd have to see him.

Mom reached over to grasp Erin's hand. "How do you feel about that?"

"I . . . don't know."

"You could leave for the night," Honor said. "We can handle the wedding without you being here."

Erin lifted her chin. "I will not be banished from my own home just because Owen is going to be here."

"So, what are you going to do?"

She shrugged. "Ignore him as much as possible."

"You have to talk to him eventually, *cailín deas*," Mom said. "Maybe you should do that before the wedding."

She felt the beginnings of a headache sliding up her temples, that familiar tension tightening between her shoulder blades. "I know I do. But not . . . right now, okay?"

"What are you putting it off for?" Brenna asked. "Just confront him. He's back from *his* honeymoon, isn't he?"

"Brenna," Mom said in her warning voice.

"Yes, he's back. He texted Jason asking about me."

"He texted Jason." Brenna slanted a look at her. "Not you. Jason."

"Yes."

"That makes no sense," Brenna said. "So he hasn't even tried to contact you?"

Erin shrugged.

"What a dick."

"Brenna," their mother said again.

"Sorry, Mom."

Erin did not want to be having this conversation, least of all with her family. At least Dad wasn't in the room. Oh, God, Dad. How was he going to react knowing that Owen was going to be here? Hopefully no one would tell him, and that night he'd be in the house watching a ball game and the whole event would pass him by without his knowledge. The last thing they needed was their father to confront Owen during Ryan and Yolanda's wedding. Talk about a disaster.

Mom's phone rang and she answered it.

"Okay, hang on a second." She muted the phone. "This is a supplier I need to talk to. I have to step out."

After Mom left, Brenna turned to Erin.

"You have to talk to Owen," Brenna said.

"I don't *have* to do anything, Brenna. I'll do it when I'm ready."

"So, what? You're just going to wait until he shows up for the wedding and then hide in the house?"

Erin lifted her chin. "I will not hide in the house. It'll be business as usual."

Brenna rolled her eyes. "Come on, Erin. You know that'll never happen. You'll be pissed off and won't be able to stop yourself from confronting him. Which will ruin Ryan and Yolanda's wedding."

"Trust me, I won't ruin anyone's wedding. And why aren't you on my side?"

"I'm always on your side. Which is why I think you should talk to him. The sooner you put this all behind you, the sooner you can move forward with your life."

She snorted out a laugh. "Oh, like you've done since your divorce from Mitchell? I don't see you doing much moving forward, Brenna."

Brenna shot visual daggers at her. "We aren't talking about me right now."

"Well, you can't offer me advice on how to live my life, considering you aren't doing a good job of living yours."

"I had a date."

"And how did that go?"

"He left the table after dinner to go brush his teeth."

Erin gasped. "Dear God. Did you report him to the police?"

"Not funny. He was rude and I didn't like him."

"You always find fault with guys you go out with so you won't have to admit that no guy is going to be good enough for a second date, and then you can continue to hide out at home."

Now it was Brenna's turn to gasp. "That's not true."

"Hey, you two," Honor said, her tone even. "Please stop. Brenna can date or not date whomever she pleases. And Erin can choose to see Owen or not."

"You've been quiet through all this, Honor," Brenna said, switching her attention to Honor. "What's your take on this whole Owen business?"

Honor looked down at her lap. "He texted me."

Erin's heart rate shot up. "What? He texted you, too? When? What did he say?"

Honor looked over at Erin. "Right when he got back. He asked how you were doing."

She couldn't believe Honor had kept that from her. "And what did you say?"

"The truth. I said you were miserable and unhappy and I asked why he did it. He said he wanted to talk to you. I told him he should text or call you, not me. He said he would. Obviously, he hasn't."

"Why didn't you tell me right away when he contacted you?"

"Because you were already upset and I didn't want to make it worse. I'm sorry, Erin."

Honor had the most miserable, dejected expression on her face. It always worked to defuse any argument the sisters were having.

Erin inhaled deeply, then let it out slowly. "You don't have anything to be sorry for. And I'm sorry, Brenna. Taking potshots at you is just my anger at Owen being misdirected."

Brenna nodded. "And I had no business butting in. I'm sorry, too."

Honor stood. "Group hug, then?"

Honor was ever the peacemaker.

They all stood and hugged it out, then took their seats again.

Erin took a long swallow of her coffee.

"So, what are you going to do about Owen?" Honor asked.

"I don't know. I realize I need to close that chapter, which means I'm going to have to talk to him, but every time I think about it I get so angry and my emotions get so jumbled that I shove the thought of seeing him aside. And then when it comes up again, the whole circle repeats itself. But you're right, I can't let this wait until the wedding. It's not fair to Ryan and Yolanda. I'll take care of it."

"It's for the best," Brenna said. "As painful as it will be, you need that closure so you can move forward."

Erin nodded. She knew Brenna was right, but she'd be just as happy if she never had to speak to Owen again.

Closure was just some word that someone made up to make themselves feel better about being broken up with.

She'd never feel okay about what Owen had done to her.

CHAPTER

······

twenty-three

JASON TOSSED HIS surgical mask in the bin, followed by his gloves. He pulled off his gown and left the surgical suite, leaving wrapping up Sweet Pea to the surgical techs. He went straight to his office and uncapped the jug holding his ice water.

What he really wanted was a large whiskey.

Losing a patient was the hardest damn thing.

Correction. Having to tell Sweet Pea's owners that their dog didn't make it through surgery was going to be the hardest thing.

He knew going in that it was going to be a difficult surgery, and had let Clyde and Frances know the odds were stacked against their terrier mix. They wanted to do the surgery anyway. Sweet Pea had gotten into a tussle with one of the neighbor dogs, and she'd suffered serious puncture wounds in several areas of her body, along with excessive bleeding. At twelve years old, it was an uphill climb, and one the poor old pup just couldn't make.

Now he had to make the hardest phone call, but it was his job and he did it, letting a crying Frances know that he'd done everything he could to save her beloved Sweet Pea's life. It didn't matter to Frances and Clyde, though, because he'd failed.

Sometimes this job was rewarding as hell. Days like today? It just fucking sucked.

Puddy wandered into his office, so he bent down and wrapped his arms around his pup. Puddy licked his face and it was just what he needed.

He ran his hands over Puddy's back. "You know just how to make me feel better, buddy."

But he couldn't hide in his office, so he did rounds, checking on the other in-hospital patients, finished updating charts and reported in to Dr. Sunderland.

"Tough loss today," Carl said.

Jason nodded and gave his report on the surgery.

"You did everything you could, but the injuries were too severe. I just finished reading your report."

"Still sucks to lose her."

Carl nodded. "Always does. That you care so much about the loss means you're in the right line of work. Now go home and shake it off tonight, and come back tomorrow ready to save some lives."

"Thanks."

But he didn't go home. He waited until Carl and Frances showed up to pick up Sweet Pea. Then he sat with them while they cried over their dog, answered whatever questions they had and hugged them both.

He'd lost pets of his own over the years, and it was always hard as hell. He knew exactly how they felt. It was like losing a part of yourself, a member of your family.

After they left, he grabbed his keys and his dog and got into his truck, went home, fed Puddy and let him outside. Then he took a long shower, trying to scrub off the feeling of utter defeat. He got out and felt cleaner, but the feeling of loss lingered. So he grabbed his phone to send a text message to Erin.

What are you doing?

She texted back. Paperwork.

He replied: You're working late. Let me take you to dinner.

It took her a few minutes to reply.

Not sure that's a good idea.

He frowned. What did she mean by that? It had been a few days since he'd seen her, and he'd been swamped with work at the clinic, but he thought things were good with them.

He sent another text. I really need to see you.

Again, it took her another few minutes before she sent her reply.

I am hungry.

He hadn't realized he'd been holding his breath until he got her response.

He sent her another text: I'll be there in thirty.

He got dressed, called Puddy in and gave him a bone to chew on. Puds happily took the bone and trotted to his blanket. Jason grabbed his keys and got in the truck to go pick up Erin.

He needed to shake off this mood, because he never brought work home.

This was more than work, though. It was devastation. He hated feeling it, hated that it lingered within him. He tried not to let any of his clients affect him personally, but he'd been treating Sweet Pea since his first day on the job—hell, even before that, when he'd started interning at the clinic before he graduated from vet school. She was a sweet dog, her tail always wagging whenever he walked into the exam room.

Dammit. His eyes welled with tears and he swiped them away. He couldn't get emotionally involved with his clients. That wasn't how this was supposed to work. He had to remain unaffected, do his job and move on, even when the outcome wasn't positive.

Which was why he needed to see Erin. She was a needed distraction, a balm to his soul.

He pulled up in front of the main house and parked, then got out. Agatha came around from the side of the house with Finn holding her leash.

"Hey, what's up?" Finn asked.

"Nothing much." He bent down to take the full brunt of Agatha's enthusiastic greeting. "Hey, baby girl. You get bigger every time I see you. And prettier, too."

"Stop. You'll spoil her."

He looked up to see Erin standing on the top step of the porch, looking exceptionally pretty in a bright yellow sundress with flowing short sleeves and ruffles at the hem that billowed in the night's breeze.

He grinned and stood.

"I'll just hand her off to you," Finn said, dropping Agatha's lead in Jason's hand.

"Thanks, buddy."

Finn walked off and Jason headed up the steps. "You get prettier every time I see you, too."

Her lips curved. "Stop. You'll spoil me."

He walked up the steps until he was on the top one with her, then slipped an arm around her.

"Don't," she whispered, and he backed away.

"What's wrong?"

"Nothing. I'm just . . . I don't know, in my head, I guess."

He didn't even know what that meant, but he'd give her some time to open up about what was on her mind. "Okay. Let's go get something to eat. I'm starving."

"Me, too."

She took Agatha from him and walked inside. She was back out in a minute or so.

"She climbed right onto my dad's lap. I think she loves him more than me."

"That's doubtful."

"It's okay. He's outside a lot during the day, and she loves being with him. He keeps her calm so she's not running amok, but she still gets to enjoy the outdoors."

"That's good for her. And the cast should be coming off soon enough so she'll be able to do that running amok."

"She'll like that. I'm ready to go if you are."

He didn't take her hand like he wanted to, just walked alongside of her and opened the door to the truck, waiting while she climbed inside.

After he got in on his side, he turned to face her. "What are you hungry for?"

"Honestly? I'd love some Thai food."

"Sounds great to me."

They hit up one of their favorite restaurants in the city. Once they were seated, Erin ordered iced tea and Jason ordered a beer.

"Rough day?" she asked.

"Really rough day."

"Tell me about it."

He told her about losing Sweet Pea, how hard he tried to save her, despite the odds against the old dog.

She reached over and squeezed his hand. "I'm so sorry, Jason. That had to be so hard."

He shrugged. "It's not like it's the first time I lost an animal. It happens in my line of work. Animals get sick, they get old, they get injured, and sometimes they don't make it. It's part of my job."

"But this one seems to have hit you pretty hard. Why do you think that is?"

"I guess because I remember Sweet Pea from my internship. She was always bright and energetic and so sweet. And her humans adored her."

"It's probably hard on them, too."

"Yeah, telling them wasn't easy." He took another long swallow of beer. "It just sucked, Erin."

"You did everything you could for her."

"This one hurts."

"I know it does, babe. I'm sorry." She rubbed her hand over his. She didn't tell him to blow it off or tuck his feelings inside or some bullshit about how tomorrow it would be better. And that actually *did* make him feel better.

He finished his beer, then they ordered dinner.

"Tell me about your day," he said, needing the distraction.

"Well." She took a sip of her iced tea. "I found out Owen texted Honor, too, to ask about me."

"Wait." He frowned, trying to catch up to what she just said. "Owen texted Honor. Not you."

"Yes."

"What the fuck is he doing?"

She shrugged. "I have no idea."

"Why doesn't he just call you?"

"Again. No idea."

He could tell from the way she tapped her fingernails on the table that she was irritated. He couldn't blame her. "Okay, I take that back. I know why he isn't calling you.

He knows you won't pick up. But I don't get the texting of other people like Honor and me. What's the purpose of that? Does he think either of us is going to fill him in on your emotional state?"

"I don't have an explanation for anything Owen does. Not anymore. I'm not sure I ever knew him."

Now it was his turn to offer up some sympathy. "I'm sorry, Erin."

"It is what it is. And to top it off, I was reminded that he's a groomsman in an upcoming wedding at the vineyard."

"Oh, shit, that's right. Ryan Phillips's wedding. I forgot all about that."

"So did I until Honor brought it up at our meeting on Monday."

He couldn't imagine what Erin's reaction to that had been, but he'd bet she'd been damned unhappy about it. "What are you going to do?"

Their server brought their plates, asked them if they needed refills on their drinks, then left.

Erin stared at her plate, then lifted her gaze to Jason. "I'm going to do my job, like always."

His lips lifted in a slight smile. "You sure a trip to Tahiti isn't warranted?"

"I'm not running."

"I was only kidding. Kind of."

She stabbed her fork into her shrimp curry. "I'm going to have to see him eventually. Which doesn't mean I have to interact with him."

He dug into his chicken satay, chewing thoughtfully as he tried to figure out a way to help Erin. After he took a swallow of beer he said, "Maybe you should talk to Owen before the wedding, then things won't be awkward.

You know, break the ice, talk things out, close that chapter or whatever you have to do to end your relationship officially?"

She shot him a glare. "My relationship with Owen ended the day he sent that e-mail breaking up with me. I don't know that there's anything left between us to say."

A smart guy would just shut up and leave things alone. Obviously, Jason wasn't smart, because he cared about Erin and in this she wasn't seeing clearly. "Come on, Erin, you know you'll never be able to get past this until you talk to Owen. That's why you're putting this distance between you and me, isn't it?"

She opened her mouth to say something, then closed it, focusing on her food instead. Deciding that he'd said enough for the moment, he did the same. Mouth shut, except to eat.

They ate their meals in silence. A tense silence that he'd caused.

Way to go, dumbass.

Maybe he should learn to keep his opinions to himself. Maybe Erin wouldn't be in such a mood.

She pushed her plate to the side and looked up at him. He braced himself for verbal fire.

"You're right, of course. I know you are. But I just can't bring myself to initiate a conversation with him, especially since he hasn't contacted me since he's been back. Shouldn't *he* be the one to get in touch with *me*?"

"Yeah, he should. I don't have a clue why he hasn't. I think he's being a dick about this, Erin. He's my best friend and I'd like to kick his ass all the way down a gravel road."

Her lips curved. "That does make me feel better. And bad at the same time. I'm sorry you feel like you're in the middle between us."

"I don't feel that way at all. I haven't even talked to him since before he ran off."

"And I feel responsible for that."

He signaled for their server, who came over. "Can I get the check, please?"

Their server brought the check and some mints. Erin popped one in her mouth and he took the other. Once he paid the bill, they got up and went outside. It was brutally hot and humid, with some dark clouds gathering.

"It could storm," Erin said.

He turned and grasped her hand. "I'm gonna get stormin' mad if you keep telling me you feel responsible for whatever rift I have with Owen. That's on him, not you. We straight on that?"

She nodded. "Yes. And thanks. I've got enough weighing on me without adding guilt to it."

He swept his thumb over her cheek. "No guilt. The only person in this situation who should feel guilty is Owen. Try to remember that."

"I will. And one more thing."

"Okay."

She leaned in and brushed her lips across his. "Thank you for always being open and honest with me, even when you know it might not be something I want to hear. You have no idea what that means to me."

That brief taste of her, the warmth of her body against his, got his motor running. He could have stood there and kissed her forever. But thunder rumbled, breaking the hazy spell that Erin always seemed to wind around him. They both took a step back and Erin scanned the sky.

"This storm looks like it could be big."

He looked around at the dark gray, low-hanging clouds. Another crack of thunder, followed by lightning. Storm was coming closer. It would be a race to get home before the rain started falling. "Could be. Want me to take you home?"

"Do you have wine at your house?"

"I always have wine at my house."

"Then let's go to your place."

"Sounds good." They climbed in the truck and he put it in gear. He kept an eye on the weather as he put his foot on the gas and hustled back to his house.

They'd beaten the rain home, and Puddy was happy to see him. His little butt wiggled back and forth.

"Hey, buddy." He lifted him and looked over at Erin. "I'm going to let him out real quick."

"While you do that, I'll use the bathroom."

He nodded and walked out back with his dog. Thunder cracked, loud and menacing, the clouds moving by faster than before. By the time Puddy finished peeing on every tree and bush in the backyard, the wind was whipping around the yard, the tree branches bowing down from the force of the impending storm. He brought the dog in and shut the back door.

He gave Puddy a toy to occupy him. The pup took the toy to his blanket and Jason went to the kitchen and poured a glass of wine for Erin.

She came out and met him in the kitchen.

"Your wine," he said, handing over the glass.

"Thanks." She took a sip, closing her eyes as she savored the taste. "Mmm. Red Moss Vineyards' sauvignon blanc vintage. That was a good harvest."

"It's one of my favorites."

She opened her eyes to look down at his hand wrapped around a bottle of beer. "And yet you're drinking a beer."

He shrugged. "I decided not to mix beer and wine tonight. I have an early surgery tomorrow."

"Okay. I'll give you a pass. Especially since I know how well stocked you are on our wines."

She took a sip and sighed. He could see her body relaxing with each swallow. He was glad to see the tension easing in her now.

She took another sip, rolling the wine around in her glass. "Oh, by the way, I have kind of a weird request."

"Yeah? Hit me."

"We're having a wedding this weekend and I need people to play paparazzi to the bride, per her rather odd request. I'd like to enlist you and Clay and Finn, along with our friends from last weekend."

He cocked his head to the side. "You ask anyone else yet?"

"Finn is in. So are Alice and Clay. And I thought if you agreed, we could see if maybe Mike and Daria and Vince and Summer want to do it, too."

He lifted his shoulders. "Sounds like fun. I'm game."

She smiled at him over her glass. "You're easy."

"I'm so insulted."

She laughed. "No, you're not."

He laid his beer down on the counter and walked over, laying his hands on either side of her hips. "And what will my payment be for this task?"

She put her wineglass down on the island. "You think I would trade sexual favors for your participation in this task?"

"Nah. I think you'll fuck me because you can't keep your hands off me."

She palmed his chest, digging her fingers in. "That sure of yourself, are you?"

"That I can make you come—several times? Yeah, I'm sure."

Erin had tried so hard to play it cool, to hold back her feelings for Jason. But one look at him earlier tonight and she could tell right away something was off.

She knew Jason well, knew he felt things deeply. He tried to downplay his emotions, but she knew him better than he thought she did, and the man had a huge heart, especially for people he held close, and for the animals in his care. It was one of the things she admired most about him. She knew that he was one of the people—outside of her family—that she could call on if she needed him, and he would be there for her no matter what.

So the idea of taking a step away from him, especially when he needed her comfort, was ludicrous. Not when they'd grown closer these past few weeks, when she was so emotionally drawn to him.

What she felt for Jason went beyond physical. It was like the two of them had become even further connected because of her breakup with Owen.

And now, as they stood there together, their bodies touching in such an intimate way, she wanted him more than she'd ever wanted another man. She swept her hands over his shoulders, then wrapped one hand around the nape of his neck, teasing her fingers into the softness of his hair. The physical contact made her senses swirl, exponentially heightening her desire to get naked with him.

"If you're going to make me come several times, don't you think you should get started?"

Thunder boomed so loud she felt the shock of it in her heart. Jason brought his mouth to hers and kissed her, bringing another jolt, an electrical pulse zinging through her. She melted against him, absorbing the full force of his hard body pressed against hers.

He lifted her and placed her on the kitchen island and she wrapped her legs around him, bringing his body even closer. She wanted that contact, needing to feel him close. And when he kissed her jaw, then started raining kisses along the column of her throat, she tilted her head back, giving him access to her neck, delighted by the goose bumps he raised along her skin.

With the storm going strong outside and the one brewing inside of her, she'd never felt more alive, more tuned in to all of her senses. Jason's muscles rolled underneath her hands as she explored his body, and the way he smelled when she inhaled a deep breath was so primally male. The way he dragged in deep breaths as he slid his hands under the straps of her dress and drew them down made her own breathing labored. And the sensual darkness in his deep brown eyes as he made eye contact with her was a pleasure she'd never felt before.

"Ever been naked and feasted on while lying on a kitchen island before?"

The sound of his voice made her body quake. Jason in sex mode, his voice lowered, and all that sizzling energy directed toward her was quite . . . something.

"Can't say that I have."

He lifted her very slightly, just to slide her dress over her butt, then off, leaving her in her bra and panties. "It's gonna happen tonight. I've had fantasies about you and this island."

"Is that right?"

He reached around her to deftly unhook her bra, then slid that off as well. "Yeah. You, naked, spread eagled, my mouth on your pussy while you scream."

She drew in a shaky breath as her mind came to grips with the visuals his words evoked. "I could get on board with that."

"Good. Lie down." He drew his shirt off and made a pillow out of it for her head. The one thing she liked about him—okay, there were a lot of things she liked about him, but this was one of those many things—was that he always thought about her comfort.

"You could climb on top here and go to town on me," she said, offering up her best suggestive leer.

"That comes after."

"I see you've thought this out in detail."

His lips curved, and that sexy smile held a lot of promise. "I think about you a lot when I'm lying in bed at night."

"Really." Despite the cool air-conditioning vent blowing out some icy air, her body flushed hot as she mentally conjured up Jason in his bed, his cock in his hand doing some serious hand job movements as he fantasized about her. Her sex quivered and she couldn't help but open her legs, inviting him in.

He smoothed his hand along the inside of her thigh, then teased the top of her sex with his fingertips. "Oh, yeah. In my mind, I've had you here, up against the wall in my bedroom, outside against the tree—" He cocked his head to the side. "And then in the tree."

She gasped as he slipped two fingers inside of her. "In the tree?"

"I haven't exactly figured out the logistics of that one, yet, but in my fantasies it works great."

Right now, she didn't care about location as long as he kept rubbing her clit with the heel of his hand and pumping his fingers in and out of her. "Yes, keep doing that. Right there."

And then he replaced his hand with his mouth, his fingers moving in her while he sucked her clit. She raised her hips off the island and bucked against his face, riding that wave of ecstasy all the way to heaven, then hell, then heaven again.

She kept her eyes closed, savoring the euphoria of that incredible high. When she opened them, Jason was naked and climbing on top of the island.

She smiled and opened her arms.

"This is not the most comfortable bed," he said.

"Hey, fulfilling fantasies here, right? Comfort isn't the idea."

Fortunately, he had an oversized island, so he lay next to her, then rolled her on top of him. He smoothed his hands along her back.

"Your comfort is important to me, though."

She sat up and ran her fingers along his stomach. "You know, when you were giving me that mind-blasting orgasm, I wasn't thinking about whether I was comfortable or not."

"Good to know."

He grasped her hips and rolled her along the length of his rigid cock. She was happy to see he'd already put on a condom, so there'd be no break in the action. And she was so ready for more. She lifted, positioned him at her entrance, then slid down on him, watching his face as he entered her.

She sighed her contentment.

"Good?" he asked.

"So good."

After that there were no words, just moans and sounds and the feel of him taking her right where she wanted to go. She leaned forward so she could look at him, touch him as she rocked against him and took them both right to the edge of oblivion. And with every thrust she moved with him, felt that innate sense of oneness she always felt with Jason that both settled and unnerved her at the same time.

He pulled her fully on top of him, gripping her hips in

a tight embrace as he ground against her in a tight fusion that left her gasping. Their gazes stayed connected in such an intimate way it nearly blinded her in its intensity, but she couldn't look away, because he was so beautiful in the way he moved, in the way he'd captured her with his body and with his soul. There was such heat in his gaze she wanted to fall into that fire and let it consume her.

And when it did, she cried out and Jason dug his fingers into her hips, going at the same time with a shudder and a groan that only intensified her climax and left her shaking in its wake. She collapsed and lay her head on his chest, absorbing the wild beats of his heart.

They lay like that for a long time, Jason stroking her sweat-soaked back. Erin was sure her limbs were useless and they'd probably have to sleep like this.

"It's like lying on stone."

She lifted her head up to look down at him. "Well, it is stone."

"Back. Killing. Me."

She laughed and climbed off of him and they both finagled their way off the counter. They went into the bathroom, slipped into the shower for a quick rinse-off, then got dressed.

Jason went to let Puddy out, so she found him outside on the patio.

"I see the rain has stopped," she said.

"Yeah. Humid as hell, though."

She'd wound her hair up in a bun on top of her head, so fortunately the humidity wouldn't mess with her hair. She leaned against him. "I don't know about you, but I could use a cold drink."

"Beer?"

"I was thinking ice water."

He grimaced. "Fine."

She laughed and they went inside. She fixed them both glasses of ice water. Jason gulped his down in a few swallows, then fixed another while she sipped hers.

"Did you work up a thirst?" she asked.

He gave her a hot look over the rim of his glass. "You could say that."

She picked up her phone and checked the time. "I should go."

He laid the glass on the counter. "Or, you could stay with me tonight, and I could bring you home in the morning."

She laid her hand over her heart. "What would the family say?"

"That you're finally out having some fun?"

No one would notice, and Agatha was probably with her dad. She knew it was fine. No one would care.

The only thing she had to worry about was her heart. Jason was dangerous, and she'd have to be on guard.

"Sure. I'll stay."

"Don't make it sound like a death sentence."

She rolled her eyes. "Jason, I'd love to stay with you tonight. But it's not bedtime yet. Whatever will we do with our time? Maybe watch some TV?"

He laughed and stalked over to her. "I've got a few ideas."

Her body instantly flared with heat. "I'll just bet you do."

Good thing she could do her job on only a few hours' sleep. She had a feeling she wasn't going to get much shut-eye tonight.

And she wasn't complaining about that at all.

CHAPTER

······

twenty-four

AT LEAST JASON didn't have to wear a suit to this thing, so he was thankful for that much.

He didn't know shit about what paparazzi did or how they did it, but he sure as hell could point a camera at someone and press a button. And if it made the bride happy? Okay, correction. If it made Erin happy? Then great.

They were all gathered in the main house, and Maureen and Johnny Bellini had barbecued brisket and corn and made a few salads. Plus, there was plenty of beer and wine. So, all things considered, Jason couldn't really consider this work. It was more like a party, especially since a lot of his friends were here. Then Finn had brought in some of the whiskey he'd made, and it had really started to feel like a party.

Brenna came through the door and stared them all down. "I smell whiskey."

"I swear she has a nose for it," Finn said, leaning over to whisper to Jason while he grinned at Brenna. "She'd be a fine whiskey maker."

Brenna narrowed her gaze at Finn, obviously having

heard him. "Do *not* get drunk. We can't have you all falling over."

Finn lifted his chin. "Irishmen do not get drunk on whiskey."

"But the rest of us might," Johnny said, laughing.

Brenna came over and took the bottle of whiskey away from her dad.

"No more. And straighten up, all of you. You're on in about ten minutes."

She walked away, muttering something about "a bunch of lushes."

"The woman needs to lighten up a little," Finn said. "Maybe think about having some fun."

Jason motioned with his head toward the door. "Maybe you could be the one to show her some fun."

Finn laughed. "I think she'd rather cut off my balls. She hates men."

"Not all men," Honor said, pausing as she came into the room. "Just one man in particular."

Finn nodded. "Yeah, that ex of hers. He did her dirty, that bastard."

Jason nudged Finn. "See? She just needs a nice guy."

Finn's eyes widened. "Me?"

"Yeah, you. You have things in common."

"Like what? The woman's a ballbustin' hellcat. I wouldn't want to be cornered by her in a dark alley when she's in a mood. And she's always in a mood."

Jason laughed and took a sip of whiskey. "Oh, come on, Finn. You like a challenge."

Finn stared after Brenna. "That I do."

"Hey, everyone," Honor said. "Time to set up for the arrival of our bride."

Finn stood, then looked down at Jason. "And besides. Who ever said I was a nice guy?"

Jason laughed as they followed Honor out the door.

Erin and Brenna were already at the entrance to the arbor. They all wandered out.

"Okay," Honor said. "Erin and Brenna will hand you cameras. We have a red carpet set up, and as soon as our bride shows up in the limo, you start crowding in—but don't crowd her too closely—and start snapping photos."

They handed everyone cameras. Nice, big, professional-looking cameras.

"These are real," Erin said. "And expensive. Please treat them kindly."

There was an actual photographer on hand who gave them a quick how-to on using the cameras, but the idea wasn't to take professional shots. The photographer would take care of that part. They just had to make it appear as if the bride was the most important person in the world.

As it should be. And if this was what she wanted on her day, then this was what she was gonna get.

They all set up off to the side.

"This is *so* fun," Daria said.

"You're gonna want this for our wedding, aren't you?" Mike asked.

Daria just slanted a sly smile in Mike's direction.

Jason tried not to laugh. He knew Daria, knew this wasn't her thing, but he wasn't about to tell Mike that. It was more fun to let him suffer.

The limo pulled down the drive, and the driver opened the door. That was their cue. They rushed up and flashes started popping. To make it seem more authentic, they started calling her name, which Erin had told them was Marie, and asking her to look their way.

Marie looked happy as hell, grinning and waving at the cameras like she was a movie star.

And then her dad came around and she slipped her arm in his and headed down the aisle.

Which put an end to their part of the show. Short, but still fun. Erin and Brenna collected the cameras for the photographer since he had to dash off to take pics for the actual wedding.

"Come on," Summer said. "There's some open seats in the back row. Let's watch the wedding."

Daria and Mike went with Summer and Vince, and Clay and Alice joined them. Jason had seen a lot of weddings, so this was his chance to leave. He helped Finn and the Bellini women collect all the cameras and box them up.

"Where do you want these?" Finn asked, his arms filled with boxes.

"Greg said we could store them in the house and he'd pick them up after the reception," Brenna said.

Brenna took the last box and Finn followed behind her. Jason moved out of the way and Erin went with him. They huddled under one of the tall trees away from where the ceremony was taking place. They could still watch, but no one could see them.

"That went so well," Erin said.

"Yeah, it was fun. Bride seemed to enjoy it."

"That's what counts. If she's happy, then we did our job."

He watched as the bride and groom said their vows. He couldn't hear the words, but their smiles pretty much said it all. "Kind of a weird request, though."

Erin shrugged. "We get odd requests all the time. If we can accommodate them, we will."

He turned his head and looked at Erin. "What kinds of requests?"

"Let me think. Someone wanted a safari-themed wedding, and asked if we could rent out a few of the animals from the zoo and have them wandering the property on their wedding day."

Jason resisted the urge to bust out a laugh. "No shit. I assume that was a hard no."

"Definitely a no. As if the zoo routinely rented out their precious babies like a commodity."

Jason couldn't imagine the balls it took to even ask for something like that. His guess was that it was either someone with a lot of money, or not a lot of common sense.

"And then someone wanted fair rides and a midway."

"Nuh-uh."

"Oh yes. With a Ferris wheel and games and booths and other rides. Oh, and goats."

"Wait. Goats?"

She shrugged. "I didn't ask, because we said no. Well, I said no. Honor tries to be more accommodating, but it was a definite no."

"I'm glad."

"And then there was the couple who asked if we'd dig up the property and install a pool and water slide, because they wanted a water-themed wedding."

He just gaped at the ridiculousness of that request.

"I know. We told them we probably weren't the right fit for them, and suggested they might want to consider renting out the water park for their reception."

If he didn't know Erin as well as he did, he'd think she was bullshitting him. "Do people even think about not only the cost of an endeavor like that, but also the fact that this is a vineyard and not an amusement park? Or a water park?"

She leaned against the tree and crossed her arms. "Tell me about it. I'm the one who has to present wedding couples with a proposed budget. And when they come up with outrageous ideas, and I calculate how much it's going to cost them, I'm the one who gets yelled at because suddenly it's too expensive."

He didn't like the idea of her clients getting mad at her, but it was her job and he knew she had it handled. "So they blame you because they're spending too much money."

"Exactly. But we always manage to come up with a way to make it work. Almost always, anyway. There are a few exceptions, of course, but we've only had a couple of occasions where a couple has canceled the venue because we've been unable to deliver what they want."

"And here I thought that putting on a wedding was easy."

She laughed. "Yes. So easy."

He put his hand above her head, resting it on the trunk of the giant oak tree. "You work hard. It's sexy."

She arched a brow. "The work I do isn't sexy, Jason."

He wrapped his other arm around her waist and tugged her against him. "The hell it isn't. You think on your feet, juggle numbers, come up with brilliant ideas. Tell me how that isn't sexy."

She breathed in and out, causing her breasts to rise and fall above the top of her dress, making him want to kiss the globes, then get her naked and taste her all over.

But she was working, and he knew as soon as the wedding ceremony was over, she'd get busy again. So for now he took the few minutes they'd have together to kiss her, to take her lips and dive inside her mouth and taste the sweetness of her. It was so easy to get lost in her.

The loud applause made Erin press her hands on his chest, a signal for him to take a step back.

She licked her lips. "I have to go."

He nodded. "Yeah, you do."

She swept her fingertips across his jaw. "We'll take up this . . . discussion . . . later?"

He gave her a half smile. "I'll be around."

"Okay."

She walked away, disappearing into the crowd that was exiting the vineyard and heading toward the barn for the reception. Jason made his way toward the house, where he knew he'd find food and beer.

Agatha greeted him at the door, her tail whipping back and forth with great joy.

"Hey, baby girl." He gave her a few pets, then she wandered off down the hall.

He made his way down the hall toward the backyard, where Johnny and Maureen were, along with Finn. Clay and Alice had reappeared from the wedding, along with his other friends.

Jason grabbed a beer and settled into a chair next to Clay.

"How was the wedding ceremony?"

"It was good."

"I don't think paparazzi is in our future wedding plans, but I do so love the vineyard," Alice said. "After all, this is where we met."

"Is that why you want to get married here?" Maureen asked.

Alice looked over at Clay, then back to Maureen. "I couldn't think of a more appropriate place for our wedding. And May will be perfect."

Maureen beamed a look of utter joy. "I know the girls are so thrilled you two are getting married here. We're all so happy."

Johnny sported a grin a mile wide. "It'll be a good wedding. Happy for you both."

"Thank you," Alice said. "Me, too."

Jason slanted a smile at Clay. He knew how much Clay loved Alice. They could have the wedding at the Henry ranch, here at the vineyard or at the courthouse and Clay wouldn't care, as long as Alice married him.

Clay smiled back at him. "So, you'll be my best man, right?"

They'd been friends forever. Clay and Jason and Owen. They'd been through some shit together. Tough times. Good times. To stand up for Clay? Yeah, that would be a highlight.

"I'd be honored."

"What are you honored about?" Erin asked as she walked around the side of the house.

"Clay asked Jason to be his best man," Maureen said.

Erin didn't look at all surprised. "Of course he did."

Jason gave her the kind of hot smile that made her go weak in the knees. She curved her lips and smiled back at him, then turned her attention back to Alice. 'We're going to plan such a fun wedding."

"And will you be my maid of honor?" Alice asked.

Erin put her hand to her heart. "I'd love to. But what about Lainie? You were her maid of honor at her wedding here at the vineyard."

"I know. I've already talked to her and she agrees that it would be too difficult for her to help me out from out of state. She said she'd love to be a bridesmaid. And I'd really love for you to be my maid of honor."

Erin grinned. "Then I'm happy to accept."

The two women hugged, then Erin poured herself a glass of wine and sat next to Alice, the two of them getting out their phones, no doubt to schedule a meeting.

"Planning your future without you, buddy," Jason said.

Clay smiled over his beer. "I'm fine with that. I'll dress up, I'll show up, and that'll be good enough."

Jason laughed.

"Hey, have you been over to the brewery to see Owen yet?" Clay asked.

Jason shook his head. "Nah. I figure if he's got something to say, he'll call me. He hasn't even talked to Erin yet."

"Still? What the hell? Why not?"

"No clue. Maybe he's scared."

Clay frowned. "That doesn't sound like Owen. Then again, none of what happened is like Owen. The guy I know wouldn't bail on his woman right before the wedding. If he wasn't happy or changed his mind, he'd man up and tell her, face-to-face."

Jason nodded. "Yeah. That's what's been bugging me all these weeks. Why did he run?"

"I don't know, man. But I'm not planning on trying to make contact with him until he talks to Erin first."

"Agreed."

"You know he bailed on being in Ryan Phillips's wedding?" Clay asked.

That news shocked him. "I didn't know that. Kind of last minute, isn't it?"

"Yeah." Clay took a sip of beer. "Fortunately they got someone to fill in, but kind of shitty of him."

Jason knew the wedding was here at the vineyard, so maybe that was a good thing? He looked over to where Erin was still engaged in conversation with Alice. Did she know? She probably did. She knew everything about every wedding here at the vineyard.

"Damn." Jason shook his head. It was like some stranger had taken over his best friend's body. He didn't know what to make of it. He'd like to talk to Erin about it, but bringing up Owen to her was never a good idea.

Erin got up and disappeared again, no doubt to help her sisters out with the wedding, so Jason turned his attention back to his friends. He figured he'd wait on Erin, and when she was finished with her wedding duties, he'd spend some time with her. But he wasn't going to bring up Owen.

So they ate and drank and told stories and had a damn good time. Some folks left, and Maureen and Johnny went to bed, leaving Jason alone with Clay and Alice. Jason was telling Alice stories about their teen years, giving her all the dirt on her fiancé.

"Then there was the time one summer when he was fifteen," Jason said. "He crawled out the bedroom window at one in the morning, thinking he could take his horse into town to meet up with a girl he liked. Only the horse wasn't that fond of having to get up that early, made one hell of a ruckus, bucking around the barn, which woke Clay's dad, who also wasn't that happy about discovering his son trying to sneak out."

Alice's eyes widened. "What happened?"

"Let's just say I didn't leave the ranch for a while, and my daily chores list was . . . unpleasant."

She laughed. "Oh, you poor thing."

"Nah, don't feel sorry for him," Jason said. "The girl he wanted felt so bad about him getting in trouble, she ended up giving him a—"

"Don't tell her everything, man."

"So, not such a poor thing, after all," Alice said, giving Clay the side-eye.

"You don't know how much I suffered, babe. Two weeks at home, mucking out horse stalls. All that horse shit."

"Uh-huh. I'd say you're feeding me a line of horse shit right now."

Jason muffled a laugh and got up to go toss his empty beer bottle. When he came back, Clay and Alice were standing.

"We're heading out," Clay said. "I've got a date with some cattle early in the morning."

Jason nodded. "I'll walk with you."

This way he could get a peek at the wedding to see if it was wrapping up. He didn't want to linger if Erin was still busy.

And it looked like she was. The reception appeared to still be in full swing. He took out his phone. It was eleven thirty. Typically, the latest a reception would go was eleven, but this one didn't seem to be even close to breaking up.

He saw Brenna heading their way.

"Is anyone still around back there?" she asked.

"No, we're the last."

Brenna blew out a breath. "This reception is insane and these people can party. I'm headed to the cellars to get a few more cases."

"Need some help?" Jason asked.

"I could use a hand or two."

They all ended up helping Brenna cart the wine into the kitchen area of the barn. Erin and Honor came in to help with the bottles, while Erin whipped out her phone to tally up the number of cases, no doubt to add it to the clients' final bill.

"Some party, huh?" Alice asked.

"They're all having fun," Honor said. "And that's what matters."

"And no one is blackout drunk and throwing up in the vineyard, so that's even better," Erin said, hoisting a few bottles of wine out of the case. "I think the entire group is dancing out all the liquor they consume."

"Need some help?" Jason asked.

"We've got the bar staff here to assist, so we're good, but the wedding party said they're having so much fun they've asked for extra time, so I think we're going to be at this for a while. Sorry."

"It's okay."

"Thanks for understanding. I'll talk to you later." She gave him a quick kiss, then disappeared back into the reception area.

He said his good nights to Clay and Alice, then climbed into his truck, looking into the barn again.

Yeah, it looked like a big party. That's how all wedding receptions should be. That's how he wanted his to go.

Someday.

With a smile, he put his truck in gear and started down the road.

CHAPTER

······

twenty-five

IT WAS A spur-of-the-moment plan, but the idea had popped into her head from the moment Alice had told her Clay had proposed to her. Since Alice's birthday was this weekend, Clay was flying in her parents to help her celebrate. The timing would be perfect.

Ever since Alice and Clay had first met each other and had been snowbound at the house during the Christmas season last year, Erin and Alice had become close friends. And now Clay and Alice were engaged and getting married—at the Red Moss Vineyards. The idea of throwing Alice and Clay an engagement party seemed like the perfect fit.

She'd already talked to both Alice's and Clay's parents, and they were all on board with the idea. And if there was one thing Erin was good at it was planning an event.

Of course, they couldn't have the party on Friday or Saturday, since it was summer and weekends were booked solid. But Sunday afternoon was available, and everyone had said that sounded great. They were keeping things low-key, but Erin still wanted to make it elegant and fun.

She'd had a couple of weeks to plan the event, which in her world was more than enough time. And fortunately she hadn't had to deal with facing Owen since he'd bailed out on being in Ryan and Yolanda's wedding. For reasons that still eluded her. Surely he hadn't done it to avoid her. Or maybe he had.

Either way, she didn't care. She hadn't had to face him, and the wedding had turned out perfectly.

And her tension level had dropped dramatically since she hadn't had the possibility of seeing Owen weighing on her. Not that she could avoid him forever, but she could for now, and that worked for her.

Fortunately, last night's wedding had wrapped up by ten p.m., which meant they could clean up and head to bed early. Not that Erin had done that. She'd grabbed Agatha and they'd gone to Jason's. He'd had wine and food ready for her, and they'd spent a couple of hours talking about their week. They'd both been super busy and had hardly seen each other. She'd missed him, and texting and talking on the phone just wasn't enough. The catching up had been good.

So had the hours they'd spent in bed.

What hadn't been fun was waking up at dawn so she could dash home and help get the barn ready for the party today. Jason was on call this weekend, so he had to run into the vet clinic early to take care of some of the sick dogs, but he showed up at the vineyard around nine, and was currently helping Finn and Dad set up tables.

Erin, on the other hand, was taking a short break to drink her eighty-third cup of coffee.

"Aww, what's the matter, princess? Up all night with

the boyfriend?" Brenna asked, sarcasm dripping all over the word "boyfriend."

"First, he's not my boyfriend. Second, I'm doing just fine."

"Sure you are. You're barely standing. You know, this whole engagement party thing was your idea. The least you can do is be awake for it."

"What's going on?" Honor asked as she stepped up to the two of them.

"I don't know," Erin said. "Ask Brenna."

"No comment."

"You can talk to us." Honor smoothed her hand up Brenna's arm, but Brenna jerked away.

Erin frowned. "What crawled up your ass today, Bren?"

"Nothing. I'd just like a day off every now and then."

"Then take one," Erin said. "If you don't want to be here, bail."

"Oh, right, like I wouldn't be judged for that."

Erin had no idea where this animosity was coming from, but she had the feeling that it had nothing to do with the engagement party for Clay and Alice. "No one judges you."

Brenna's look was filled with anger and some kind of frustration that Erin hadn't known her sister was holding on to. "Don't they? I'm the oldest, so I'm supposed to set the example for you and Honor. You're the organized one, Erin, so you never screw anything up, and Honor is the baby so she's like . . . perfect."

Whoa. "You really think that?"

"I am *not* perfect," Honor said.

Brenna just snorted. "Whatever. I've got work to do. So do both of you."

She walked away, leaving Erin and Honor looking at each other in bewilderment.

"What was that about?" Honor asked.

"I have no idea. She came at me saying I was falling asleep on the job today, and then it escalated."

Honor looked over to where Brenna was directing the setup crew.

"Something's upset her," Honor said. "She hasn't talked to you about anything in particular?"

"You know Brenna. She keeps things to herself. Always has. When she broke up with Mitch she had already filed for divorce before we even knew they had split."

"I know." Honor breathed in and blew it out, her frustration evident. "I wish she'd open up and tell one of us what's bothering her."

"Me, too." Despite her irritation at having taken the brunt of Brenna's ire, she loved her sister. If she was unhappy, then Erin wanted to fix it. But she couldn't fix what she didn't know.

"Let her cool down," Erin said. "Then we'll talk to her together."

Honor nodded. "Good idea."

Whatever it was that had made Brenna flash up had apparently passed, because after that the rest of the morning moved along smoothly. The one thing the three sisters could do well together was run an event. They had tables and wine set up, food was cooked and ready to serve, and everything was in place an hour before the guests were due to arrive.

Erin dashed into her bathroom to take a shower, dried her hair, then put on a light touch of makeup so she wouldn't melt into the heat. She slipped on her cotton sundress and her tan sandals.

She walked out of her room at the same time Brenna did—and her sister was wearing the same copper-colored sundress.

Brenna scrunched her lips. "Well, shit."

Erin laughed. "I'll go change. You look amazing."

"No, I'll do it."

"No, really, it was a toss-up between this one and the yellow one."

Brenna tilted her head. "The yellow one looks amazing with your dark hair."

"Thanks. Yellow it is."

Brenna started down the steps.

"Bren?"

"Yeah?"

"You know you can talk to me—and to Honor—about anything."

"I know. And I'm sorry I was such a bitch earlier. I had a bad day yesterday. I shouldn't have taken it out on you."

"It's okay. That's what sisters are for. You want to talk now?"

Brenna shook her head. "Not really. Maybe."

Which to Erin meant yes. "Okay. Spill it."

"I had a terrible date."

Erin frowned and walked over to Brenna. "What happened?"

Brenna shrugged. "I had high hopes, you know? On the surface, he seemed like a nice guy. I thought we had a lot in common. But then it all fizzled out over dinner and I was just so . . ."

"Disappointed?"

Brenna waited a beat before answering, but Erin could read her sister's face.

"Yes. I mean, how hard is it to carry on a conversation over a meal? It's not like I'm a physicist or anything. I just want to talk about wine and books and gardening. I find out about his likes, he finds out about mine."

"But?"

"Oh, I found out all about his likes, all right. He was only interested in shoveling food in his mouth and talking all about himself and all his major life achievements. His big house, his bitchin' car."

Erin winced. "He did not say 'bitchin',' did he?"

"Oh, he did. And then he expected that I'd come over to his place after dinner for some hot after-dinner sex for dessert. Even though he hadn't asked me one single question about who the hell I was."

Erin wrinkled her nose. "How revolting. I'm so sorry, Bren. What a waste of a night."

"I got a good meal out of it, so it wasn't a total waste. But still, how hard is it to find a decent man?"

"I wish I had a good answer for that one. But please don't give up. The right guy for you will come along."

"Yeah. Sure he will. Anyway, I'm really sorry I snapped at you." Brenna hugged her.

"It's okay. Sometimes you just have to let it out. But not at us next time, okay?"

Brenna laughed. "Yeah, I'll make a mental note. And I'll find Honor and apologize to her, too."

"Okay. I love you."

Brenna smiled. "I love you, too."

She watched as Brenna walked down the stairs, feeling awful for her. Bad dates were a big deal, especially since her sister was trying to get out there again. But nothing good came from holding your pain inside. No one knew that better than Erin. She hoped this wouldn't derail Brenna from dating. In fact, she'd make sure to encourage Brenna to keep her toes in the dating pool.

Her heart feeling lighter as she walked into her room, Erin changed into the yellow sundress, then switched her sandals as well. The white ones would go better. And the copper dress Brenna wore made her sister's hair look like fire. So all in all, it was a good decision on both their parts.

She ran into Jason at the foot of the stairs. His hair was damp.

"Took a shower in the guest bath. I got a little sweaty setting everything up."

She leaned into him, breathing in his fresh clean smell. "You smell good, but you know, I also like you sweaty."

He looked around, saw that they were alone, then pulled her close and kissed her. It was a long, lingering kiss, the kind that made a woman weak in the knees, one that was filled with passion and promise.

When he pulled back, she breathed deeply. "That was very nice."

He waggled his brows. "More where that came from."

As he walked away, she sighed. She hoped so. It had been a long week without him and her body ached for his touch. She missed sitting and talking with him, discussing their days together. Talking on the phone just wasn't enough. She needed to see him, to touch him while they were talking, to look into his warm brown eyes so she could read his emotions.

Whoa. That had been deep. Way too deep for her liking. Where had light and fun gone? Where had all these . . . feelings come from?

She didn't like it. Not one bit. She wasn't supposed to be feeling anything. This thing she had going on with Jason was supposed to be easy and breezy and lusty and sexy. Not deep and emotional and needy. She was using him to get over Owen. Not falling in . . .

Nope. She shook her head and stalked down the stairs.

She was never going to L-word again. L-word made you stupid and unable to see when the guy right in front of you didn't L-word you back. That wasn't going to happen to her. Besides, Jason didn't even feel the same way. He was in this for the same thing—good times and hot sex.

"Good times and hot sex."

"What are you muttering about?"

She looked up to find herself standing right in front of her mother.

Shit.

"Uhh . . . that we needed to make sure to have plenty of cooled wine and hot crab dip."

Her mother frowned, then arched a brow, studying her. "You're acting strange. And your cheeks are pink." She lifted the back of her hand to Erin's forehead. "You're not coming down with anything, are you?"

Yeah, a case of the mumbling stupids. "No, I'm fine, Mom. I really do need to go check on the food."

"The food is already being set out, and I just saw Clay's parents pull up. That's where I was headed."

"Okay. I'll go to the barn and make sure everything's ready."

"You do that." Her mom started to walk away, then stopped. "You're sure you're all right?"

She could never slide anything past her mother. "I'm good, Mom, really. But thank you for always looking after me."

She kissed her mom on the cheek.

"Okay. If you need me for anything, you know I'm always here."

It must have been written on Erin's face—the indecision, the emotion—because her mom had always known when something was off with her. But this? This she couldn't talk about with her mother. Not when she didn't even really know how she felt.

"I know. Thank you."

Her mother walked out the front door, and Erin

slipped out the side, heading over to the barn. It was simply decorated because Alice insisted that they didn't go overboard for the engagement party. It was more important to both Alice and Clay that it just be a joyful get-together to celebrate their engagement, not a fussy party.

Erin was all about fussy parties, but she and her sisters also knew to give the clients what they wanted. Not that Clay and Alice were clients. This event was being done out of love for Clay and his family, and for Alice, their new friend.

Erin's new best friend. She and Alice had shared so much since they met six months ago, and it was like they'd known each other forever. It was funny how that had worked out. She had friends from childhood and from college, but she wasn't as close to them as she'd grown with Alice.

She dashed into the house to grab the fresh flowers and took them over to the barn, setting two vases down at the main table where Alice and Clay would sit with their families. They looked so pretty. Alice would love that. Then she went back to the main house to wait on the porch for Alice and Clay to show up. Her nerves were on high alert and she didn't know why. They had everything set up, and it was all going to be fine. But she wanted so much for this day to go well.

She'd done weddings for a couple of her high school girlfriends, and she'd never felt jittery about it. Of course, after high school and moving on to college, those friendships had lost that closeness they'd once had.

Maybe it was because Erin was so close with her sisters, shared so much with Brenna and with Honor that she had never formed intimate bonds with any women beyond her sisters. Until she had met Alice and forged an immediate friendship with her.

Which was why she wanted this engagement party to be everything for Alice. She knew they could have thrown hot dogs on a grill and had beer available and Clay would have been happy, because Clay was all about family and friends, which was one of the reasons Erin liked him so much, knew he was the perfect guy for Alice. He wasn't fussy, didn't care all that much about his own needs. But he'd bent over backward to carve out a life for himself and for Alice, to make sure Alice's career came first, that she could make a life with him and still be able to do the work she did. He prioritized Alice in a way that made Erin see what had been missing in her relationship with Owen.

Not that Owen had begrudged her her career. He'd always been supportive, even if it meant they couldn't see each other as much. It was just that the two of them had been so focused on their own careers—Erin with her job and Owen starting up the brewery. But had they really taken the time to focus on each other like they should have? Had they gotten engaged because it was what had been expected out of both of them?

She took a seat on the front porch steps and wondered why they hadn't ever had a conversation about that, about whether either of them was ready for marriage. If they were really in love with each other, or were just following expectations.

Maybe she'd been so blinded by the proposal and the ring and the planning and the whole wedding experience that she'd never taken the time to explore her feelings. But now that she'd had the time to take a step back, she wondered if she'd ever felt the whole wonder of it, the magic of falling in love, that feeling of "Oh, God, this man is my whole world."

Maybe she was feeling it now, and that was why she was questioning why she'd never felt it before.

Her face flamed hot and she pressed her palms to her cheeks.

Oh, God. That could not be what was happening.

Could it?

"Hiding out?"

Jason opened the front door, looking magnificent in a long-sleeve button-down white shirt, a stark contrast against his dark, tanned skin. He had on crisp jeans and his cowboy boots and just looking at him in this simple attire took her breath away.

He frowned. "What? You said we didn't have to dress up."

"You look . . . fine." She cleared her throat past the lump of realization that had seemed to settle there.

"Okay. You look gorgeous, by the way. I like the color of that dress."

"Thank you."

His compliments were never empty. She saw it in the sincerity of his look, in the way he always said something specific about her clothes or her hair or even a bracelet she might be wearing.

He sat next to her, picked up her hand and kissed the back of it. "I missed you this week."

"Same." How could she not see that she was wrapping herself up in Jason, letting her emotions lead the way instead of keeping herself firmly cut off from getting involved? She'd tried so hard to make it just about fun, but somehow she'd opened her heart.

Then again, how could she not? She'd known Jason practically her whole life. They'd been friends forever. It wasn't like she could just have sex with him and not feel anything for him.

This was such a mess. She could not fall in love with him. It was ridiculous to even think she could fall in love again. Not so soon after Owen. What she was feeling wasn't at all realistic.

She was rebounding. That's what it was. She was taking all her messed-up feelings about Owen and projecting them onto her crush on Jason.

"Everything okay?"

She looked up. "What?"

"Normally we talk, and you're over there silent as dirt."

"Oh. Just going over today's activities in my head."

"Uh-huh. You have it planned out to the millionth degree already. So what's going on, Erin?"

She couldn't even wrap her own thoughts around how she felt right now. How could she talk to Jason about them?

Fortunately, she was spared having to answer when Clay and Alice pulled down the driveway. She stood, brushed off her skirt and smiled, heading down the stairs to greet them.

Alice looked beautiful in a long slate-blue flowered maxi dress, her happiness evident on her glowing face. She was letting her hair grow out, and the dark brown waves fell just to her shoulders. Clay was, as usual, in his jeans, cowboy boots and a button-down shirt, wearing his cowboy hat. But together? They made a striking couple.

She went over to them and hugged them, whispering to Alice that she loved her dress.

"Thank you," Alice said. "And you, that dress, I love your hair, half up like that with those curls falling down. Why do you always look stunning?"

She blushed under her friend's complimentary perusal, though she always thought Alice underestimated her own beauty. "Thank you." Then she led the couple into the barn, where they were greeted with cheers and applause.

When she threw a party, Erin liked to take a step back and watch the expressions on the couple's faces.

Clay only looked at Alice, which made Erin's heart squeeze. Alice's eyes sparkled like diamonds as she took in the champagne sparkling in golden buckets on the tables, the gold and white decorations, the rustic touches that made the barn look like an actual barn for a change, and the bits of California décor that spoke to Alice's home state.

Alice turned to Erin and mouthed *I love you* before being swallowed up by all her guests.

Erin couldn't be happier for her friends. They all ate and drank and celebrated Clay and Alice, and it turned out to be a perfect day. Erin and her sisters stayed busy making sure every guest was accommodated, which turned out to be beneficial, because Erin was trying her best to avoid Jason.

Not that she didn't want to see him anymore. She absolutely did. She just had to get her riotous emotions under control first. Once she worked it all out in her head, she'd be fine and they could go on the way they were.

Fortunately, Jason was occupied with Clay and some of their other friends, and she had taken organizational point, which meant she was on the run most of the day, which suited her just fine.

Until her mother grabbed her by the arm and hauled her out of the barn.

"What are you doing?" her mother asked.

She frowned. "Making sure the food trays stay full and we don't run out of wine or beer or iced tea or water. And that our guests are happy. You know, my job."

"We hired caterers for the day. That's their job. There's plenty to drink and we only need to check periodically. You haven't sat down in three hours and I'm sure your friend Alice would love for you to spend time with her to help celebrate her engagement."

She looked over and saw Alice sitting with Clay and Jason. Alice looked up at her with an expectant smile.

"Oh, well, I was just going to—"

"You were just going to go over there and sit with Alice."

Mom gave her *that look*.

"Mom."

"Go sit down, Erin."

When you got *that look* plus the *tone of voice*, you did not disobey. Erin had to admit defeat.

"Yes, ma'am."

She walked over, immediately catching sight of Jason tracking her with his gaze.

The man's smile could light up a city. Maybe even a universe. For sure it lit up her heart, making it trip over itself as she made her way to the table.

Apparently, she hadn't gotten her emotions under control during all that time she'd been avoiding him. And she still had no answers on how to do that.

But Alice pointed to the chair next to hers, which was on the other side of the table from Jason.

"Come sit next to me and we'll catch up," Alice said. "Have some wine. You've been working the entire time."

"I'm sorry. I wanted to make sure you and Clay had a good party."

"The party is amazing, Erin. More than I could have ever imagined. My parents are thrilled. Clay's parents are so happy. We couldn't have asked for more. I didn't even expect this. It's just . . . everything. Thank you."

Alice threw her arms around Erin and hugged her. Tears pricked Erin's eyes and she forced herself not to burst into tears. Instead, she squeezed her friend tight.

"You're welcome. You deserve this."

When Alice pulled back, her eyes shimmered with unshed tears, too. She laughed. "Well, no more of that. I can't wait to plan the wedding."

"May will be here before you know it."

"I know. And I have to get a dress. The venue is set, of course, but there are so many details."

"Hey," Erin said, laying her hand over Alice's. "We're both planners. We can manage all the details."

"You're right. I just started thinking that it's less than a year away and had a minute of panic."

"No panicking. You've got me as your maid of honor now. I've got this. And I'll make sure you do, too."

"Thank God. Because I'm in LA next week, and then when I get back? All the planning."

She gave Alice a confident smile. "Already on my schedule."

"So tell me what's going on with Jason," Alice asked.

Erin frowned, trying to avoid looking across the table at the subject of their conversation. "What do you mean? Everything's fine."

"Is it? Because it seems to me every time he tries to approach, you turn and nearly run in the opposite direction. Are you two fighting?"

She couldn't resist. She took a quick glance across the table. Jason had gotten up and was at the bar at the other end of the room chatting with Finn.

"No, we're good."

Alice cocked her head to the side. "You know, a good friend of mine once told me that I should face my feelings. Are you in avoidance?"

Alice was a good friend. A friend who was right. But now wasn't the time.

"You do realize this is your engagement party, right?"

"And you do realize that we're friends, and I'm here for you, no matter what or when. So spill it."

She sighed, realizing she wasn't going to be able to back her way out of having this conversation with Alice. "Okay. I've got some mixed emotions going on. Feelings that I don't know what to do with or think about. You know how you get into a relationship that starts out one way, and then suddenly it turns out another way entirely—a way you didn't expect at all?"

Alice beamed a smile. "Oh, yes. I'm marrying that guy."

That answer hit like a building falling on top of her. "Okay, that's not what's happening to me."

"So what is happening? Are you saying you don't have feelings for Jason?"

"Well, I'm not saying that, either."

Alice shrugged. "I'm confused."

"Me, too. Let's just say I'm still trying to reconcile the past relationship, while trying to juggle the current one. And I think my feelings are getting tied up in the mix between the two."

"So you still have feelings for Owen."

"Oh, God no. In fact, I'm second-guessing if I ever had the right kind of feelings for Owen. Which means how do I even know what love really is?"

Alice laid her hand over Erin's. "Oh, honey. When it's real love? You'll know it."

"I thought I knew it before. That's what I'm saying. Was I caught up in the romance of . . . romance? The whole proposal and wedding planning thing? Because while I'm pissed as hell that Owen dumped me right before the wedding, to be honest, Alice?" She looked around to make sure no one was within hearing distance. They weren't, so she continued. "To be honest, I don't miss Owen. I'm not heartbroken over losing him, and I should be. If I loved him, I should be nursing heartbreak. The only thing I've been nursing is my feelings of anger and rejection."

"Ohh, okay. Now I'm getting it. You're comparing your feelings for Owen versus your growing feelings for Jason, and it's confusing you."

"Like you would not believe." She was so happy to have a friend who understood her dilemma.

"That is a problem. And one that's probably not resolved easily. But, honey, I don't think avoiding Jason is the answer."

"Probably not. But I need some space to sort out my thoughts. My feelings. Every time I get close to Jason it's like everything inside of me . . . short-circuits."

Alice laughed. "That's not necessarily a bad thing."

Erin quirked a smile. "Okay, not a terrible thing. But it is if I'm trying to think clearly."

"I don't know," Alice said with a slight shrug. "It sounds like you might be falling in love. Is that so bad?"

Was it? She didn't know. Maybe because she was trying to have a fling, not fall in love. And what the hell did she really know about falling in love? She'd thought she was in love with Owen. She'd been so wrong.

So was she really falling in love with Jason, or was this another round of lust and fun and infatuation and the romance of it all? Or was it hiding her feelings of rejection and turning them into something that wasn't even real? How was she supposed to know when she wasn't thinking with a clear head?

Until she could sort it out logically, gain some perspective, she had to keep her distance.

But it sure helped to have Alice's counsel.

The party lasted until early evening, and then everyone headed out. Alice had to pack and Clay and his dad and some of the hands from the ranch had to see to the cattle.

Alice and Clay thanked them for the party.

"We owe you a big one," Clay said, shaking everyone's hands and hugging Erin, Brenna and Honor, who he'd always treated like sisters.

"I'll talk to you when I get back," Alice said.

"When you get back? I'll be texting you next week. I have some dress ideas."

Alice giggled. "Fantastic."

Everyone disappeared after the guests of honor left. Everyone except Jason, who lingered at the barn while Erin supervised the cleanup from her position at the entrance to the barn. Of course, the crew they'd hired had it all under control and she really didn't need to be there. She still just felt . . . unsettled. And having Jason standing only inches away from her wasn't helping to settle her.

"You've been avoiding me today," he said, leaning against the doorway, his thumb hooked in his belt buckle in the most natural, sexy way, which disturbed her greatly.

"I was busy."

"No, you were avoiding me. Wanna tell me why?"

"I've got a lot on my mind, Jason, and it can't always be about you."

"So what you're saying is I'm on your mind a lot?"

She'd laugh if she wasn't so miserable. "I'm tired."

He pushed off the wall and came over, stopping in front of her. He smoothed her hair away from her face with his fingers. Just that modicum of touch was enough to send her senses haywire. Then his fingers trailed down her temple and across her cheek until his thumb brushed her bottom lip.

Every part of her quivered with awareness. She wanted him to kiss her. She didn't want him to kiss her.

"You do look tired," he said, taking a step back. "You should get some rest, babe."

She'd never been more relieved. Or more regretful.

"Good night, Erin."

She watched him walk away, her body—her entire soul—still vibrating from his touch.

Damn.

CHAPTER

······

twenty-six

Bᴀᴛʜʀᴏᴏᴍ ᴡᴀs ꜰɪɴɪsʜᴇᴅ, painting had been done, all that was left was putting the flooring in the bedroom. Finn had offered to come over to lend a hand tonight, as he had on a few other occasions during this project. Jason was glad for any help he could get. In return, Jason offered to toss some steaks on the grill and supply all the beer Finn wanted.

"These are good floors, man," Finn said as they were nearly three-quarters done with the bedroom.

They'd taken a time-out to drink some water and stretch, because laying floors was backbreaking work, especially when you'd already put in a full day's work on your regular job.

"I plan to lay the same hardwoods down the hall so they match the ones that I've laid throughout the entire house. So I'm almost there."

"It's lookin' fine." Finn looked it over. "Not too dark or light, just the right color. And the grain has those grooves that'll wear well."

"Thanks. I thought it was a good choice, especially with Puddy and his nails."

Speaking of Puddy, he currently sat between Jason and Finn, his ball in his mouth, waiting for someone to play with him.

"Soon as we're done here, buddy. When we're grilling we'll throw the ball."

"He's a good boy."

"Yeah, he is," Jason said. "You should get a dog."

"Erin's dog Agatha is like the vineyard dog now. Keeps us all on our toes. Besides, I only have the one-room cabin on the grounds. Not like my own place."

He could listen to Finn talk in that Irish accent all night long. Even though Finn had been in the US since he was eighteen, he hadn't lost that lilt to his voice.

"You thinking about moving out?"

Finn shrugged. "The Bellinis are the only family I have now. Maureen's like my mum. When I'm ready to settle down I'll move on. For now, I have the cabin and it's convenient. Far enough away from the main house to give me some privacy, and close enough that I can walk to the vineyard."

Jason's lips curved. "It's a damn good cabin, right there near the pond."

"Yeah. Good fishin' there."

Jason finished off his water, so they got back to work. Within an hour they had the rest of the floor done. Damn, it was good to have that project finished. It was great having Finn there. He worked his ass off, didn't slack off on the job or bullshit around. When there was work to be done, it got done well and fast.

They washed up and Jason pulled a couple of beers out of the fridge, handing one to Finn. The cold brew was just what Jason needed after that hot, sweaty job.

Jason grabbed the steaks and some corn on the cob, put them on a plate, and covered the plate to keep the flies away. They went outside and he fired up the grill.

"Thanks for your help," he said, tilting his bottle toward Finn.

"Happy to do it."

"I hope I didn't take you away from something important."

Finn laughed. "If I'd had something more important to do, I'd have said no."

One of the reasons Jason liked Finn was his brutal honesty. The guy wouldn't lie about anything even if it hurt your feelings.

"Besides, someday I'll have my own house and I'll have to do all this shit. So you taught me a few things."

"I doubt there's much I can teach you. You know woodwork, you know your way around a saw and hammer, and when you're not doing that you're making your own whiskey. Is there anything you can't do?"

Finn pondered the question for a bit while he drank his beer. "I dunno. I'll try just about anything. Though my grandad once had me help him put up a roof when I was a lad. Hated that. Hot as fuck up there."

Jason took a couple of long swallows of beer, then nodded. "Yeah, I've done that, too. That's like last on the list of things I'd want to do. I was glad when I bought this place that the roof had been recently replaced and it was at least one thing I didn't have to do."

"You're lucky. I'd have said no if you asked me to help you."

Jason laughed. "I wouldn't have blamed you. Another beer?"

"Yeah."

He turned the steaks and the corn, then went inside to

put potatoes in the microwave to cook. He brought the beers outside.

"Surprised Erin's not here tonight," Finn said. "You two seem tight lately."

Jason took a long swallow of beer. "Yeah, well, I'm not sure where her head's at right now."

"What does that mean?"

"I don't know. One minute she wants to be with me, the next minute it's like she can't wait to get away from me."

"I was in a room with you earlier, man. You do smell, so I feel sympathy for her."

"Yeah, well, you don't exactly smell like a bar of Irish Spring, either, asshole."

Finn laughed. "Seriously, though. You have feelings for her, then?"

"Yeah."

"That's too bad. That's gonna mess with your head."

Understatement. When the food was done, he took the steaks and corn off the grill and they went inside. Potatoes were done so they piled food on their plates and sat at the table. They were both hungry so they dug in and ate without saying much of anything, which suited Jason just fine.

"Have you tried talking to her about how you feel?" Finn asked.

Jason pulled his attention from his plate and onto Finn. "Indirectly."

"What the fuck does that even mean? Indirectly. You either tell a woman how you feel or you don't."

"It's . . . complicated."

"No it's not. I don't know how far those feelings you're havin' have gone, but maybe you could have it go something like this. 'Erin, I love you. Oh, and I worked my ass off on this great bedroom so I could share it with you for the rest of my life.'"

He stared at his friend. "That kind of sucked, Finn."

Finn shrugged. "Never been in love with anyone. How the fuck should I know how you tell a woman you love her?"

"Just for future reference? Not like that."

"Whatever. If you love a woman, as long as you're sincere and it comes from the heart, it doesn't matter what words you say."

Okay, he had a point there. "I'm not sure she's ready to hear those words yet. I'm not sure she feels the same about me."

"Is she still hung up on Owen?"

"I don't know. Maybe. She hasn't talked to him yet, so the fact that he's still hanging out there, unresolved, is a big issue for her."

Finn waved his fork at Jason. "Then you've got a problem."

"Yeah." A big one. And one that he had no control over.

He wasn't all that damn happy about letting other factors decide his future. But there wasn't much he could do about it other than wait.

Or maybe continue to be the friend he was to Erin before all this started between them. Because she probably needed one right now.

CHAPTER

......

twenty-seven

ERIN HAD JUST put the finishing touches on the financial component of a proposal for a couple they'd met with this morning when her phone pinged. She picked it up to see a text from Jason.

Feel like a picnic?

She studied her phone, her brows knit into a frown.

No, she didn't feel like a picnic. She felt cranky and out of sorts, like she had been for the past two weeks. Even Agatha was avoiding her, preferring the much happier disposition of Erin's father. Not that she could blame the pup.

"Hey, I was just going to ask—" Honor started, popping her head in, but then stopped and asked, "Why are you shooting an evil glare at your phone?"

She tossed her phone on the table. "No reason. What's up?"

Honor walked in and pulled up a chair. "Don't give

me that. You were frowning so hard I was afraid your face was going to freeze that way."

Erin laughed. "One of Mom's favorite lines."

"Very effective, too, especially now when we have to worry about wrinkles."

"Please. You have the best skin out of all of us."

"I do not. And you're beautiful. Now tell me why you made an ugly face at your phone."

"Jason texted me to ask if I felt like having a picnic."

Honor gasped. "The horror. How could he, that bastard."

"You don't understand."

"Obviously. So explain it to me."

"I don't know. I'm . . . cranky."

"Yes, you are. And you have been for a while now. Is this still about Owen? Because if that's the case then you're totally entitled."

"Partially. But I think I'm more upset that I'm not as upset as I should be about him dumping me."

Now it was Honor's turn to frown. "What?"

"I know, it doesn't make sense. But I've had some distance from it now. And along with spending time with Jason, I've had the chance to feel . . . to feel . . ."

Her sister's face changed into an empathetic smile. "To *feel*? Something for Jason that maybe you didn't feel for Owen?"

Her sister was nothing if not utterly succinct in her summation. "I guess. But I don't know, Honor. How do I even know if what I'm feeling for Jason is real? I thought I was madly in love with Owen, and look what happened there. Am I even a good judge of what love is? I've never been more confused about anything in my life."

"There's no time limit on falling in love, is there? Can't you just be with Jason and let things happen naturally? See if what you're feeling is real?"

Her sister had a point. "I guess so."

"Then go have a picnic and quit being so grouchy."

Erin finally dropped her shoulders, letting some of that tension go. "Fine. I'll go picnic."

"Good. And did you send those financials?"

"Yes. The document should be in your e-mail."

Honor stood. "Awesome. Thanks. I can finish off the proposal and get that sent off tomorrow morning. Have fun."

"I will. I guess."

Honor turned in the doorway. "No 'I guess,' Erin. You will."

"Fine, I will. Get out."

Honor laughed on her way out. Erin retrieved her phone and typed a reply to Jason.

A picnic sounds fun.

It took him about thirty minutes to send his response, likely because he was busy with a client.

Pick you up at six thirty. I'll take care of everything.

Of course he would, because that was the kind of man he was.

She sighed, then went back to work for the next few hours until it was time to end her day and go get ready for the picnic. Of course, she'd forgotten to ask Jason if it was a park kind of picnic, or if he was just going to bring her to his house and they'd have fried chicken. Not that it really mattered. Oh, who was she kidding? The right outfit always mattered. She pondered her closet while Agatha chewed on a toy.

"Dress or capris, Agatha?"

The pup cocked her head to the left.

"Capris it is. You have such good taste." She crouched down and ruffled Agatha's fur, which made the pup roll over, so of course she had to rub her belly.

She changed out of her dress and into capris and a sleeveless top, then slipped on her tennis shoes and wound her hair into a bun on top of her head. She stopped in the dining room to talk to the family while they ate, snatching a bite or two of her mom's caprese salad, which was delicious.

"So, a date tonight?" Brenna asked, offering up a sly smile.

"No, just a . . ." She had no idea how to describe the picnic she was going to have with Jason. She'd meant to come up with a way to make it sound casual, and now that she'd paused, the entire family was staring expectantly at her.

"She's going on a picnic with Jason," Honor finished for her.

"Oh, nice," her mother said, then resumed eating.

In fact, everyone just nodded or mumbled "Great" or "Have fun" and went back to eating as if it were No Big Deal.

Which, apparently, to her family, it wasn't. She was the only one making it A Big Deal. Of course, she was the only one whose emotions were involved.

Agatha took a spot next to her dad, circling then lying down at his feet. He absently patted her head, then resumed eating. Erin shook her head, but was grateful her puppy was so well loved and taken care of.

She said her good-byes and went to the door, deciding to wait outside. A storm had passed through earlier in the day, and though they were heading toward July, it had cooled down some. The air felt fresh and clean and it was still cloudy outside, which made her happy since it suited her mood.

Erin took a seat on the porch swing, enjoying the respite from the heat. Winds that had been furious earlier during the storm had died down, so now it was perfect.

She didn't sit long, though, because she saw Jason's truck pulling down the long drive toward the house. Just seeing his truck pumped up her heartbeat into a fast rhythm.

Calm down, girl.

It was ridiculous how this man got to her. She walked down the steps as he stopped in front of the house. He got out of the truck, coming around to greet her with a smile, looking ridiculously hot in jeans, boots and a tight brown T-shirt that molded to his sculpted shoulders and biceps.

"Hi, beautiful."

And still, those words that he'd been saying to her for years, even when she'd been with Owen. She'd always brushed it off as funny. Now she took it to heart, especially when he made eye contact with her, when he smiled at her in that way that always caused her stomach to do that funny flip.

"Hey. Thanks for the picnic invite."

She climbed into the truck and he closed the door. He'd left the motor running and it was nice and cold inside, helping to cool her down.

Would she ever stop having this chemical reaction around him? Or maybe it was her emotions, the way she felt about him that had added to this meltdown she felt whenever she was around him lately.

Whatever, it was damned disconcerting.

He pulled into the park by the lake and drove to a spot shaded by a thick grouping of tall trees that seemed to be bent over on purpose to provide shade. They got out and he grabbed a bag and a blanket, leading her to a nice grassy spot near the water.

"So you really did mean a picnic," she said, watching him spread the blanket out.

He looked up, tilting his head. "What did you think I meant?"

"I don't know. I thought maybe you'd grab a bucket of chicken and we'd hang out at your house."

He frowned. "That's not a picnic."

"I don't know. If we ate on the floor it would be."

He reached for her hand and tugged her down on the blanket. "If we ate on the floor, we'd be fighting Puddy for our food."

She laughed. "You're probably right."

"Besides, it's nice right now. We're in the shade, not too hot, and we're by the lake. Perfect night for a picnic."

She slapped her arm, killing a mosquito. "Except for the bugs."

He reached into the bag and pulled out mosquito repellant. "Got that covered."

The man was always prepared. She put on the repellant, mentally cursing the bug bite that would likely drive her crazy for the next week. Damn bloodsuckers.

Jason pulled out turkey wraps, hummus, chips and carrot sticks, as well as a jug of water and a bottle of wine. He uncorked the wine—a Red Moss Vineyards brand, of course—and poured it into plastic wineglasses.

He handed a glass to her.

She took a sip, enjoying the mellow smoothness of the rosé. "You thought of everything."

"I figured you needed an easy night."

He had no idea how much. "Thanks for this. It's really nice."

The view was incredible, both of the lake and of the

gorgeous man next to her. She drank her wine and let her body relax.

"Tell me about your day."

She looked over at Jason. "Not much to tell. Just routine."

"That's a good thing, right?"

She inhaled, let it out. "For me? Definitely. How about yours?"

"Nothing eventful."

"And for you that's good, too, right?"

"Yeah." He cracked a smile, and there went those twinges in her belly again.

"Good."

"Oh, I finished the master bedroom and bathroom."

"You did? That's great. Have you moved back in yet?"

He shook his head. "Not yet. I still have to buy new furniture. Wanna come shop with me?"

Her eyes widened. "I'd love to. When?"

"As soon as possible. I'm tired of sleeping in that double bed."

She ran her fingertip over the rim of her wineglass. "If I recall correctly, we didn't have a problem in that double bed together."

His lips curved in that hot smile that never failed to make her toes curl. "It was close quarters, but we managed. Now imagine how much rolling around we could do in a nice, king-sized bed."

"I definitely can't wait to shop now."

"Good. How about tomorrow night?"

She pulled her phone out of her bag, swiped and studied then looked up at him. "It turns out I'm free tomorrow night."

"Good. Consider it a date."

"A shopping date," she said with a grin. "And if you want my furniture expertise, I'll expect dinner, too."

He rolled his eyes. "Of course you will."

They ate their food, then packaged it all up in the insulated bag and drank another glass of wine. Or, rather, Erin had another glass while Jason had water.

"Thank you for this," she said. "It was exactly what I needed."

"I'm glad you came."

They took everything to the truck and put it in the back, then Jason locked it up and they took a stroll around the lake, watching the sun set. Jason hadn't even held her hand, which Erin found curious.

She stopped midway through their trek to face him. "Are you mad at me?"

"What? No. Why would you ask that?"

"You haven't hugged me or kissed me or held my hand. You've mostly kept your distance, physically."

"Because last time we were together you said you had a lot on your mind, and I got the idea you wanted some distance."

"Oh." He was right about that. She had been throwing off some signals that night. "I'm sorry about that."

"Don't be sorry for feeling how you feel. You have that right."

He always managed to say the perfect thing to make her feel better. She slid her hand in his, and just that contact made her whole world tilt normal again.

She leaned into him. "I don't need distance. I need you."

He drew her close and kissed her. Right there on the sidewalk, with people walking and jogging past them. She didn't care, not when his mouth was on hers, his body touching her, and all that heat and muscle pressed to her. She wanted to rub herself against him in the most inappropriate way for a public place. Instead, she gripped his biceps and held on while he made her dizzy with lazy, slow kissing.

She pulled back. "Shouldn't we take this somewhere a little more private?"

"Why? No one's paying attention to us."

She looked around to discover he was right. People were going about their business. Walking and running by, sitting by the lake, and not a single person was staring at them. Maybe she was the one feeling exposed. "I guess you're right."

He ran his thumb over her cheek. "You feel self-conscious letting me kiss you on the sidewalk."

"Maybe a little." Though she'd lost herself in that kiss for a few minutes, not caring where they were. She'd fallen deep into the feel and taste of him and forgotten where they were. Something that happened far too often with Jason.

"Okay," he said. "Let's walk."

They set off on the walk again, but this time Jason took hold of her hand. Her heart tumbled at the gesture.

By the time they had made their way around the lake and back to the parking lot, the sun had almost set, leaving a beautiful orange glow on the horizon.

"Ready to go?" he asked.

"Sure."

She thought he'd take her to his place. That kiss had warmed her up considerably, and she was ready to show him she'd moved past her indecision. So she was surprised when he exited the highway not toward his place, but toward the vineyard.

He pulled up in front of the house and got out to come around to her side. She fought back her disappointment and smiled at him when he opened her door.

"Can I walk you up?"

"Sure."

He took her hand again and walked up the steps, stopping before they got to the door. He turned her to face him. And then he tugged her close, wrapping his arms around her.

"I wanted to take you home with me, but I've got a complicated surgery that starts early tomorrow morning. If I brought you home with me, I'd want to take my time with you, spend all night making love to you."

Her nerve endings went a little haywire as he then went into descriptive detail of all the things he'd do to her.

She sighed. "I'll hold on to that until we have some time."

"I'm off this weekend."

She grinned. "That's very good news, because I have a few ideas of my own."

His brow arched. "You do, huh?"

"Yes." She lifted on her toes, then whispered a few things that popped into her head, listening to the way his breathing quickened.

He took her hand and started down the stairs. "Sleeping's overrated."

She laughed and tugged on his hand to stop him. "And your job is important. Go home and get some sleep."

He looked at her. "Sleep? After what you just said to me, you expect me to sleep?"

She brought his head down to hers and kissed him, a deep, passionate kiss that ended up lasting a lot longer than she intended. It was a good thing none of her family were around, because he'd grabbed her butt and suddenly she was backed up against the porch rail, his erection rubbing against all the soft, needy parts of her. By the time they pulled apart they were both breathing heavily.

"This is unfair," he said.

She stared up at him, lost in the dark depths of his beautiful eyes. "At least I won't be the only one suffering tonight."

"Trust me, I'll have to take care of business before I sleep."

Her sex quivered. "So will I."

"And that'll make jacking off easier, because I'll be thinking of you naked, your legs spread, you touching yourself while you're thinking of me."

"You'd better get out of here or we'll be doing it in your truck like teenagers."

"If I had a condom on me right now we would be."

She bit down on her lip, then looked toward the house. She had no idea where everyone was, but the house was dark. Maybe they were all out. If she was lucky they'd all gone somewhere together tonight.

She pondered that thought for all of a millisecond, then laid her hands on his chest. "Don't. Move."

She dug through her purse for her keys, opened the door, listened fast for sounds or motions but heard nothing. She ran upstairs, again not seeing her sisters, thankfully. She grabbed the condom, then, thinking quickly, shimmied out of her capris and into a short skirt, and ran back downstairs.

Jason was leaning against his truck with his arms folded and a smirk on his face.

"Nice skirt."

"Shut up and get in the truck."

He put the truck in gear.

"Where are you going?"

"Somewhere not in front of the house."

"Oh. Good idea."

He drove a short distance to the side of the vineyard, where it was dark and oh so private. As soon as he'd put the seat back, she straddled him and kissed him. And then his hands were under her skirt. Touching her bare skin. Driving her past the point of reason.

He pulled his lips from hers, his gaze hot. "You took off your underwear."

"I'm in a hurry."

"Damn, woman."

She reached for his zipper and then he helped her, shoving his jeans and underwear down, releasing his hard, throbbing cock into her hands. She tore off the wrapper of the condom and slid it over his shaft, then climbed on top of him.

When she seated herself on him, feeling that heat and energy pulsing inside of her, she stilled, absorbing the sweet pleasure for a few seconds before she began to move.

"Like that," he said. "God, I love the way you move."

His voice, so dark and deep, heightened her senses, sent thrills of excitement through her. She rocked against him, gripping his shoulder for support. He snaked his hand under her shirt, pulling her bra cup aside to tease her nipple.

"You're soft everywhere," he said, coaxing her nipple to a hard pebble, shooting exquisite pleasure all the way to her sex.

She was already pent up, so ready to explode. The excitement of location, the forbidden nature of possibly being caught here, and having Jason thrusting into her made her pulse quicken, made her body quiver against him.

"Jason. I need . . ."

"Shh. I know what you need." He had hold of her hips and helped her as she rose and fell against him. "I'll get you there."

Yes, she was right there. So close, so maddeningly close as she rocked her pelvis against his body. And then he reached down, teasing her clit while she rode him straight to heaven.

She saw his jaw tighten as he drove into her. She tilted her head back as she came, as her climax crashed through her. Lost in the hazy fog of release, she dug her nails into Jason's shoulders, listening to the sounds of his groans. He shuddered and thrust against her and she fell forward, laying her head on his shoulder, and rocked through the remnants of one incredible orgasm.

Out of breath, she held tight to Jason, their heartbeats coming back down to normal together.

"Dammit, Erin."

She lifted up. "What?"

He swept a loose hair away from her face. "You make me lose control."

Her lips curved. "That's not a bad thing, is it?"

"With you? No. Never."

He wrapped his hand around the nape of her neck and brought her forward for a soft kiss. Then they disengaged and righted their clothing. Erin felt warm and satiated and very happy that they hadn't said good night earlier. This had been so much better.

He drove her back to the house and walked her to the door.

"I want you to know that my legs are shaking," he said.

She laughed. "Mine, too."

He kissed her again, this time longer, deeper and with just as much passion as earlier. But she stepped back.

"Get some sleep," she said.

"I'll sleep good now."

She smiled. "Good night, Jason."

"Night, babe."

She waited while he got in his truck and drove off.

Then she went inside, locked the door and made her way upstairs. She ran into Brenna in the hall.

Brenna cocked her head to the side. "You weren't wearing a skirt when you left the house earlier tonight."

"What? Sure I was."

"No, you had capris on. And where's your purse?"

"I . . . Who are you, Mom?"

Brenna quirked a knowing smile. "You had sex outside."

Erin rolled her eyes and brushed past her sister to head to her room. A few minutes later, Brenna popped her head in the door, followed by Honor.

"So where did you do it?" Brenna asked. "In the vineyards?"

"You weren't wearing that skirt earlier," Honor said. "And Brenna said you had sex outside. Did you?"

It was definitely time to get her own place. She studied her phone, hoping to hide the deep blush she knew her face was wearing. "I don't know what you're talking about."

"Her cheeks are pink," Brenna said. "She's guilty."

"For sure," Honor said with a laugh, then came over and sat on the edge of the bed. "Tell us everything."

Erin looked up. "I'm not telling either of you anything. Mind your own business."

"I think she had sex with Jason, out in the vineyard." Brenna looked to Honor.

Honor nodded. "Definitely sex with Jason. But I think it was in his truck."

Erin rolled her eyes. "This isn't a game of Clue, you know."

Brenna looked smug. "Which means one of us is right."

"Clue sounds fun," Honor said. "We haven't played that game in years."

Erin rolled her eyes. "Both of you. Out."

Brenna laughed and grabbed Honor's arm. "She's just pissed because she got caught in the act."

Still staring at her phone, Erin said, "If you'd caught me in the act, you wouldn't be trying to guess when and where, would you?"

"Aha!" Brenna wagged a finger. "So you did have sex with Jason somewhere outside."

She smiled sweetly at her sister. "I admit to nothing."

Honor laughed. "Come on, Brenna. We don't want to ruin Erin's afterglow."

Her sisters left and closed the door. Erin put her phone to the side and lay back on the bed, replaying the hot moments she'd shared with Jason in his truck. She had no idea where her sisters had been, but they hadn't been in the house when she'd dashed upstairs to get the condom and make a quick change of clothes. Maybe they'd all been out and had come in the back door.

She shrugged. Either way, she'd had a great time.

Her phone pinged and she picked it up.

The text was from Owen.

Can we talk?

She bolted to a sitting position, those three words on her phone making her stomach churn.

She stared at her phone until her eyes burned, until tears formed, trying to find meaning behind those innocuous three words.

How dare he ruin her perfect night like he'd already ruined her perfectly planned wedding? She'd been doing so well. She'd tried so hard to move on, had hardly been thinking about him at all. And now this?

Why now, after all this time?

Then again, why had he bailed instead of talking to her face-to-face?

She stared at the text message, her fingers hovering on the keys.

She ended up tossing her phone to the end of the bed.

"Dammit, Owen. Why are you suddenly back in my life?"

She knew how she was going to handle this.

She . . . wasn't.

She got up and went into the bathroom, getting as far away from her phone—and from Owen—as she could.

CHAPTER

······

twenty-eight

WITH ERIN'S HELP, Jason now had a completed bedroom, furniture and everything. The bathroom looked shipshape, too, with a rug and stuff on the counter, but not too much stuff, because according to Erin, he wouldn't like too much clutter.

She was right. He'd put a vanity in with drawers, which meant he had a place for all his things. So the counter was mostly clear and he liked it that way, plus it made it easier to clean. She'd put a basic, non-floral-smelling candle and a cute blue ceramic dog on the counter to match the dark blue rug on the floor, and then they'd hung one picture of a foggy lake on the wall that he'd really liked. He'd had to agree that the bathroom had needed something, and Erin had known just what that "something" had been. She had a good eye. Not that he was surprised.

Erin had also helped him choose his bedroom furniture. Not too dark, she'd told him, because it would make the room appear smaller. He'd gone with a gray tufted headboard and awesome gray antique nightstands, and a silver dresser that went well with the off-white walls. Fortunately, he had the French doors that led out to the backyard along with a couple of windows that let in a lot of light, so the room was bright.

He'd let Erin run with choosing sheets and blankets, because that wasn't in his area of expertise, and since he wanted her comfortable in his bed, he figured whatever she liked was fine with him.

She'd chosen a dark gray duvet cover and some soft-as-hell sheets. And hey, as long as they weren't rough and scratchy, he didn't care. Plus, everything looked good. He knew Erin would get it right.

Tonight they were having a housewarming party, which Erin had talked him into because the house was mostly finished, and mainly because he rarely had people over. She told him he should celebrate all the work he had put into the house.

Maybe she was right.

Besides, he had the weekend off, so why not have people over and do a little partying?

Erin had told him the vineyard had an afternoon wedding today, so she'd have plenty of time to come over and help him set up for the party.

He'd gotten up early this morning to clean the house. Once that was finished, he went to the grocery store to get all the stuff they'd need. He made a couple of snacks that would need to chill, and when he was putting those in the fridge, the doorbell rang.

He frowned and looked at his phone. Way too early for Erin to be here, so he went to the door and opened it, shocked to see Owen standing there.

He just stared, not knowing what to say. He hadn't expected to see him.

"What are you doing here?" Jason asked.

"Can we talk?"

"I don't know that I have anything to say to you."

Owen tilted his head to the side. "Come on, man. We're friends."

"Are we?"

"It's hot as fuck out here, Jason. Can I come in?"

Jason thought about closing the door in Owen's face, but the guy looked like he was about to pass out. Sweat ran down his temple and he looked pale, so he stood to the side and Owen walked in.

Jason shut the door and led Owen into the kitchen.

"You want some ice water?"

"That'd be great, thanks."

Owen climbed onto one of the barstools and took a seat while Jason fixed them both something to drink. He handed Owen the water and waited while he took several gulps. While Owen drank, Jason noticed how pale Owen looked. He'd lost some weight, too. Maybe stress.

Or guilt.

"Why aren't you tan? I thought you were in Aruba. On the honeymoon you and Erin were supposed to go on."

Owen set the glass down. "Yeah, about that. There's a lot I need to tell you. About why I didn't marry Erin."

Jason rested his hip against the island. "You talk to Erin yet?"

"I've tried. I texted her a couple of times in the past week. She won't answer my texts."

Jason didn't know whether to be happy Erin hadn't answered him or upset that this thing between them wasn't settled yet. "You could go over there."

"And face the wrath of her entire family? No, thanks. I'd rather meet her on neutral ground."

Jason took a sip of water. "I've known you since we were six years old, Owen. We fought those eighth graders together that knocked over our bikes. You were never a coward. Until now."

Owen looked down. "It wasn't cowardice, Jason. There's something I have to tell you."

Jason held up his hand. "It's not me you have to tell. It's Erin. Until you talk to her, I don't want to hear it."

"Come on, Jason. I have to talk to someone."

"Then talk to her."

Owen let out a breath. "You're right. I know you're right. I just thought maybe you and I being best friends and all . . ."

"That maybe you could have come to me weeks or months before the wedding or whenever it was you thought you didn't want to marry Erin and talked to me about it?"

"It wasn't like that."

Owen's voice had gone soft with . . . what? Regret? Did Owen regret what he'd done? Did he still love Erin? Did he want another chance with her?

The thought of it caused a knot to form in Jason's gut.

How would Erin feel about it if Owen fell on his knees and begged her forgiveness?

Would she take him back? She had been in love with him. Maybe she still was.

Shit.

"You gotta talk to Erin first, Owen."

"Yeah."

"And then after you do that, you and I can talk. Because I have some things to say."

Owen slid off the barstool. "I know you do."

They headed to the door. Owen turned. "You were there for her, weren't you? When I . . . after I, you know."

"You know damn well I was." In ways he wasn't about to tell Owen right now.

"Thanks for that. You've always been a good friend."

He'd never seen Owen look so beaten down, so defeated. So in need of a damn hug.

But he couldn't be that guy for Owen. Not right now.

"I'll see you later, Owen."

Owen gave a short nod. "Yeah."

He turned and walked out the door. Jason shut the door, feeling like the shittiest friend ever.

But right now, it was more important that he was on Erin's side. And he knew he was right. Owen had to talk to Erin first.

AFTER WORKING THE wedding, Erin had changed into something less formal, then whipped up a couple of things for tonight's party. Honor and Brenna would meet her over there later, but she wanted to get to Jason's early so she could help him set up. After all, this whole party thing had been her idea. She didn't want to leave it for him to do all the work.

She'd brought Agatha with her since Jason had told her bringing her dog would keep Puddy occupied. Agatha pressed her nose against the window, loving the adventure of a car ride. She was going to enjoy hanging out with Puddy. The two of them got along so well.

After arriving at Jason's house, she grabbed Agatha's leash, all of her stuff, and went to the door. Jason had left a note for her that said he was in the shower and she should come in, so she did.

Puddy greeted them at the door with enthusiastic barks and tail wags. She bent down to pet him and he and Agatha led the way into the main part of the house.

The house was spotless, smelled like he'd scrubbed it stem to stern, and the kitchen was shining.

Wow. Okay, so she'd planned to help him clean it, but it was obvious that wasn't going to be necessary.

She tucked the snacks into the fridge and fixed herself a glass of ice water, wandering around to see if there was anything that needed to be done. Agatha grabbed one of Puddy's toys and the two dogs wandered off, play growling at each other.

Satisfied the dogs were happy, she turned away and saw Jason rounding the corner wrapped in a towel, his body shining with moisture from his shower.

Jeebus. She needed his body, in a painting, on her wall, so she could ogle him every day.

"Oh, you're here," he said, offering up a smile. "I was hoping it was you. I heard barking."

"It's me. You look hot. Metaphorically and literally."

He laughed. "Thanks. So do you. Every damn day."

He made her blush. All the time. How did he do that? "How's the new shower working?"

"Great. You should try it out with me."

Looking at him with that towel slung low on his hips made her want to push him into the bedroom and get sweaty with him just so they could try the shower out right now. "I intend to."

He walked over to her and brushed his lips across hers. She inhaled the smell of freshly showered male.

"Too bad we have people coming over."

She sighed, then laid her palms on his chest. "Yes. Too bad."

But he stepped back. "I'll go get dressed."

"Anything you want me to do?"

He gave her a lazy smile. "You wanna come watch me?"

"You want people to find us naked when they get here?"

He sighed. "Fine. I'll be right back."

While he did that, she went to the refrigerator and got out the stuff she'd brought to make a charcuterie board. She got out the cutting board and started slicing meats and cheeses and laid them on the board, then spread out the fruit.

"What are you doing?" Jason asked as he came out of the bedroom. He was wearing shorts and a sleeveless shirt. She took a moment to admire his tan skin, his still-damp hair and his gorgeous smile.

"Making charcuterie." She assembled the crackers, jams and nuts she'd brought on the board as well.

Jason grabbed a cube of cheese and popped it into his mouth. After he swallowed, he said, "You have amazing talents."

She tilted her head back so he could give her a kiss. "Thanks."

"I have chicken and steak marinating in the fridge."

She paused. "When did you have the time to do all that, and clean the house?"

"I had the day off. Lots of time."

"Such a Renaissance man."

He laughed. "Yeah, baby, that's me."

"Truly. You're like a unicorn. You cook, you clean, you've renovated your entire house . . ."

"Almost. There are still a few things left to do."

She rolled her eyes. "Never satisfied, are you?"

He shrugged. "I like projects."

"You like to stay busy."

"True that." The dogs were at the back door wiggling their butts, so Jason went over there and let them out, then closed the door. "Hot as the seventh level of hell out there. I thought about setting up table and chairs out there, but I don't know that anyone's going to be interested in sitting out there, even after the sun goes down. What do you think?"

"I think I'm enjoying your air-conditioning and everyone else will be, too. But some of the guys might want to hang out with you while you're grilling, and you've already got that covered with the lawn furniture you have out there, right?"

"Yeah."

"So you're good, I think."

"Perfect."

The doorbell rang, and Jason went to answer it. Suddenly a crowd of people were in the house. Their friends from the boat—Vince and Summer, Daria and Mike— followed closely behind by Clay and Alice.

And, of course, like a lot of parties, people congregated in the kitchen. Jason passed out beers and opened bottles of wine. Erin finished the salsa and set it in the fridge to cool, then pulled out the guacamole she'd made before she left the house, along with some shrimp dip she'd made as well.

She also pulled out the sangria she'd made.

Jason came up behind her. "When did you make all this?"

"Today. Some before work, some after."

"Thank you. I'm glad you're my partner." He pressed a kiss to the side of her neck, causing tingles to shoot down her arm.

Partner. Such a strange word. She shouldn't read too much into it since he'd just said it in passing. But he didn't say girlfriend, either. He probably just meant partner in this event tonight, and he didn't mean anything else.

Fortunately, she didn't have time to obsess over it because other people showed up, including her sisters.

Honor brought a date, some guy named Walter who

Erin didn't really care much for, but Honor was all hopeful about this guy.

Erin hoped it was a casual thing because Walter was a know-it-all. If you said you'd done something, he'd done it already. And better. If you claimed to know something, Walter knew twice as much about the topic as you did. Honor had met him at one of the weddings they'd thrown. He was a deejay and had worked the wedding, and Erin would bet the guy wouldn't know monogamy if it bit him in the ass.

Right now, Walter was staring at Daria's ass. She would've liked to say something to Honor, but since her sister claimed it was just casual, she'd let it go.

For now.

"Walter's a class-A douchenozzle," Brenna said, coming up to stand next to Erin as they both sipped glasses of sangria.

"You noticed, too, huh?" Erin asked.

Brenna nodded. "Total windbag. I don't know what Honor sees in him."

Erin sighed. "He's smart. Good-looking, for sure."

Brenna shrugged. "Good looks only go so far. Man has a roving eye."

He'd moved on to checking out Alice now.

"For God's sake," Brenna said. "Can't he keep his eyes on Honor for five minutes?"

"Apparently not."

Brenna started forward. "I'm going to say something."

Erin laid her hand on Brenna's arm. "Don't talk to Honor."

"Oh, I'm not talking to Honor."

Brenna moved through the crowd. Erin hung out at the kitchen island. One, to make sure drinks stayed refilled, and two, to keep an eye on Brenna.

Honor was distracted, talking with Alice and Clay, so Brenna pulled Walter aside. Erin had no idea what her sister said to Walter, but whatever it was made Walter's skin go pale. He nodded in rapid succession. When Brenna left, Walter made his way to Honor and put his arm around her. Honor looked up at him and smiled.

Brenna came back and offered up a smug smile.

"Did you threaten his life?"

"More like his livelihood. I told him to stop checking out the ass of every woman in the room, that I know every event planner in this state, and if he didn't knock it off I'd make sure he never booked a gig again."

Erin's brows knit together. "*Do* you know every event planner in the state?"

"Of course not. But he doesn't know that."

Erin laughed. "Well done."

"I still think one of us should warn Honor away from that jerkoff."

"You're probably right. We'll talk to her tomorrow."

She hated that her sister was much too nice to weed out the bad guys. Poor Honor always gave her dates the benefit of the doubt, always went in with such high hopes, and her hopes were always dashed. She dated such losers.

Erin's gaze gravitated to Jason, who was definitely one of the good guys. Who cared about one chosen word? She was lucky to have him in her life, to know he cared about her.

Everyone destroyed her charcuterie board, which made her very happy. There wasn't one grape or nut left. Not even crumbs. Clearly everyone came hungry.

And dinner was great, with fajitas and rice and salad and watermelon. Everyone hung out inside and seemed perfectly happy to stay in where it was cool. Except the guys, of course, who had to "help" Jason grill the meat outside, where it was a million-degrees hot.

"Dudes," Alice said as they sat around the table and ate. "I don't understand their need to hover in groups over a steamy hot grill and drink beer."

"Harkens back to their caveman days, I think," Erin said.

"And they say women travel in herds," Daria said. "I can guarantee you that you'll find a larger group of men huddled together at a gathering like this than you will women."

Summer nodded. "Whereas women tend to mingle with everyone."

"Probably because we're better at conversation with both sexes," Erin said.

"Wait." Jason looked over at her. "You're saying women are better at something?"

"Yes." She arched a brow for emphasis. "Care to argue the point?"

He looked at her for a second, then shook his head. "No, ma'am."

"You're a very wise man," Mike said.

Erin laughed.

Once dinner was over, the guys all piled into the living room to argue over a baseball game. The women congregated in the kitchen to drink. Erin thought their activity was way more fun.

She was currently at the kitchen island refilling her wineglass when Jason came in to grab two beers. "Are you doing okay?"

"I'm great, thanks. Dinner was good."

He gave her a quick kiss. "It was. Thanks to you."

He walked away and she couldn't help but sigh as she

made her way back to the kitchen table, where they'd set up a multitude of chairs for everyone to sit and relax.

"I swear you have hearts popping out of your eyes whenever you look at Jason."

She turned to Alice. "I do not."

"You totally do. You've got that love look."

"I do?"

"Absolutely. No sense in denying it."

She couldn't very well deny it since it was true. "Okay. I won't."

"Have you told Jason how you feel?"

"No. Mainly because I haven't closed off the whole ex-fiancé thing yet."

"Oh." Alice frowned. "Why not?"

"I don't know. Probably because I don't want to talk to him."

Alice laid her hand on Erin's arm. "I can't blame you for that. But you can't move forward with your life until you close that chapter."

Not the first time she'd heard that.

"I know. And it's a barrier that's preventing me from telling Jason how I feel about him."

Alice gave her a sympathetic look. "So what's stopping you?"

She wished she had an answer for that. "Nothing, really. Other than not wanting to face him."

"I can't blame you for not wanting to see him, Erin. What he did to you was awful. And I hate using the word 'closure,' but in this case, you do need it, if for no other reason so you can put the past behind you and have the future you deserve."

That did sound good. "You're right. I'll make it a priority."

Because she knew what she wanted. And who she

wanted it with. But she couldn't take those steps until she closed the door on her and Owen.

The party broke up around one. Erin had already had a full day, and she was exhausted. But she wanted to talk to Jason, needed some alone time with him. Fortunately, they had great friends who had helped clean up.

Jason closed the door when the last person left, then turned to face her. "Fun night, huh?"

"Great night."

They walked together into the living room. Puddy and Agatha were passed out on the floor together.

"Those two had fun."

"They wore themselves out, plus soaked up all the love they got from everyone. I know Agatha will probably sleep all day tomorrow."

Jason pulled her down on the sofa. She curled up next to him, wishing the two of them could just be silent like this, soaking each other in. But she had important things to say.

She straightened. "We need to talk."

"Uh-oh. That's never a good conversation starter."

"Owen texted me a couple of times asking to talk."

He nodded. "I wanted to talk to you about that. He came by here this afternoon."

Her pulse skittered. "He did? What did he say?"

"He wanted to talk about you. About his decision. I wouldn't let him. I told him he had to talk to you first."

She didn't know if she was relieved or disappointed. If he'd told Jason his reasons, maybe Jason could have prepared her for the conversation she was going to have with him. Then again, that would have been unfair. And Jason had just been looking out for her—taking her side— which was why she loved him. "Okay. Thanks. I'm . . . I'm going to talk to him."

"I think you should. I know it won't be easy, but don't you think it's time?"

She let out a soft laugh. "I don't ever want to talk to him again. But yes, you're right. It has to be done. I have to finish this. Or we can't . . . you and I can't . . ."

He smoothed his thumb over her hand. "Yeah. I know."

She loved that he understood, that she didn't have to say the words.

She laid her head on his shoulder and just breathed, content to be in the moment with him.

Tomorrow she'd think about what she'd say to Owen when she saw him.

CHAPTER

······

twenty-nine

COMING TO OWEN'S apartment made Erin equal parts sad and furious. They'd planned a future together. And that future had evaporated in a single e-mail.

But she wasn't as angry or upset as she'd been the day she'd read that e-mail. Now she was more determined to get this over with, say what she needed to say so she could walk out and be done with Owen.

She'd told her parents and her sisters that she was meeting with Owen today. Her father wanted to go with her, and she'd explained that this was something she had to do on her own. Her mother had agreed, and then added if she needed her, she was only a phone call away.

She'd always had her parents' support, and she was so grateful for that. And for her sisters, who were angry again on her behalf. Brenna and Honor had also offered to go with her. She'd turned them down, too.

The only one who hadn't offered to accompany her had been Jason, who seemed to understand that she had to handle this by herself.

She was going to be fine. One short conversation and this would all be in the past.

All she had to do was get out of her car and go to the door. She'd been sitting in the car for fifteen minutes, frozen to the driver's seat, unable to move.

You're past this. Past him. Get out, have the talk and be done with it.

She knew she was right, that this was going to be uncomfortable and unpleasant, but it had to be done. And sitting here wasn't making it happen. She turned off the engine, grabbed her keys and got out, walked to the door and rang the bell, her heart pounding so hard she could hear her blood rushing in her ears.

She took several deep, calming breaths.

The door opened and there was Owen. She'd expected him to look tanned and smug. Instead he looked pale. He looked ill. Not the nervous kind of ill, but really sick.

Her stomach dropped and everything she'd planned to say, every angry feeling she had, disappeared.

"Dammit. Owen. Are you all right?"

"Come on in, Erin. It's hot out there."

She walked in and as he closed the door she took in the sight of him. His clothes hung on him and he looked like he'd lost weight. And he hadn't needed to lose any.

"Would you like something to drink?" he asked.

"No, I'm fine. What's wrong, Owen?"

He gave her a wry smile. "Oh, you would know as well as anyone that the past couple of months have been kind of stressful. More for you than me."

That was bullshit. He should have been tanned. He should look healthy, even if he did feel guilty about dumping her. What he looked like wasn't normal. Not even for a guilty man.

She wanted to be angry. She wanted to shout at him

and tell him how he'd broken her heart. But looking at him now, he wasn't the same Owen she'd always known. Something was definitely wrong with him and she needed to know what it was.

He sat next to her on the sofa, not close.

"I hurt you," he said. "Let's talk about that first."

She shook her head. "No, you tell me what's going on with you."

He shook his head. "My guess is you've had a big speech built up in your head awhile now, and you want to let me have it. I deserve it."

He was right about that, but just seeing him made her anger dissipate. How could she scream at someone who was so obviously ill?

"I'll save the histrionics for later. Please tell me what's wrong."

He blew out a breath. "Fine. So, I'm sick."

Her stomach clenched. "Define sick."

"I have cancer."

Oh, God. Her heart started drumming that fast rhythm again. "Cancer."

"Yeah. Hodgkin's lymphoma."

"Okay, I don't know anything about that."

"It's a cancer in the lymph nodes. But totally treatable, so I'm gonna be fine."

"That doesn't make me feel better." The pieces started to fall together. "You knew. Before the wedding."

"Yeah."

"Why didn't you tell me? We could have faced it together."

"Come on, Erin. I didn't want you to have to deal with that."

Now she *was* angry. "Oh, you think I only wanted to marry a healthy guy? The 'in sickness' part of 'in sickness and in health' didn't mean anything? How little do you think of me?"

He shook his head. "That's not what I meant. I didn't want to burden you with what might come down the road."

At her look, he raised his hands. "I know, I know. In retrospect, I realized I should have told you. I should have told everyone. But I didn't. I didn't understand what was going to happen. I had just gotten the initial diagnosis. I panicked. I didn't even tell my parents. My friends. Anyone. You. I thought we couldn't start our lives together like that."

"So, what? You went through all this alone?"

Owen was always a happy, upbeat guy. But the look of utter defeat he gave her made her heart crumble. "Yeah."

"Why didn't you confide in anyone? At least your parents?"

"I didn't want to worry them. Not until I knew more. I figured I could maybe get through this without anyone knowing."

She stood and started to pace. "Are you kidding me? Cancer is not something you just 'get through' by yourself, Owen. You need a support system. You need people around you who care about you, to help care *for* you."

"I've kind of figured that out now." He dragged his fingers through his hair. "I didn't have my shit together before. I told you I panicked. And while you thought I bailed and left to go on our honeymoon, I was getting treatment. I kind of lied to you in that shitty e-mail I sent you."

Which made her even angrier at him. "I could have been with you. You do realize we could have canceled the wedding. Hell, I *did* cancel the wedding. The only difference was that you dumped me and decided to go through all this without me. And why? Because you didn't love me enough. You didn't trust me enough to see it through with you."

He picked up the glass of water on the table and took a long swallow, then set it down. "We hadn't been talking much. Your head was filled with wedding things. You were so happy. If I'm being honest, I wasn't sure about us."

Now the truth was coming out, and she couldn't deny how much that hurt. "You weren't sure about us? About how you felt about me, you mean."

"Yeah. I mean, no. I don't know how to explain it."

After all this time, all her reflection about the two of them, she knew exactly what he meant. "You don't have to. But why didn't you talk to me, tell me how you felt?"

"I wanted you to be happy."

"At the expense of your own happiness? A marriage doesn't work if only one person is happy, Owen. You have to know that."

"Yeah, I know. But I was just so damn tired all the time. I didn't know what was wrong with me yet. I just felt like I was walking around in some kind of fog. I didn't have it in me to have that conversation with you, knowing what would follow." He managed a smile. "You're kind of a force to be reckoned with, Erin Bellini."

She blew out a breath of frustration. "I would have been pissed. I *was* pissed. But we'd have gotten through it. I wish we could have talked about it. I wish I'd known about your diagnosis. I wish I could have been there for you, even if we weren't together." Her eyes filled with tears. "Are you going to be okay?"

He nodded. "The doctors say my prognosis is really good. It's stage one, only one lymph-node area. They caught it early."

Despite her terror, a measure of relief fell over her. He'd beat this. Owen was young and strong.

"Did you tell your parents? Please tell me you have a support system."

"I did tell them, finally. And yeah, they're going to help me."

"That's good."

"They were really pissed at me about not telling them. And for not being honest with you about everything."

Her lips curved. "That's good, too."

"I'm glad you came over. I've been anticipating and dreading this conversation for a long time."

Despite his illness, part of her was kind of glad he'd been uncomfortable about talking to her. She knew it was petty, but there it was. "Same."

"I still feel like I owe you a lot in the way of explanation."

"You don't have to give it all today. But I think we both know where we stand. How we both felt. It took me a while to figure things out after . . . well, after that e-mail. At first, I was devastated, and then angry as hell with you. But then I had a lot of time to think, to come to some conclusions. I was blind to how I felt because I was so caught up in the wedding planning that I wasn't seeing our relationship for what it was. Or what it wasn't."

"So you realized it, too. I thought it was just the illness making me question everything. But you felt it, too?"

She nodded. "I'm sorry I didn't see it. I was so caught up. Stupid of me."

"No, it wasn't. And I should have talked to you. About everything. About this, about how I felt. I'm really sorry, Erin. I fucked this all up."

"Yes, you did. But the only thing you need to be thinking about right now is getting well."

"I'm gonna be okay."

"I know you will."

And she was going to help him. They might not be together anymore, but that didn't mean she was going to abandon him. Now that she knew the truth, she wasn't going to walk away.

They talked awhile longer and she got some information about his treatment.

"Do you want me to go with you?" she asked.

He shook his head. "Nah. I've got this covered. But thanks."

"Okay." It felt weird, talking to him, but not being with him anymore. They'd been through years of friendship, then years of being a couple. And now they were just . . .

She didn't know what they were anymore, but she just felt empty. She thought this meeting would go differently. She thought she was going to walk away from him with a clean slate, a new start.

And now?

Now everything was different.

"Let me know if you need anything, okay?"

"I need you to quit being nice to me. Not after what I did."

Through all this she'd learned that everything wasn't such a huge deal, and if life didn't turn out like she envisioned, her world wasn't going to come to an end. So as Owen walked her to the door, she turned to face him and smiled. "Sometimes life throws us a curve we didn't expect. We deal with it and adapt, you know?"

"Do I ever."

"Okay, so you and I? We're dealing. And we'll both be fine."

"Yeah, we will."

She did something she hadn't expected to do. She put her arms around him and hugged him. "I'll talk to you soon."

He hugged her back. "Okay."

When she pulled away, she held on to his forearms. "Call me if you need me."

"Sure."

She felt the insincerity in his answer. "I mean it, Owen."

"I will."

She left, not feeling at all like she thought she would. She thought she'd feel free and light. Instead, she felt devastated and out of sorts. She couldn't talk to Jason because he didn't know, and he should hear the news from Owen himself.

So, instead, she went home, snuck up the stairs so she didn't have to talk to her family and closed the door to her bedroom so she could think. Her mind was whirling with all that Owen had told her. All her feelings were a jumbled mess now.

Did she still love him? No. She already knew that. But she felt so bad that it had all turned out this way.

She had to do something to make it better. She didn't have that closure she'd gone for.

So now what?

CHAPTER
......
thirty

Jason couldn't figure out what was going on, but something was definitely off with Erin. She'd texted him and told him he needed to talk to Owen, that she couldn't tell him what they'd talked about. And then she'd told him she needed some alone time to think.

It was odd, and left him feeling like something major had happened between Erin and Owen. He left her alone that night, but she hadn't called him or answered his calls the next day. He'd expected her to come see him. Instead, she was avoiding him and it was making him crazy not knowing what was going on.

Since she wasn't talking to him, he was going to have to talk to Owen. He called Owen, who said he should come over, so Jason made his way over to his apartment that day after he got off work. Owen was there by himself, which was good because Jason intended to get to the bottom of what went down between Erin and him yesterday.

Only he hadn't expected the outcome he got after he and Owen had a detailed conversation about exactly why

Owen had called off the wedding. He'd gone in a little wary, maybe even more than pissed off, and had been reduced to devastation and tears.

He swiped at his eyes. "Why didn't you tell me?"

Owen shrugged. "Man, I was a mess. I didn't tell anyone. Not even Erin, the one person I should have told."

"How did she take it when you told her?"

"Not good. She was upset, and worried about me. And we had a long talk about our relationship."

Jason felt a twinge in his gut, part of it jealousy and the other part hoping that they'd both gotten closure.

He shouldn't have been thinking about himself at all. Not with what Owen was going through, and knowing how upset Erin likely was after she'd found out about Owen's diagnosis.

"And?"

"We both realized our relationship had run its course, but neither of us had recognized it at the time. I had wanted to talk to her about how I felt, but this disease had wrecked me, left me confused and foggy, so I didn't know what the hell I was feeling. And Erin was so caught up in all things wedding that she couldn't see the forest for the trees, ya know?"

He felt bad as the relief washed over him. "Yeah. I'm sorry for the way things worked out for you and Erin."

"Thanks. I'm just sorry I hurt her. I was a mess and I didn't handle the diagnosis well. I hurt a lot of people. You included."

Jason shrugged. "How the hell do you handle being told you have cancer? You did the best you could, man."

"I guess. I don't know. I'm struggling with this."

He didn't know how to help his best friend. "I'm here for you. If you want to just come over to my house and throw rocks, we'll do that."

Owen studied him for a few seconds, then said, "There's a new axe-throwing place in town. I'm thinking of adding that feature to the brewery."

Jason laughed. "Yeah, just what you need. A bunch of drunks throwing axes at your head."

"You might have a point."

But now that he'd mentioned his brewery and pub, something occurred to Jason. "What about The Screaming Hawk? Do you need help with the brewery or the pub?"

Owen shook his head. "Nah, I've got it covered. I still intend to work, and my people there have been awesome about stepping up since I've been sick."

"You also have friends who will step up when you need it. So don't be afraid to ask."

"Thanks. I'll let you know."

And maybe Jason wouldn't wait to be asked.

Because that's what friends were for. Something he needed to be better at. Especially for Owen. Because with one conversation, everything had changed. And right now, no matter what had happened, or how he felt about Erin, it was Owen who needed him.

CHAPTER

······

thirty-one

ERIN HAD SLIPPED out of work a few hours early on Tuesday to go with Owen for his treatment appointment. She'd finally told her family everything about what had gone down with Owen, and even her father had mellowed.

"If that boy needs anything, we'll do it," her dad had said, which was completely different from his earlier sentiments of wanting to throttle Owen.

"Does he want you to go with him?" Brenna had asked as Erin packed up a tote bag filled with healthy snacks.

"Well, no, but he might like some company. And his parents both work, so the more people diving in to share the load, the easier it'll be on everyone. Plus, I can spare a few hours."

"We all could," Honor said. "So if you need me to pitch in, just let me know."

"Thanks."

She knew Owen hadn't asked for help, but she couldn't just sit by and do nothing. And she'd already talked to Owen's mom, Gwen, and gotten all the info on his cancer treatment. After, they'd both cried with each other on the phone.

Gwen had told her she appreciated how forgiving she was about how Owen had handled abruptly canceling the wedding. And they'd both talked about how angry they were with Owen about him not coming clean with them about his diagnosis. At least Erin and Gwen were on the same page about that. But that was a done deal, and couldn't be changed. Erin had to put that part in the past. The most important thing now was to get Owen healthy again, so he could have a future.

Owen was shocked to see her when she showed up in the waiting room at the cancer treatment center.

"I thought my mom was meeting me here."

"She has a meeting. And I'm helping you out today."

He frowned. "You know, I don't need a babysitter. Treatment days are typically fine."

"Uh-huh. I've done a ton of research, and sometimes you get nauseated, plus this is your long treatment day, and you need food."

He cocked his head to the side. "There are vending machines."

She rolled her eyes. "Snacks don't count. I brought you a sandwich and soup and some healthy snacks."

His lips curved. "You? Did extensive research? I'm so shocked, Erin."

"Funny."

They called Owen's name, so she followed behind as they entered the treatment area. She watched closely as the tech took his vitals and weight. He'd lost twelve pounds since before the wedding. Wow, that was a lot. Owen was tall, but always a bit on the lean side, so the weight loss was noticeable.

They went to a cubicle, where he had a nice comfortable lounging chair. She took a seat in the available chair
while his nurse, Layla, hooked him up to the IV. He'd get
a bag of fluids first, then the chemotherapy drugs. Erin
had been doing a lot of research, plus, she asked Layla a
few questions and she was nice enough to answer them.

"How many of these have you had?" she asked after
Layla left.

"I do a longer treatment, then the following week a
shorter treatment. Then I have a week off to recover. I've
had two complete rounds so far."

"How have you been reacting?"

"Good. A little tired. Some nausea. Not too bad. This
week where I get the longer treatment seems to be the
one that wears me down the most. But I'm still able to get
through work. Then I go home and pass out."

"But you need to eat."

"Mom takes care of that. She's been bringing dinner
over to my apartment."

She studied him. "Maybe you should consider moving
back home for a while. Just while you're undergoing
treatment."

His lips curved. "You've been talking to my mom,
haven't you?"

"Why?"

"Because she suggested the same thing. And, no, I'm
good at the apartment for now. I like being by myself."

"You shouldn't be alone. Not right now."

"If it gets too hard to do it alone, I'll hang out with my
parents. But I've got this, Erin. My oncologist seems to
think I'll only have to do one full course of treatments.
He has high hopes that'll take care of it."

"I hope so."

"Hey, no one told me we were having a party here."

Erin looked up, surprised to see Jason at the entrance to the treatment cubicle. "What are you doing here?"

"I decided to take part of the day off and hang out with Owen while he was loafing."

Owen laughed. "Yeah. Loafing. Thanks for coming by. You don't have to do that. I know how busy you are with work."

Jason shrugged. "I don't mind. Hey, Erin."

She nodded, feeling so incredibly uncomfortable now that Jason was here. She hadn't yet told Owen about her relationship with Jason, and now certainly wasn't the time. She hoped Jason didn't plan to.

They hadn't talked, hadn't seen each other. She'd been wrapped up in her emotions about Owen and hadn't been able to face talking to Jason about how she felt.

She didn't even know how she felt right now, other than confused. And sad. And upset.

Owen smiled at both of them. "Just like old times, isn't it? Except for the toxic-drugs thing."

Jason grinned. "Yeah, that part kind of sucks. But we're here to keep you from running amok and annoying the nurses."

Just then Layla came over.

"Got a fan club, I see," she said with a smile as she removed the fluid bag and set up the chemotherapy bag.

"Yeah, I'm super popular," Owen said.

"I'm not at all surprised," Layla said, then turned to look at Jason and Erin. "He's very charming."

Owen gave a smug smile. "See?"

"Really, Owen?" Jason asked. "Hitting on the nurses?"

Owen let out a weak laugh.

"If you need anything, just let me know," Layla said, then left.

"I think she had her eye on you, Jason," Owen said.

Jason looked over at Erin, who did her best to give him a passive stare.

"Yeah, she seems nice."

"She's very nice. And single. So are you seeing anyone?"

Jason scratched the side of his nose. "Well, actually— Ow, dammit!'"

Owen frowned. "You okay?"

He bent low to grab on to the ankle Erin had kicked.

She smiled sweetly at him. "Yes, Jason. Are you all right?"

"Fine. Just got a cramp."

The last thing Owen needed right now was to hear about her and Jason. Surely Jason knew that. She gave him a look, but apparently he'd grabbed a clue because he launched into mundane conversation with Owen. At his request, Erin got a warm blanket from the nurse, and Owen eventually fell asleep. Erin and Jason stepped outside.

"Are you crazy?" she asked. "You weren't going to tell him about us, were you?"

"He's going to find out eventually."

"I know, but not right now, and definitely not while he's in the treatment room."

"So maybe we can go over there together sometime this week and tell him."

"Tell him what, exactly? That we've been sleeping together while he was having cancer treatments?"

Jason gave her an incredulous look. "And how were we supposed to know that since he didn't tell anyone? Surely you don't feel guilty about that. About us."

"I . . . I don't know. I don't know how I feel right now. But I don't want to say anything to Owen yet. Let's give him some time to feel better."

"And when do you think the right time will be, Erin?"

"I don't know. I don't have a crystal ball. I've never been through this before."

"So, like . . . never?"

She frowned, unable to fathom what was going through Jason's head right now. Why couldn't he understand she was trying to help Owen? "What are you talking about?"

"Are you still in love with Owen?"

"What? No. I just . . . want to be there for him right now. He needs me. He needs all of us. You're here, aren't you?"

"Yeah, but that's different."

He wasn't even making sense. "Oh, come on. How is that different?"

"Because I wasn't the one that was going to marry him. I wasn't in love with him."

"It's not like that." How could she make him see what she felt, the pain and confusion? She reached out to touch him, but he took a step back.

"I'm going back inside. I'll see you in there."

She watched him walk away, and knew that things between Jason and her were not okay anymore.

What had just happened?

CHAPTER

······

thirty-two

"IT'S LIKE SHE'S there with Owen all the time," Jason said to Clay and Alice. "Like the breakup never happened."

Clay lifted his beer and took a sip, then looked over at Jason, the three of them enjoying some happy hour time at Owen's brew pub, where they'd been pitching in to help. Now that all the stock was loaded and the brewery was clean, it was time to sit back and enjoy the fruits of their labor. Right now, Jason was enjoying a dark APA that was going down nicely.

"Define all the time," Alice asked.

"It's been two weeks, and as far as I know she's been over there almost every night."

"Huh," Clay said. "You think they're back together again?"

"I don't know. She's at his place as much as she can be, helping out with his laundry and feeding him meals and taking care of him. And I try to talk to her, but she's been vague, saying she's busy juggling things and she doesn't have time to see me right now."

Alice came over and rubbed his shoulder. "Do you

think it's because she feels some sense of responsibility for Owen? They were engaged."

"Yeah. And Owen was the one to break it off."

Alice gave him a sympathetic look. "Because he was sick. Because he didn't want Erin to feel obligated to him. Her loyalties are divided right now, and she's likely feeling confused and emotional. Give her some time to come to terms with how she feels, Jason."

Clay leaned back against the chair and nodded. "Yeah, I agree with Alice. You pressuring her right now is only gonna get her riled up and make her push back. You don't want that."

No, he didn't. He took another swallow of beer and let his conversation with Clay and Alice sink in.

Maybe they were right and he was worrying for nothing. Then again, maybe they didn't know Erin like he did. When she went in, she went all in. It was the reason she'd ended up with Owen in the first place.

She'd always had blinders on with Owen.

But he'd back off and give her some time to figure out her own heart. Because if Jason wasn't the guy she wanted to be with, Erin was the one who had to make that decision. He couldn't make it for her.

And he couldn't force her to love him, either, especially if she was still in love with Owen.

Just the thought of that stayed with him for the rest of the day as he made his way over to Owen's. Owen had asked him to come over and hang out with him that night. Jason stopped at the store and picked up groceries for dinner. Owen answered.

"Hey. You look pretty good."

Owen laughed. "So what you're saying is I normally look like shit?"

"Yes. That's exactly what I meant."

They walked into the living room. Owen had the baseball game on, so Jason put the food in the fridge, then fixed himself a glass of ice water and came in to sit next to Owen.

"It's my off week, treatment-wise, so I tend to build up strength and weight during this week."

"So you're feeling good this week."

"Yeah, I feel great. Almost like normal again. Or my new normal, anyway."

"Hey, you'll be normal again as soon as you're finished with treatment. Then you can go back to your life the way it was before."

Owen looked over at him. "Ya think?"

Jason gave him an encouraging grin. "I don't think. I know."

"Yeah. That's what I think, too."

"So was Erin here today?"

"No, she had a wedding this afternoon that was going to last until late. She said she'd try to come by tomorrow after work."

"That's good." They watched the game for a while.

"Do you think you and Erin will end up back together?"

Owen glanced at him. "Why?"

Jason tried to shrug nonchalantly. "Just curious."

"Huh." Owen slid off the couch. "Let's cook some dinner."

"Okay."

Jason had brought chicken breasts to grill, along with vegetables and some fruit to make a salad. He wanted to make sure Owen ate healthy food, so he and Owen sliced and seasoned the zucchini and squash and put them on the grill pan. Owen started on chopping up the fruit while Jason went outside and fired up the grill and cooked the chicken and vegetables. By the time he brought the food inside, Owen had the fruit salad made and was popping grapes in his mouth while talking on his speakerphone.

"Yeah, Jason's here and we're grilling chicken and veggies."

"Oh. Well, that sounds fun. Say hi to Jason for me."

Jason recognized Erin's voice. "I'm right here. Hey, Erin."

"Hey. How's it going?"

"Good. You?"

"Fine. Busy here. Well, I've gotta go. Talk to you later, Owen."

Owen gave Jason a frown as he said, "Yeah, later, Erin. Bye."

He tucked his phone into the pocket of his shorts. "That was weird."

"What was weird?"

"You. And Erin. It was tense."

"No, it wasn't." It had been tense as hell, but he didn't want Owen to pick up on that. He plated their food and they went back into the living room to eat and finish watching the game.

Owen was silent while he ate, and Jason kept his focus on the game, hoping Owen would forget about that earlier phone conversation.

"What's going on with you and Erin?" Owen asked when he put his empty plate on the table in front of the sofa.

Guess he hadn't forgotten. "Don't know what you mean."

"Come on, buddy. I know I've been missing in action for a while. Tell me what went down with you and Erin."

He took in a breath and blew it out, then laid his plate on top of Owen's. "We've been spending time together. It started out with her wanting revenge on you dumping her."

Owen laughed. "That sounds like something Erin would do."

"And then we started seeing a lot of each other."

"And now it's turned into something more?"

Jason shrugged and stared at the TV, trying to downplay it.

"You're in love with her."

He shifted his gaze, looking at Owen. "Yeah. I am."

"Does she feel the same?"

"I don't know. We didn't get that far."

"Okay. Thanks for telling me."

"I don't know how she feels now, Owen. She thought you were over her, that you dumped and ran. She didn't know—about all this. This changed everything."

Now it was Owen's turn to shift his attention to the TV. "Yeah, I know it did. But, honestly? Everything changed with us even before I got sick."

Jason didn't know what he meant by that.

He supposed he'd have to let Owen and Erin figure it out together.

And he'd just have to wait.

CHAPTER
······
thirty-three

"So WHAT HAVE you been doing?" Jason felt like he was sitting across the table from a stranger instead of from the woman he loved.

"Oh, you know, just working and stuff."

She kept her focus on her salad, didn't even meet his gaze. They were having dinner, and he'd had to push to get her to agree. She'd been spending so much time with Owen it was like he'd almost had to beg to get some time with her.

"I spent some time with Owen today."

She lifted her head. "You did? How's he doing?"

"Good. Seems stronger."

Her lips curved into the first smile he'd seen from her since he'd picked her up at her house. "I'm glad to hear that."

His stomach twinged at that smile, because it wasn't for him. It made him feel guilty. She should smile about Owen feeling better. So why did it make him feel so shitty?

He scooped his French fry into the ketchup, eating his

food without even tasting it. Everything was bland without the joy of Erin's smile and laughter in his life. They were out of sync, off kilter, and he didn't like it.

"I thought maybe after whatever wedding you have on Saturday you might want to come over and spend the night at my place."

"Oh. I, uh, was going to go over to Owen's. There's a movie marathon we were going to watch together."

Again, that knot in his stomach. "Okay."

"You could come over and watch with us. It's a comedy marathon and I know you and Owen would enjoy watching that together."

"Yeah. Maybe."

She reached across the table to touch his hand. "What's wrong, Jason?"

It wouldn't be fair to ask her to see less of Owen. He was the guy she was going to marry. If she was still in love with him, what was he supposed to do? Ask her to back the hell off? Owen was sick. He needed her more than Jason did right now.

"Nothing. Everything's fine."

"You sure?"

"Yeah. Just fine."

Except it wasn't. And he didn't know how to fix it.

Someone was going to get hurt, and he had a feeling it was going to be him. And just like all those years ago when Erin chose Owen, he was going to have to just suck it up and take it.

So after dinner he drove her back home and walked her to the front door. He wanted to pull her into his arms and tell her how he felt, but in the end he just brushed his lips across hers. It wasn't enough.

"Night, Erin."

She gave him a curious look. "Good night, Jason."

He walked away without looking back.

ERIN STOOD ON the porch and watched Jason climb into his truck, feeling so empty inside she wanted to drop to the floor and cry.

She didn't know what to do, how to make everyone happy.

Owen needed her. And she knew Jason was upset about all the time she was spending with Owen, but what was she supposed to do? Abandon the man she was going to marry? She felt . . . obligated. All that anger she'd held inside for so long was gone. Now she felt like it was her purpose to help Owen feel better. And in doing so she'd put her relationship with Jason on the back burner.

She felt as if she were being pulled apart, and no matter what decisions she made, they were going to be the wrong ones.

She was doing the best she could right now. It was all she had.

When she saw Jason's taillights fade from view, she turned and went inside.

CHAPTER

· · · · · ·

thirty-four

ERIN HAD FINISHED off the last of her work for the day, then went up to her room to change clothes.

She was just winding her hair into a ponytail when she heard a knock.

"Come on in."

Her mother came in and leaned against the doorway, studying her. "Are you seeing Jason tonight?"

"Jason? No. I'm taking dinner over to Owen's."

"So, you're back with Owen?"

"Not exactly. I'm just helping him out while he's having treatment."

Her mom went silent. When Erin finished her hair, she turned to face her mother's inscrutable expression.

"What?" she asked.

"For a while there, I had a feeling you had fallen in love with Jason."

She didn't know how to answer that, and every mention of Jason made her stomach clench in anxiety. "I . . . I just need to help take care of Owen right now."

"Why is Owen suddenly your responsibility?"

She tilted her head. "Mom. He's sick."

"Yes, he is. And I feel awful about that. Gwen and I have had several long conversations about his treatment and prognosis. She seems to think he's going to bounce back from this in no time at all."

"Yes. I agree." She had to believe that.

Her mother came into the room and sat on the edge of Erin's bed, then patted the spot next to her, giving Erin no choice but to come sit down. She did, and waited for her mom to speak.

"Do you love him?"

"Who?" she blurted, realizing she had no idea which man her mother was referring to.

"Owen, honey. Are you still in love with Owen?"

"Oh. No. I care about him. I feel awful about him being sick, and I feel somehow responsible for helping him."

"And in doing so, you're losing the man you do love."

Tears pricked her eyes. "Jason."

Her mother grabbed her hand. "Yes. So you need to figure out how to handle this. You're not responsible for Owen anymore. He freed you from that responsibility when he broke up with you."

"But, Mom, he broke up with me so I wouldn't feel responsible for him. What if he still loves me?"

"Then you need to have an honest conversation with him, and tell him that you're in love with someone else now."

She shuddered in a sob. "How can I do that? How can I break his heart like that when he's so sick?"

Her mother smoothed her hand down her back. "I don't know. But even if I was sick, I'd want the person I cared about to be honest with me."

She closed her eyes, realizing her mother was right. She owed Owen the truth. And she owed Jason the truth.

It was time to suck it up and stop trying to be every-thing to everyone. She couldn't do that anymore.

"Thanks, Mom." She threw her arms around her mother and hugged her tight. "I needed this."

"That's what I'm here for."

After her mother left her room, she cleaned up her face, fixed her makeup, then headed out. She picked up chicken salad sandwiches and some soup for dinner for Owen and her tonight, and thought about what she was going to say to him on the way over.

By the time she arrived at Owen's apartment, she still had no idea. She supposed she'd just have to wing it.

Owen smiled as he opened the door. "Hey there."

She leaned in to give him a quick hug. "Hi. How are you feeling?"

"Pretty great this week."

"I'm glad to hear that. I brought dinner."

"You didn't have to do that." He led her into the kitchen. "I was actually thinking we'd go out."

"Really? Are you feeling up to that?"

"Yeah. I can leave the house, you know."

"Of course. I can put this all in the fridge."

"Great. Then I'll have food to eat tomorrow and Tues-day when I don't feel like cooking."

"Aww. You know I'd bring you food then, too."

"My mom will be over. She hovers."

Erin laughed. "She loves you."

"Yeah, she does."

They ended up going out to eat at Hidalgo's Mexican restaurant since Owen was craving carne asada. His ap-petite was definitely perky. He even finished off Erin's chimichanga.

"It's good to see you more like yourself."

"Once I finish treatment, I'll be all like myself."

She smiled. "I like this positive attitude."

He shrugged. "I have to believe I'll beat this. Plus, my doctors all tell me I have a ninety-six percent chance. I like those odds."

"They're pretty great odds, Owen."

She didn't want to be a downer when he was feeling so upbeat, plus they were in a public place, so now wasn't the time to talk to him about her feelings. They could wait.

After dinner they took a walk in the park by the lake. A rainstorm had hit earlier and despite it being humid, it was at least a bit cooler. Plus, there was a nice breeze, making it feel wonderful, especially since the sun had gone down. And she knew exercise was good for Owen, even if it was in the heat of summer.

"Let's take a seat here," Owen said, motioning to a bench that looked out over the water.

They sat in silence for a few minutes, then Owen shifted to face her, picking up her hand in his.

"Erin, I need to talk to you about something serious."

Uh-oh. "Okay."

"I don't really know how to say this without just coming out and saying it so it's clear. I don't need you to babysit me."

She blinked, then frowned. "What? That's not what I'm doing."

"Yeah, it is. I don't know if you feel some kind of misplaced guilt or whatever, but honestly? I've got this. I'm going to be okay. And nothing about what happened to me has anything to do with you. You're not responsible for me."

It took a minute for the words to sink in, but when they did, she said, "Okay. So you don't want me to come around anymore?"

"No, I don't. It's not good for either of us, and it's definitely not good for your relationship with Jason."

She frowned. "What does this have to do with Jason?"

"He loves you."

Her heart skipped a beat. "He told you that?"

"He tried not to. But it's kind of obvious. He's got it bad. Hell, he loved you even before you and I started dating."

Erin held up her hand. "Wait. What?"

Owen shrugged. "I kind of knew he wanted you. And I stepped in. Not because of some competition thing, but because I wanted to go out with you. He's just more of a gentleman than I am and he backed off."

She didn't know. Even then, she didn't know. She was such an idiot. "Owen. I'm sorry."

"Don't be sorry. You and I both know we were over before the wedding, we just didn't see the signs. We weren't meant to be. And this thing you're doing with me right now? Coming over to be with me, to take care of me? I appreciate it and all, but I've got this."

"You know I don't mind. I'm happy to help you."

"I know. You and Jason and Clay and all my friends have been awesome, and I'll never be able to repay the kindness. But the next time you come to my house? It had better be with Jason."

She sighed, realizing how much she'd screwed this up. "I've kind of ignored him lately, wanting to be here for you. I'm sure he thinks . . . oh, God, I don't even know what he thinks. Probably that I don't care about him anymore."

"Then go fix it. He loves you, Erin. The forever kind of love. And I can guarantee you that he's not at all second-guessing his feelings for you."

Her eyes welled with tears. She threw her arms around Owen and hugged him tight. "Thank you for understanding. And for continuing to be my friend. I'd hate to lose you."

"We'll always be friends, Erin. You're never gonna lose me."

She pulled back and squeezed his hands. "I'm holding you to that. And we did love each other, once."

"Yeah, we did. It just wasn't the forever kind of love. We were just too blinded by other things to see that."

She nodded. "You're right."

"Erin."

"Yes?"

"I'm so sorry. For everything I put you through."

She reached for his hand. "I forgive you."

He let out a sigh. "Thanks. I needed to hear that."

They made their way back to Owen's apartment and she said good-bye. Not a forever good-bye, but a definite end to their relationship. She felt much clearer.

Now she had to go to Jason and fix the colossal mess she'd made of her relationship with him.

CHAPTER

· · · · · ·

thirty-five

IT HAD BEEN a long, tiring day, and Jason was exhausted. One more client and he could go home. He walked through the hall and saw his dog, Puddy, had found a nice quiet corner to curl up and sleep.

"I know exactly how you feel, bud," he said to his dog as he made his way to the room in the back. He lifted the chart, frowning as he saw the name.

What the hell was she doing here?

He opened the door and Erin was in there with Agatha. Agatha's tail whipped back and forth when she caught sight of Jason, and Erin's face lit up with a bright smile.

Jason's gut tightened, but he was at work, so right now he was Dr. Callum. His personal feelings didn't count.

"So, what's going on with Agatha?" He took a quick glance at her leg. Her cast had come off two weeks ago, and as far as he knew she was running like a champion.

"It's her heart, doc," Erin said, coming over to stand close to him.

Jason breathed in Erin's fresh scent, trying his best not

to be affected. Wasn't gonna happen. He could never be close to her and not feel anything.

He frowned. "What's wrong with her heart?"

"She's brokenhearted without you. As is her human." Erin laid her hands on his chest. "I miss you. I love you. Just you. No one else but you."

Her words sank in. She said she loved him. But could he believe in that? Believe in her? Did she even know what she really wanted? "You made an appointment to tell me that?"

"Well, it was important. You see, I realized that you've always stood on the sidelines, waiting for me to open my eyes and see the wonderful man in front of me. And sometimes—okay, more often than sometimes—I'm clueless. But not anymore." She stepped forward and took his hand in hers. "I see you. I see your kindness, how you've always been there for me. I see the amazing, wonderful and thoughtful things you've done for me. I see how unselfish you are, how you always put others first. I see the only man I will ever love for the rest of my life. And I need to apologize for not seeing all of that sooner. Much, much sooner."

"What about Owen?"

She sighed. "I'm sorry about that. I had this misplaced sense of guilt and responsibility when I heard his diagnosis. And I felt like I needed to take care of him."

"And now?"

"Now you're my priority. Not that we're abandoning Owen, but if we see him, we'll do it together, provided you agree with that. Since he's our friend. But I can't make this about Owen anymore. I need this to be about you and me. Just you and me from now on. I'm sorry I didn't do it much sooner."

Relief flooded him as her words sunk in. Relief, and a whole lot of love for this woman. He scooped his arm around her waist and tugged her closer. "That's okay. You can spend a lifetime making it up to me."

"Yeah? How will I do that?"

"Just love me." He kissed her, telling her with his kiss how much he'd missed her, how much he needed her. He deepened the kiss to tell her how much he loved her.

The door opened and Casey, his tech, came in. "Dr. Callum, do you need—"

He pulled away and turned to Casey. "Busy here kissing the woman I love. I think I've got this."

Casey grinned. "I can see that. Sorry, Doc."

She inched the door closed and Erin laughed, tangling her fingers in his hair. "So that's a 'Yes, I forgive you'?"

"Yes. I forgive you."

She laid her head on his chest and just feeling her close to him healed the gaping hole in his heart.

She pulled back and looked up at him with tear-filled eyes.

"I had a long talk with Owen. We're friends. We'll always be friends. All of us. But there's nothing between him and me. I need you to know that nothing happened between us after he got back. I just felt a need to help him and I had some momentary confusion about what that was all about."

"I believe you. And I understand. You went through hell with all of that. It's understandable you'd be confused. But let's make something clear. In the future, when you're confused about your feelings on things? You talk to me. I'm always going to be here to help you."

She laid her head on his chest. "I love you, Jason."

He wasn't sure his heart could contain all the emotion he felt for Erin. But he sure as hell was gonna try. "I love you, too, Erin. Now I need you to do two more things for me."

She lifted her head to meet his gaze. "What's that?"

"Pack up your things—and Agatha—and come live with me. Because I don't want to go another day without you. And marry me. Because I've waited long enough for you."

She sucked in a deep breath, and he saw the shimmer of tears. "Yes." She let out a soft laugh. "And most definitely yes."

He kissed her again, and this time Agatha poked her nose in between them to let them know she was part of the family, too. They left the exam room and Puddy made his way to Agatha, the two of them happily greeting each other.

They didn't say anything to the staff about the engagement. First, he was going to get her a ring. And then they'd tell their families first before anyone else.

He left the office and headed for home, Erin following behind him.

He smiled as he caught sight of her car in his rearview mirror. She was following him home. To their home.

Oh, yeah. This was going to be the start of one hell of a great adventure.

ACKNOWLEDGMENTS

· · · · · ·

Huge thanks to my editor, Kate Seaver, for brainstorming the creation of this series with me. Boots and Bouquets wouldn't exist without you and, as always, I'm so grateful for your willingness to be part of the creative process.